Country Love Song

BETTY GOSSELL

Riverview Press

info@riverview-press.com
www.riverview-press.com

Other Books by Betty Gossell

Gate to Gate Trilogy - Boarding Pass series with Karen Pickens (2018)

A Home for Molly (2019)

Serenity Secrets (2021)

A Life of Devotion (2022)

Oh, To Be Like Him! (2023)

Lizzy's Journey (2024)

Dedication and Thanks

While writing Part III of my previous novel *Gate to Gate Trilogy*, I introduced my readers to the character of Lucy Armando. I felt she had an interesting story to tell and considered writing more about her. Several of my friends and family encouraged me to explore the idea further, and *Country Love Song* is the result.

At the top of the list of cheerleaders are my mom Wanda (who has passed away since I first started writing) and my sister Rosemary. Always interested in the story and pushing me to continue, I doubt this would have been completed without them. Thanks also to my daughter, Karen, who helped with the musical aspects of this book. Numerous friends provided encouragement as well, plus many others who enjoyed my previous writings. Thank you everyone.

Life, as often happens, managed to get in the way to delay this book's completion, and a global pandemic certainly did not help. I appreciate those whose love and support got me through the tough times.

Contents

Prologue

Winning a nationally televised singing competition puts Lucy Armando on the fast track to fame and success. It's a dream come true, but she quickly learns that all that glitters isn't gold, and that not everyone who flocks to her side has her best interests at heart. Will she be able to hold onto her Christian values and conservative beliefs in the fast-paced but cutthroat music industry? And will she learn who she can trust before it's too late?

Verse 1
The Meeting

Chapter 1

Standing in the center of the stage, the studio lights nearly blinding her and the crowd screaming at the top of their lungs, Lucy Armando squeezed the hand of her competitor Julia Buchanan. She could barely breathe and felt like she was going to faint. She closed her large brown eyes and tried to slow her pounding heart.

Over the noise of the crowd and the raucous studio music, she could barely hear the host yell, "Well, here we are on the final night of our competition. You remember that we started out with ten talented singers and are down to the final two. We received a record number of votes overnight, and now the announcement we have all been waiting for...the winner of Season Four of *Rising Star* is..."

Lucy felt her legs trembling and worried she might fall. The crowd continued to scream and stomp their feet. The spotlight was hot on her face, and she felt sweat trickle down her back. She knew the host's long pause was for TV effect, but she wasn't sure how much more she could take.

"Lucy Armando!" the host finally shouted, and she felt Julia squeeze her hand and then give her a giant hug. Confetti rained down and she heard what sounded like fireworks. The other eight competitors rushed onto the stage, hugging her and gushing congratulations. Everyone was crying, including Lucy herself. Somehow, the host pushed his way through the crowd and presented her with a large trophy and a plaque listing her as the winner. He also gave her a giant fake check in the amount of $500,000 and announced she had won a recording contract with Star Records.

Eventually the cameras were turned off, and Lucy was whisked backstage by the show's producer for a series of media interviews. Still in shock that she had won, she tried to answer the reporters' questions coherently. The network photographer appeared again, and she posed for promotional photos and did a short video. Finally, she was able to return to her dressing room and sank exhaustedly into the chair at her makeup table.

Alone for just a moment, Lucy looked in the mirror, hardly recognizing herself. Her long jet-black hair was styled in big curls held in place by vast amounts of hairspray. The makeup artists had layered more color to her cheeks and lips than she had ever worn before in her life. False eyelashes and layers of blue and bronze eyeshadow made her brown eyes appear even larger than normal. She was wearing a very short and very tight-fitting denim skirt and a low-cut paisley blouse covered in sequins and fringe. On her feet were pink cowboy boots that were cute but horribly uncomfortable. How vastly different she looked now as compared to the outfit she wore when she auditioned: well-worn jeans, a flowery peasant top and her favorite scruffy boots. Her hair had been pulled back into a loose ponytail and she had on only a little lip gloss and mascara. Things sure had changed in the ten weeks she had been on the show – and she had a feeling the changes were just beginning.

She had barely caught her breath when there was a firm knock on the dressing room door. Lucy took one last look in the mirror and then rose to open the door. She found one of the stage managers who skeptically said, "This young lady says she's a friend of yours and wants to see you."

He stepped to one side and Lucy saw her best friend from high school Sonya Vasquez. After confirming that it was ok, Sonya scooted past him and gave Lucy a giant hug. Lucy pulled her into the dressing room and shut the door. Hugging Sonya again, Lucy started shaking and sobbing.

"Is this really real? Did I actually win? This can't be happening!"

"You were so amazing on stage!" Sonya gushed. "And so brave! There is NO WAY I could sing in front of so many people, plus the millions at home."

"I just couldn't think about it! The lights were so bright that I really couldn't see past the judges and the first few rows of the audience. The strangest part was the noise! The crowds, the music – everything was so amplified. I could hardly hear anything the host was saying. And then there's *this* thing..." she said as she pulled out her earpiece and unclipped the battery pack from the back of her skirt. "This drives me crazy – hearing the band or backup singers while I'm on stage, or one of the stage managers giving directions."

"So, what happens next?" Sonya asked. Although she was nearly a year older than Lucy, they looked almost identical and people were certain they were twins, or at least sisters.

Before Lucy could answer, there was another knock on the door, and they were soon surrounded by record label executives and more media. One of the gentlemen extended his hand and introduced himself. "I'm Josh Bradford, from Star Records. I've been assigned as your Manager for the next year. We'll be working very closely – recording your first album and doing some videos, plus lining up dates for your tour. Your hometown is near St. Louis, right? You need to fly home in the morning and pack up as much as you can and come back here to Nashville on Sunday. I've rented a furnished condo for you, and we start work on Monday. Got to hit the ground running and make the most of the publicity, you know?"

It was then that he noticed Sonya sitting beside Lucy. His eyes went back and forth between them. He looked at Lucy quizzically. "I thought you said you are an only child. Is this your sister?"

"No, Josh, this is Sonya Vasquez, my best friend. People often get us confused."

"Wow, you aren't related? Well, anyway – head back to the hotel and try to get some sleep if you can. Your flight home is at 9 AM tomorrow. I'll see you Monday."

Josh left the dressing room and Lucy looked at Sonya with wide eyes of disbelief. This was suddenly VERY real, and her life was about to change forever.

Chapter 2

Lucy locked the door of her efficiency apartment and carried the last of her belongings to her overloaded Honda Civic. The few days she had been home had been a whirlwind of celebrations, farewell parties and giving notice at her telemarketing job. Here she was, just two months into her 21st year, ready to embark on the biggest adventure of her life so far.

Growing up in Chesterfield, Missouri, a suburb of St. Louis, Lucy had lived a quiet life as the only child of Antonio and Marissa Armando. She had a smattering of friends, but her greatest passion was music – singing in her high school choir and at church and playing in the school band. After graduating, she decided to take online music theory classes along with voice lessons while working at a call center. Prior to auditioning for *Rising Star*, the largest audience she had ever sung for was when she performed the National Anthem at a Division II college basketball game. Nothing in her past had prepared her for the craziness of the recent weeks of auditions and then the show itself.

As she got into her car and adjusted the mirrors, she smiled at her reflection. Gone were the false eyelashes and layers of makeup for the TV show. Her long hair hung loosely down her back and the overly tight (and overly revealing) clothes were replaced by a pair of cutoff jeans, a Willie Nelson T-shirt and Converse tennis shoes.

She backed out of her parking spot and took one last look around before driving to the apartment rental office where she dropped her keys into the night deposit slot. After filling up with gas at the Mobil station and grabbing an early lunch at Wendy's, she embarked on her five-hour drive to Nashville. Josh had forwarded detailed maps and instructions for the best route to her new condo, but she wanted to arrive before dark and have a chance to unload her car and unpack. Her mind was spinning at the thought of beginning her professional music career tomorrow. Tomorrow!

She had driven to Nashville several times in the past few years – attending concerts and going to FanFest. But this time she was going as a *performer*, and she was exceedingly nervous and excited.

Just as she was about to merge onto the highway, her dad called from Florida. He put her on his speaker so her mom could be on the line, too. They apologized again for not being there to help her pack and see her off, but her mom's cancer had progressed to where her dad didn't want to leave her alone. Their trip to the Florida Cancer Center had already been extended twice as she was having side effects from the chemo for her lymphoma. Lucy promised to call once she got to her condo and hopefully, they could Facetime later in the week.

She stopped on the outskirts of Nashville to stretch her legs and get a cold drink. The drive had gone quickly, and she had enjoyed singing along with the latest CD from her idol Travis Jones. She checked her email on her phone to see a flurry of messages from friends and family. One particular email caught her attention – it was from Josh and the subject line said "URGENT."

With fear in her heart and trembling hands she opened the email to read, "Hey, Lucy, hopefully your trip is going well, and you are almost here to start your new life! I wanted to let you know that I have a few guys lined up to help you unload your car and do anything else you might need. I took the liberty of picking up a few groceries for you – bread, milk, coffee – you get the idea. I left some documents in the condo for you and a map to the nearest grocery store, pharmacy and bank. Text me when you get to town, and I'll arrange for the guys to meet you. See you in the office at 10 tomorrow. Sleep well, and congrats again!"

She double-checked the condo address on her GPS and drove the remaining 15 miles with both hands firmly on the wheel. It was a Sunday afternoon in July, but the Nashville traffic was crazy. Thankfully, her GPS led her directly to her new home, and soon she was staring at the gates of a luxury condo complex. She entered the gate code Josh had provided into the keypad and the majestic gates slowly opened. Driving around to the back of the second building, she parked near the pool. She sent a quick text to Josh and then decided to get out and walk around while waiting for the moving guys. Much to her surprise and delight, she found that her condo was on the ground floor with a patio or garden that was shaded by numerous large oak trees. She was excited for the chance to see the inside.

She didn't have long to wait. She went back to her car and had just pulled out her phone to check messages again when a blue F150 pickup pulled into the space next to her.

"Lucy?" a young man asked in a friendly voice. "I'm Eli – Josh sent us."

Lucy smiled and climbed back out of her crowded car. "I really appreciate the help. You can see, my car is pretty loaded."

"No problem. My friend Jimmy and I can handle this in no time. Here's the keys – go in and make yourself at home in your new place!"

Eli pressed the keys into her hand in an almost fatherly way. Probably only ten years older than her, he carried himself with an ease and confidence she hoped to possess someday.

She walked up the three steps to her new front door and inserted the largest of the keys into the lock in the door. She figured the tiny key was for her mailbox but was confused about the medium-sized gold one. She gently opened the door, then her eyes grew wide in amazement. Off to her left was a large kitchen with stainless steel appliances and granite counter tops. Across the bar area was a gorgeous living room with a fireplace and French doors that opened to the patio. Light was streaming in through the massive windows along the back of the house.

Down the hallway to her left was a nice sized bedroom and large bathroom in the hallway. Pleased, she came back to the kitchen just as Eli and Jimmy came in with their first load from her car. Turning to the right, they moved into a section of the house Lucy had not seen yet. Confused, she followed them into a HUGE bedroom that was almost the size of her old apartment. There was a king-sized bed and a dresser along with a sitting area with a desk and recliner. The colors were muted brown and gray with accents of a deep burgundy. One wall had floor-to-ceiling windows, and another wall had a door to the patio. She had a two bedroom condo? Wow.

The guys put her suitcases and a few boxes in a corner of the bedroom and went outside for another load. Lucy stepped into the massive bathroom that had a giant soaker tub and separate spa shower. There was a nice dressing table with a lighted mirror, then she saw the walk-in closet that was almost large enough to be a third bedroom. The few nice clothes she had brought with her would take up maybe one-fourth of the closet.

The guys quickly finished unloading her car, gave her the keys and wished her a good night. She walked back to the kitchen and found a note from Josh. "Lucy – welcome! I hope you find the condo to your liking. There's a bit of food in the fridge, but I left you some takeout menus from a few of my favorite places. Have a great evening, and I'll see you tomorrow. Oh – the Wi-Fi password is LucyStar, and there is a bit of wood in the fireplace if you want to start a fire later. Kick back and relax, order some food, and get a good night's sleep."

Lucy thumbed through the menus and her rumbling stomach reminded her that she had only had a few snacks in the car since leaving home. One of the menus was for a sandwich shop only a few blocks away, so she called and ordered a ham and Swiss on rye, some potato salad and a chocolate chip cookie for dessert. While waiting for the food to be delivered, she opened the fridge to find the usual staples – milk, butter, eggs, cheese and some bottled water. The pantry held bread, coffee, peanut butter and a variety of paper products. The cupboards were stocked with plates, cups, pans and silverware. Everything she would need was here: was this really true?

The food was delivered in just a few minutes, and Lucy transferred it onto a paper plate so she could eat outside. Carrying her plate and a bottle of water, she opened the French doors and stepped onto the patio. Totally shielded from the other residents by a high fence, she sat at the table and ate hungrily. Once finished, she picked up her phone and called her parents. No one answered, so she left a short message and promised to call again in a few days. Then she dialed Sonya's number who she answered on the second ring.

"Hey, girl!" Sonya said excitedly. "I've been waiting for you to call. How's everything?"

"Oh, it's better than I ever could have imagined! I'm in a two-bedroom luxury condo, fully loaded with all the amenities. Once I get settled, you have GOT to come down and see me!"

"I hear birds in the background……where are you?"

"Sitting on my patio. I just finished a little dinner. I'll take some pictures and send them to you later. This just doesn't seem real."

"Well, it is, Miss Superstar! Better get used to it. Just don't forget us little people, OK?"

They chatted a little longer, then Lucy remembered that she still had all her possessions to unpack and needed to decide what to wear tomorrow.

"I want to look nice, you know? But not like I'm trying too hard."

"Well, I'm no fashion expert, but would suggest jeans and that cute purple shirt with embroidery down the front. That always looks so nice on you. And leave your hair down: you know I'm so jealous of how fast your hair grows."

They said their goodbyes and Lucy promised to call the next evening. She cleaned up her mess in the kitchen and put the leftover potato salad in the fridge, wrapping the cookie in a napkin to carry it to her bedroom. Sitting on the edge of her bed, she nibbled on the cookie and tried to imagine what the next few weeks would bring. After unpacking her suitcases and taking her toiletries into the bathroom, she decided a long hot bath was just what she needed to relax and unwind.

She was about to undress when she realized she wasn't sure if all the doors were locked. Lucy had always been a little bit afraid of staying in strange places, and on the verge of a panic, she raced through the condo – double checking all the doors and windows. Satisfied that all was safe and secure, she turned the hot water full blast and added some of her favorite lavender bubble bath that she had brought with her. Stepping into the tub, she leaned back, closed her eyes and felt the tension and anxiety fade away into the warm bubbles. She had some soft music playing on her phone, and soon she realized she was about to fall asleep. *"Oops – not a good thing to drown in the tub on her first night in town!"* she thought.

She climbed out of the bath and wrapped herself in one of the fluffy towels she found in the linen closet. After slipping into her favorite pj's, she took her guitar from its case and softly strummed a melody that had been haunting her for months. She had no lyrics yet, but the chords spoke of heartbreak and pain. She felt that she did not have enough authentic life experiences to do the music justice - things were so right in her life right now. She prayed she wouldn't have those tragic experiences any time soon.

Chapter 3

Lucy opened her eyes to bright sunshine streaming in the large bedroom windows. Momentarily disoriented, she looked around the room in confusion. Suddenly the memories of her move to Nashville yesterday came rushing back, and she looked at the clock in a panic – it was 7:51 A.M. and she needed to get up and ready for her first day as a professional musician. How in the world did she oversleep?

After a quick shower, she pulled on her favorite jeans and the shirt Sonya had recommended. She had a small breakfast of scrambled eggs and toas, and was on her second cup of coffee when she got a text from Josh.

"Just checking in. The condo OK? Did you sleep well?"

"Yes, perfect," she answered, *"I'll see you at ten."*

She set her dishes in the sink and went into the bathroom to finish getting ready. Gazing again at her reflection, she applied just a hint of makeup and brushed her hair one last time. She picked up her purse and opened the front door to her new life. She noticed that there was a newspaper lying on her neighbor's lawn and made a mental note to subscribe. Her friends teased her that *no one* read the newspaper anymore, but she enjoyed taking her time, especially on Sundays, thumbing through all the sections. She locked the door and climbed into her car for the short drive to the studio. Josh had left her a map (she made another mental note to thank him for all the little things he had done for her) and in just a few minutes she parked in the employee lot behind the studio building.

She paused outside the front door. Star Records – she glanced at all the people going up and down the sidewalk, totally oblivious of her and what was about to happen. She took a deep breath and pushed open the door. The reception area was strangely quiet – very different from what she expected, although she was not really sure what she was expecting. The receptionist was on a call, and she motioned for Lucy to have a seat. Perched nervously on the edge of a small sofa, she looked in awe at the signed pictures that lined the walls of singers who were her heroes and idols. Was it possible that she would be joining them?

"Lucy, you made it! And right on time!" Josh said enthusiastically as he walked briskly into the lobby. "Let me give you a short tour and then we'll head to my office for some additional paperwork"

He took her through a myriad of hallways that led past studios and conference rooms. They stopped outside one studio that was being used to lay down some background vocals, and another where a group of string players were recording a beautiful ballad. Josh explained that each of the studios was booked weeks in advance, and cancellations were strongly frowned upon.

He led her to an elevator that took them to the 7th floor. He opened his office door, and she gasped as she looked out the expansive windows at the Nashville skyline.

"Quite a view, isn't it?" he said as he motioned for her to sit in a chair opposite his desk. "I've just got some formalities for us to wrap up, and then I'll take you to HR for the usual paperwork. They'll go over your paychecks and give you more information about the condo. I hope you like it – it comes with the option to buy at the end of the year."

"Really? It's amazing. I love it."

"Good. I did want to go ahead and give you an advance on your pay. I know there are a lot of expenses to moving and you will need to transfer your car title, get a new driver's license, and open a bank account. Do you have a passport? If not, you need to start that paperwork, too, since we anticipate some international travel in the future. There's lots to do while we are working hard on your album and lining up your first shows."

He handed her several $100 bills and a check made out to her for her next few weeks' pay. It was more money than she had ever seen in her life. She looked at him with wide eyes.

"My *strong* suggestion to you as your manager is that you open a bank account *today* and also set up an appointment with a financial advisor. This is a major opportunity for you, but I would hate for you to be careless and blow it all."

Things has been so crazy this past week that Lucy had not really taken the time to think about the money as far as a monthly paycheck. Everything just seemed so unreal.

"Star Records is making a HUGE investment in you, Lucy. We are confident in your talents and your unique singing style will captivate your fans. We just want you to be careful and make the most of this opportunity."

"Of course," Lucy said softly, suddenly overwhelmed and very worried that she would not live up to their expectations.

After visiting a bit more, Josh took her to the HR department on the 4th floor and introduced her to a lovely older woman named Paula. He told Lucy to come back to his office when they were finished, and they would go to lunch with a few producers and studio musicians. After their working lunch she would be free to run her errands and get settled in at home. They planned to hit the ground running tomorrow, listening to some songs for her to start recording later in the week.

Lucy was trembling as she sat opposite Paula. She closed her eyes and tried to concentrate on the W4 and how to fill out the direct deposit form once she opened her bank account.

"Speaking of banks," Paula said, "do you have a preference? If not, I would suggest First Tennessee. It's where we have our corporate accounts, and we refer many of our clients there. Here's the card of one of the managers who can help you. It's not far from your condo, so you can stop by on your way home.

"Also, here is a copy of the lease for the condo. We are paying the rent for the first year. After that, you will have the option to stay on as a renter or purchase it if you want. Josh left you three keys, right? A door key, a mailbox key, and one to the clubhouse. There's a small work out room there and access to the pool."

"Oh, I was wondering what that other key was for."

"Internet and basic cable are provided," Paula continued. "You are welcome to upgrade at your expense if you want, but I would wait to decide on that, since you will be touring a lot once your album is released. Other condo guidelines are in the folder."

"One last thing," she said softly. "I know that this is all new to you, and a bit overwhelming. My friendly advice is that you be very careful about who you trust and how much access you give to anyone regarding your personal life. People will come out of the woodwork, wanting to be your friend. Just be aware and pay attention – if it feels wrong, it probably is."

"I don't mean to scare you," she continued. "The vast majority of the people you meet will have your best interests at heart. Just keep your eyes open, OK?"

They finished their paperwork, and Paula escorted her to the office door. Putting a friendly hand on Lucy's shoulder, she said, "Enjoy your lunch, then get that bank account opened. I need the direct deposit form back as soon as possible to give to payroll. See you soon."

Lucy stepped into the hallway and leaned against the wall. She felt like she was in way over her head and had no one to talk to.

After composing herself a bit, she stopped at the ladies' room and then made her way back to Josh's office. He introduced her to Darren Russo who would be producing her album. They took an UBER to the Midtown Café where there was a room reserved for them in the back. Lucy mostly listened while Josh and Darren explained the recording process. Soon drummer Blake McKenzie joined them, and they struck up a conversation about her musical influences. He told her how much he had enjoyed her performances on *Rising Star* and was looking forward to working with her on her album.

After lunch, they all went back to the office and then Josh walked her to her car.

"Any last-minute questions? I hate to rush, but I have a conference call in a few minutes."

"No, thanks for everything, Josh. I mean it. It's all pretty overwhelming."

"Well, I'm here 24 hours a day, if you ever need anything."

"Thanks, I really appreciate it."

After opening an account at the bank and making an appointment to come back to talk to a financial planner, Lucy went to the DMV to find out about getting a new driver's license and transferring her car title. Exhausted, she stopped at the grocery store to pick up a few things to tide her over until the weekend when she would have more time to shop.

Almost back to the condo, she saw a boutique with a gorgeous leather jacket in the window. She quickly turned her car around and found a parking spot nearby. She walked up to the display window and gazed at the mannequin modelling the most beautiful pearl pink jacket she had ever seen. Opening the door of the store, she was hit with the intoxicating aroma of leather and hardwood. There were a few other shoppers in the store, but a friendly clerk approached her and asked if she needed help. Pointing to the window, Lucy asked if she could try on the jacket. The sales lady looked at Lucy's figure, then found what she guessed was the correct size. Of course, it fit like a glove and Lucy fell in love instantly. She cringed when she saw the price – she had never paid that much for an article of clothing in her life! In fact, her entire current wardrobe probably cost less. She gently handed the jacket back to the clerk but said, "I'll be back – I promise!"

Lucy unloaded her groceries and then sank into a recliner that looked out the patio door towards her garden. Her brain was spinning with all she had learned today. She still had the folder of paperwork from HR to go through, and she wanted to call Sonya. But she was hungry and realized her lunch had been hours ago. She couldn't decide what she was hungry for and wondered if she had the energy to fix anything, anyway. She thought about the takeout menus on the counter but knew that would be a bad habit to get into. Plus, she had just spent quite a bit of money at the grocery store, and didn't want things to go to waste. She opened the fridge and saw that she had all the ingredients for a big salad with grilled chicken and strawberries. She poured herself a glass of wine (still getting used to being 21 and of legal drinking age) and nibbled on her salad. As she finished, she realized her breakfast dishes were still in the sink, so she quickly washed and dried everything.

Satisfied that the kitchen was spotless, she turned on the TV for some background noise and curled up on the sofa with her folder of paperwork. She was surprised to learn that the rental of the condo included housekeeping twice per month. All she had to do was call the cleaning service and make arrangements. All the utilities except the cable and Internet would be put into her name and she would be responsible for those. But everything else would be paid for.

She opened her purse and took out the money Josh had given her this morning. She was not comfortable carrying around so much cash and wondered what she should do with it. She was startled when her cell phone rang but was relieved to see that it was Sonya. They chatted for over an hour, with Sonya asking endless questions and Lucy filling in all the details. They ended the call with Lucy asking if Sonya could come down for the weekend as Lucy was feeling overwhelmed and a bit homesick. Sonya was scheduled to work Saturday at her job at the animal shelter but would try to get the time off.

Lucy turned off the lights, locked the doors, and set her alarm for seven – she needed to be at the studio the next day at nine. She thought about the song she sang in the finale of the show… *"If only you would listen, If only you could see. You would understand this message, You would know the real me."*

Lucy knew they planned to record this song first and release it ASAP. But she wondered – would she be able to stay true to herself and her values? Would the world be able to see the person she really was on the inside?

Chapter 4

Lucy sat in the corner of studio 5B, fascinated to watch Darren at the control board while Blake recorded drum tracks for three upcoming songs on Travis Jones' new CD. Was it just two days ago that she listened to him while driving to Nashville? And now, here she was, watching the magic happen.

It wasn't until Wednesday afternoon that the studio was free, and it was her turn behind the mic. She found herself even more nervous now than when she was on TV, if that was possible.

They did some basic guitar tracks first, and then she started on the vocals. It took several tries for her to feel comfortable enough to really let go and *sing*, but once she did, the group in the booth (Darren, Josh, Blake, and a background vocalist named Cheri) looked at each other and smiled – they knew the song would be a hit.

They spent the rest of the week in the studio – only interrupted when Josh needed her for a media interview or to meet with songwriters to choose the final songs for the album. It was all going together very quickly! It was fun and exhilarating, but she came home exhausted each evening.

Sonya called Thursday night to let Lucy know she was able to get off work and would be in town early Saturday afternoon. Lucy was excited and had lots of fun things planned for them.

Friday afternoon Josh called her into his office to discuss scheduling with her. He had lined up several local radio station interviews for the following week, but the most exciting news was that he had arranged for her to sing '*If Only*' at a local club Saturday night (tomorrow!) It was a small club but would be great exposure and practice for her. Local media would be there, of course. He wanted her to meet with their stylist before she left for the day to pick out something appropriate. And then he gave her a paycheck for the week.

"Payroll had to do a test on your direct deposit today, so this should be your last actual paper check. I suggest you stop by the bank on the way home, though."

Lucy looked at the check and almost fainted. She had spent virtually nothing this week and still had most of the cash Josh had given her on Monday. This much money just seemed crazy and unreal.

She drove to the bank and deposited the check, then finished the short drive home. She checked her mailbox to find a welcome letter from the condo association and some junk mail. How did they find her already? She carried the outfits from the stylist to her bedroom and laid them on her bed: two shirts that were fairly skimpy and low cut, a denim skirt and a flowing peasant skirt. They said she could wear her own jeans if they were new and without holes. She had been instructed how to do her hair and makeup. It would not as extreme as on TV, but much more than she normally wore.

She paced around the condo, feeling restless. It was a beautiful Friday night and she was in Nashville. Why was she sitting home alone? She quickly brushed her hair and freshened up her makeup a bit and dashed out the door. She was scheduled to sing at The Stage on Lower Broadway tomorrow. Maybe she should run by and see what the atmosphere was like and check out the stage setup?

She entered the address into her GPS but soon got bogged down in heavy downtown traffic. It took her almost an hour to find a parking spot that did not involve walking a mile. A light rain was falling – maybe tomorrow she and Sonya should take an UBER?

Lucy stepped into the club and found a table in the back. She realized she hadn't had dinner, so she ordered a grilled chicken sandwich and a side salad, along with sweet tea. She looked around the room, trying to gauge if they would accept her tomorrow.

It wasn't long before a middle-aged man stepped onto the small stage. "Happy Friday everyone!" he said loudly into the mic. "I'm glad you are here, because you're in for a real treat. We have a surprise substitution to the lineup tonight. You picked the right night to be here, for sure! Y'all know how Nashville is – you never know who you'll run into just walking down the street. Well, I just happened to run into this young man at lunch today. He's in town doing some recording but agreed to hang out with us for a while tonight. Let's give a big Stage welcome to............TRAVIS JONES!"

Lucy could not believe her eyes - standing on the stage (the same stage where she would be singing tomorrow) was her all-time favorite singer – her idol, her hero!

"Thanks, Joey! You know I wouldn't miss the chance to stop by if I could arrange it. What most of you don't know is that Joey was one of the first people to be supportive of my music career and used to let me sing here long before anyone else would give me a chance. And I can't thank him enough for that. But enough talking – would y'all mind if I sang a little?"

The crowd was small but jumped to their feet, clapping and cheering. Lucy couldn't take her eyes off him – he was quite tall with shockingly blue eyes and tussled reddish hair that hung down almost to his shoulders. He had a scruffy beard that only made him more handsome.

He sat on a stool with his guitar and started softly strumming, and the crowd instantly fell silent as he sang the opening line from his latest hit single. Lucy sat there enthralled, taking it all in. At one point she felt he was singing just for her.

After four songs he took a break and went out into the crowd to chat with the individual audience members. Lucy was about to leave when he approached her table to say hello. She blurted out a few nervous comments and then slipped out the door. She chastised herself all the way back to the condo. What a babbling fool she must have looked like to him.

Chapter 5

Lucy stretched and pulled the covers up under her chin. She opened one eye and looked at the clock – 9:37 A.M. Wow – she hadn't slept that late in ages!

After a quick shower and a cup of coffee, she was about to walk out the door when she got a text from Sonya stating she had a flat tire, but AAA was on the way. She thought she would get to the condo around two. This gave Lucy plenty of time to go to the grocery store and stock up, plus she wanted a bit of time to practice her song for tonight.

She stepped out of her door into the bright summer sunshine. After a short drive to the store, she pushed her cart up and down almost every aisle, loading it with not only groceries but more paper goods and cleaning products. Lucy was proud about how clean she had kept the condo this week (something she had always struggled with previously) and wanted it to stay that way. She also picked up a big bouquet of fresh flowers and a lovely crystal vase. While not terribly expensive, it did seem odd to not have to watch her budget and to be able to buy whatever cut of meat she wanted, or an vase and flowers.

Driving home, she passed the boutique where she had seen the leather jacket on Monday. It was still in the window, and there was a perfect parking spot right in front. Totally on impulse, she stopped and dashed inside. The tantalizing scent of real leather again met her at the door. The same friendly clerk approached her.

"You probably don't remember me, but I was here the other day and fell in love with that pink jacket in the display window."

"I remember," she said sweetly. "You said you would be back."

"And I am!"

"Well, you are in luck. We only have one left in your size."

"I'll take it!" she gushed as the clerk rang up the purchase. Lucy slid her debit card across the counter and watched as the transaction processed quickly. Did she really just spend that much money on a jacket?

Once home and with all the groceries put away, Lucy laid the new jacket on her bed alongside the blouses the studio stylist had given her. One of them had a pale pink and white check pattern that looked perfect under the jacket. The club had been a bit cool last night, so she wasn't overly worried about getting too hot, especially for just one song. She hung the jacket neatly in her closet next to the borrowed items from the studio.

She walked back to the living room and made sure everything was tidy, and before long there was a knock at her door. Looking through the peep hole, she saw Sonya outside holding a giant balloon that said "Congrats!"

Lucy quickly opened the door and wrapped her arms around her best friend. "You have no idea how much I have missed you," she said, almost on the verge of tears. "Get in here!"

Sonya walked into the kitchen and was amazed at the size of the condo and how nice it was. "You weren't kidding when you said this place is fantastic. The pictures you sent don't do it justice. All of this is yours?"

"For the next year, anyway. Here, let's take your things to your room and I'll give you a tour."

They put Sonya's small overnight bag in the 2^(nd) bedroom and then Lucy showed her the rest of the condo. Sonya was speechless during most of the tour, but once they got to the giant master bedroom and bathroom, she couldn't keep silent.

"Holy Moley girl – this is amazing! I mean, my room is great and the bathroom is really nice, but this? Wow!"

"You haven't seen the best part," Lucy said as she opened the door of the walk-in closet.

"Are you kidding me?" Sonya gushed. "This is huge!"

She was about to leave when she saw the pink jacket and the other borrowed clothes hanging off by themselves. "What's this?" she asked. "Buying new things already?"

"Just the jacket. The other things are from the studio for tonight. That's the other news I have for you – I'm performing at The Stage tonight!"

"You what? Your first weekend here? Just you? A whole concert?"

"No, just one song, and a couple of band members will be there, plus Josh and maybe Darren my producer."

"This is crazy! They aren't wasting any time, are they?"

"Nope. They want to take advantage of the publicity from the show."

"So, what's our schedule? What time do you need to be there?"

"I go on at eight thirty, but I need to be there by eight. It's not far but I figured we should hire a car. Traffic is crazy downtown all the time, but I hear it's even worse on the weekends. Will you help me with my hair and makeup? I'm so nervous."

"Of course! How about we have an early dinner and then we'll get you all dolled up. I'm so glad I got to be here. How long have you known about this gig?"

"Just yesterday afternoon. I didn't even get a chance to practice with the band, but they are pros and Darren told me not to worry. I actually drove over there last night and you'll never believe who was there…..Travis Jones! I even got to talk to him a bit!"

"Rubbing shoulders with the big boys now! I'm impressed!" Sonya gushed in awe.

They decided to have a light dinner on the patio, then Lucy went in to shower and started getting ready. Sonya worked her magic on Lucy's hair and makeup, and soon they were out the door and headed to The Stage. Josh was already there when they arrived and introduced her to Joey, the same emcee as last night. They found a table off to the side and before long, Darren and Blake arrived, along with a keyboard player named Adam. Lucy got out her guitar, stroking the strings lightly to calm her nerves.

"You look great," Blake said. "Pink leather looks good on you."

"Thanks, I'm so nervous. Does it show?"

"Nope, not at all. I've been here dozens of times, and the crowds are great – really receptive toward new singers."

Joey stepped onto the stage and was met with cheers and whistles.

"Ok, simmer down. I know y'all aren't that excited to see me. I have something really special for y'all tonight. How many of you watched the TV show *Rising Star*? You probably remember that part of the prize was a recording contract at Star Records here in Nashville. Well, the winner, Lucy Armando, is already here in town recording, and we convinced her to stop by and sing her signature song '*If Only*'. You loved her on the show, so let's give a big Stage welcome to Lucy Armando as she performs live for the first time since winning *Rising Star*! Lucy – come on up here!"

Lucy rose to her feet and walked the short distance to the stage. Blake and Adam took their places behind her.

"Thanks so much everyone, and thanks Joey for the kind words. I'm very excited to be here! It's been quite a crazy time since finishing the show, and we've been busy in the studio. I can't wait to share lots of new music with you. 'But tonight, I want to sing one of my very favorite songs……..'*If Only*'.

The room fell silent as she softly strummed the first chords, and the guys joined her after a few measures. She glanced at Sonya who was watching with pure pride and respect. Darren had his eyes closed and was nodding his head in time to the music. She was nervous, but the crowd was listening intently, swaying and smiling. She poured her heart into the song – the words felt like they were written by her soul. The final notes faded away, and a moment of silence hung in the air. Lucy started to panic. Did they hate it? Why was no one clapping? Then in the back of the room a young woman about her age rose to her feet and applauded. One by one, the crowd all stood, and the applause increased to an almost deafening roar. She glanced over at Sonya and Darren, both of whom appeared to have been crying. She brushed a sudden tear from her own eyes and leaned in closely to the mic.

"Thanks everyone. Your support means the world to me. Really, it's hard to find the words to express how grateful I am. I can't wait to be back and sing for you again! And thanks to Blake here on drums and Adam on keyboards," she said as she pointed in their direction. "Thanks again!" And with that she went back to her seat.

Darren gave her a big hug and Josh looked like a proud father. Sonya squeezed her hand and whispered, "Wow – I've heard you sing that song a dozen times, but never like that!"

Joey stepped back onto the stage, visibly shaken. "That was amazing, Lucy. Please come back as often as you can. There will always be room for you here at The Stage. One song or twenty, promise you will be back?"

Lucy nodded, and the crowd continued to clap and cheer. She had never felt so loved.

The rest of the night was a blur of music and fans wanting to talk to her, take pictures and get autographs. The main act of the evening was a brother-sister duo, and Lucy listened with awe. There was so much talent here in Nashville. It was hard to believe that she would stand out in the crowd.

Once back at the condo, Lucy changed out of her borrowed clothes and slipped on pj's. Sonya poured them each a glass of wine and found some crackers and cheese for them to snack on. They talked late into the night, rehashing the evening at The Stage and reliving old stories from home. Finally, way past midnight they decided to head to their separate bedrooms and get some sleep.

About nine the next morning Lucy awoke to sounds coming from the kitchen and the smell of coffee and bacon. A bit confused, she sat up in bed just as Sonya appeared at her door, coffee cup in hand.

"Oh, good, you're awake! Here's some coffee. I've been having fun playing in your gourmet kitchen."

Drinking her coffee deeply, she said "You are amazing, you know that? How am I going to survive once you go back home?"

They walked into the kitchen and laid out on the table was one of the biggest breakfasts Lucy had ever seen: scrambled eggs, biscuits and gravy, bacon, French toast, orange juice and fresh fruit. "You did all of this? What time did you get up?"

"Oh, I've been up for a while and decided to surprise you."

"Well, you did! I haven't eaten like this in ages!" Suddenly very hungry, Lucy filled her plate and ate with enthusiasm, praising Sonya's cooking and enjoying every bite.

After their leisurely breakfast, they decided to drive around and do some sightseeing, eventually ending up at the Grand 'Ole Opry for a tour. They listened intently while their guide explained the history and importance of the Opry. The tour ended with a chance for each of them to stand center stage and get their pictures taken beside a microphone. Lucy looked out at the empty seats and imagined being there in a few years, singing for a packed crowd. They exited through the gift shop and Lucy purchased their pictures. She knew exactly where she would hang hers at home for inspiration when the days seemed long, and she felt like giving up.

After Sonya left to go home, Lucy sat outside on her patio, letting the warm summer sunshine lull her into a short nap. She was jolted awake to the sound of her cell phone ringing.

"Lucy, it's Josh. Got a minute?"

"Sure, what's up?"

"I hate to bother you on a Sunday afternoon, especially since you have company."

"It's OK, she left about an hour ago."

"OK, cool. I have some news for you, and I just couldn't wait for tomorrow."

"Really? Good news?"

"Amazing news! Do you know who Jeremy Lane is?"

"The name sounds familiar – a record executive of some sort?"

"Close, he's a producer like Darren, and has worked with some really successful singers, including Travis Jones."

"Travis? Wow. But what does that…."

"Hold on – I'll tell you. It seems that Jeremy was at The Stage last night and heard you sing. He recorded part of it and sent it to Travis. Turns out they are working on a duets album, and he wants you to sing with him!"

"No way! Me, sing with Travis? You must be kidding me!"

"I'm totally serious! He wants you to record a new song he just wrote; says it will be perfect for the two of you. They will be emailing the music to Darren this afternoon for you to start in the morning!"

"Oh wow. I think I'm going to faint!"

"Please, no fainting. Just get some rest and be ready to go at nine tomorrow. Travis is in town, you know - there's a good chance he'll stop by to meet you."

Lucy hung up the phone and started shaking. She suddenly realized that she had nothing cute to wear tomorrow. In fact, she had done no personal shopping other than the pink jacket. She had plenty of money – maybe it was time to spend a little.

Three hours later she was standing beside her bed, looking at the mound of bags and boxes. She had found three new pairs of jeans, seven tops, cute new boots and some silly platform shoes. Two new purses and some pretty earrings and bracelets rounded out her purchases. It was fun to be able to get whatever she wanted and not worry about the cost, but she could see how this could quickly get out of control.

Not wanting to jinx anything, she resisted the urge to call Sonya or her parents. Instead, she put her new things away and then pulled up Travis' latest album on her phone. Relaxing in a hot bath, she closed her eyes and tried to imagine singing with him. Two weeks ago, she was rehearsing for the finals of the TV show. Now she was preparing to sing a duet with Travis Jones!

Chapter 6

"Ok, Lucy, let me explain how this will work," Darren said the next morning. "Travis' producer Jeremy sent the files over last night. Travis has recorded a demo of the song, along with a separate track of the vocals he wants to sing - harmony in spots, lead at other times, you know. We'll listen to the demo a few times to get familiar with where he's going, then just his part so you can sing along. I sent the lyrics to your email. Did you get them?"

"Yes, thanks," she answered softly, totally in awe of the process.

"Ok, let's get started." Darren pressed several buttons on the control board and soon the studio was filled with Travis's signature guitar. One by one, background instruments joined in: bass guitar, keyboard and drums. Then he started softly singing *"I was alone, lost and afraid…"*

Lucy couldn't breathe – it was the most beautiful ballad she had ever heard. The melodies faded and she looked at Darren, who was watching her reactions with wide eyes. Pulling himself together, he cleared his throat and said, "Wow, lovely. Let's listen again, and then switch to the solo track."

Lucy followed along with the lyrics on her phone and found herself instinctively harmonizing. Then it was time for the second version, and Lucy took notes when Travis was singing melody or harmony, which was when she would need to sing the lead. Travis was very generous and had given her lots of places to shine.

After about an hour, Darren wanted to see how she sounded, so Lucy went into the booth and Darren played the solo track. Lucy closed her eyes and sang the haunting words *"Never have I felt so loved, so wanted. Never had anyone like you to care…"* Once the music stopped, she opened her eyes to look at Darren to see if he approved, and was shocked to see Travis standing behind him, tears glistening in his eyes. She smiled at him, took off the headphones, and left the booth.

"I hope you don't mind me stopping by, but I really wanted to meet you. After the video Jeremy sent to me Saturday night, I knew you would be perfect for this song. Here, please sit next to me and let's chat a bit."

Lucy was stunned, unable to say much at all. She sat with him on a small sofa in the corner of the studio, finding it hard to breathe or swallow.

"You OK?" he asked softly. "Need anything? Water?"

"No, no, I'm fine," she stuttered. "I just had no idea you were coming today, at least not so soon. I hope I didn't butcher your song too badly."

"No, actually it was beautiful. There are just a few little things we can work on, but overall, it was just as I imagined."

"I'm so glad. This is all so new to me."

"You would never guess that, and you have such a soulful voice, so full of love and longing. It's very compelling."

Lucy blushed a bit and had no idea what to say. She just stared at her trembling hands in her lap.

"Why do I get the feeling that we've met before?" he asked. "Something about you is really familiar."

"We did, sort of. I was at The Stage Friday night, and we said hello during your break."

"I remember now! You were way in the back and left right away. You look very different from what you did on the show."

"I'm sure I sounded like a blabbering fool. It's just that I am such a big fan – I have all your CD's."

"I appreciate that. And now we'll be on one together. Darren, I hate to monopolize your time, but do you think we could go through it once together? Then I'll leave you to work your magic."

"No problem," Darren said as he cued up the solo track again.

"Actually, there's one more file with just the instruments that I would like to try. Ready, Lucy?"

She shook her head 'yes' and tried to swallow one more time, but her throat was just too dry.

Soon Travis was singing the first verse, and she came in on the chorus, naturally harmonizing in a way that seemed to startle them both. Their voices blended perfectly, and she followed his lead on phrasing and when to breathe.

The second verse was her solo verse, and once again she had to close her eyes to focus. Here she was, just inches away from Travis Jones, singing a love song with him!

When they reached the chorus again, she opened her eyes to see him looking intently at her, nodding his approval.

They finished the song together and the last notes seemed to hang in the air.

"That really was stunning," Darren said. "I swear your voices were just meant to sing together."

"I hate to rush off, "Travis said as he stood. Holding out his hand to Lucy, he helped her stand as well. "I know you guys have lots to do and this duet threw a kink into your schedule. Lucy, you are amazing. Thanks for doing this with me." He gave her hand a friendly squeeze and smiled, his blue eyes lingering on her face.

"No, truly, thank you for the opportunity. I'll do my best to make you proud."

"You already have. See y'all soon." And with that, Travis walked out the door.

"What just happened?" Lucy asked in a daze. "Did I just sing a duet with Travis Jones?"

"You sure did, and it was beautiful. Why don't we take about a 15-minute break and then see if we can't knock this out before lunch?"

Lucy left the studio and went around the corner to the ladies' room. Her cheeks were flushed when she glanced at the mirror, but she also noticed how cute she looked in one of the new outfits she bought last night.

Returning to the studio, she found Darren deep in conversation with Josh.

"You had quite a morning I hear!" Josh said once he noticed she was in the room. "Darren says it was great and just needs a little fine tuning. After you finish, can you come up to my office? I just got some more paperwork for you to sign."

"Sure, hopefully I won't mess this up too much."

Josh left, and Darren turned to Lucy. "I know this is all very new to you, but you have no idea how amazing you are, how eagerly you take instruction and how intuitive you are musically. Please don't sell yourself short. Travis Jones is lucky to have you."

They finished recording around eleven and Darren sent the files to Jeremy for review. Lucy went upstairs to Josh's office and knocked timidly on the door.

"Come on in – how did it go? You got done pretty fast."

"We fixed it in four tries, I think. It really is a beautiful song but not that hard to sing musically."

"I can't wait to hear the final version. In fact, the duet is what I needed to talk to you about. Your original contract states that we are keeping 100% of royalties for this first year but are paying you a salary. However, this only applies to any material we produce or originate. The duet with Travis falls under a different set of rules, ones we never really considered before yesterday. Travis and his manager are insistent that all royalties from the new album including physical sales and online streaming be divided 50/50 between him and the artists involved. I've been talking to our corporate lawyers all morning, and they have drawn up an addendum to your contract. Basically, it says what I just described, but feel free to take a minute and read it over."

Lucy read over the two-page document and signed it at the bottom.

"Just to be clear, this doesn't change our original agreement between you and Star Records; it just allows you to collect royalties from Travis for this project. I'm sure they will be in touch with you when that time comes."

"Thanks for explaining. This all happened so fast, I hadn't even thought about it."

Lucy went back down to the studio where she ran into Blake who was just heading out to lunch.

"Come grab a bite to eat with me. I hear you had quite a morning!"

"It was unbelievable, but I don't want to be gone too long. This put me way behind with Darren."

"Oh, I wouldn't worry. Everyone is still reeling from your duet. I listened to your track, by the way. You really have an amazing voice and to record a song you just got this morning – unreal!"

They grabbed a sandwich from a shop around corner and Lacy rushed back to the studio. Determined to put Travis and the duet out of her mind to focus on her own album, Lucy was all business the rest of the day, and the rest of the week.

About three on Friday afternoon, Darren leaned back in his chair and said, "Lucy – it's a wrap! We have lots of post-production stuff to do, but you, my friend, have just recorded your first album! I know Josh is on his way down to talk to you and discuss what comes next, but congrats!"

Lucy looked at him in amazement: her first album was done, less than a month after winning *Rising Star*. She couldn't wait to tell Sonya and her parents.

Josh arrived to escort her to a conference room to meet with a stylist and photographer. There were also people from marketing and concert promotions.

"Well, first off," Josh said as he started the meeting, "let's have a big round of applause for Lucy completing her first album in record time, plus slipping in a duet with Travis Jones!"

After the clapping died down, Josh continued, "Now, on to the next stop – album cover and promotions. Nathan, what are your thoughts?"

"Hi, Lucy, I know we haven't met yet. I'm Nathan Roberts, in-house arts and graphic designer. We plan to use your song '*If Only*' as the title. I was thinking about cover design. I've listened to your tracks for most of the album and I love it. I was thinking something fresh and new, the 'excitement to be in Nashville' type of vibe. Of course, we couldn't use any identifiable places without permission. Toby, what do you think?"

"Maybe looking out at the skyline at night? Or outside the city, looking in? I know of a few locations that have the look you want. Oh, sorry Lucy. I'm Toby Watkins, and I'll be your photographer."

Lucy smiled and wondered if it was appropriate for her to have an opinion. Best leave it to the professionals, she figured.

"Great Toby," Josh said. "Once you have a few locations, I want Lucy to work with Elizabeth our stylist to pick something appropriate. Lucy, do you have any questions?"

"Not a question, but a request. I realize that I don't know anything about the music business as a business, but the outfits I had to wear on the TV show were very uncomfortable – not just physically but emotionally as well. Whatever we choose, I really need it to not be too tight or too revealing. That's not who I am as a person. I take my Christian values seriously and I hope everyone can respect my feeling on this."

The room fell silent, and a few people looked nervously around. After a pause, Elizabeth spoke up first.

"Lucy, of course we will work with you. The things we choose will likely be more colorful or flashy than you are used to, but you are a beautiful girl with gorgeous eyes and amazing hair. There are ways to accentuate your features without sacrificing your standards. Actually, it is refreshing to see a young person wanting to be different. Toby?"

"We are not going to ask you to do anything you aren't comfortable with, don't worry. We all want what's best for you while still attracting an audience. There's lots of ways to do that."

Josh motioned to a young man who was sitting off to one side and who had not said anything yet.

"Lucy, this is Michael Brown, and he has started arranging venues for you to perform and other promo appearances. Michael?"

A young man in his early 30's rose to his feet and moved to a laptop that was set up to project onto a large screen on the wall.

"Hi Lucy, good to meet you. As you can all see from the schedule here on the first slide, we have several local TV appearances lined up starting in a few weeks. The next slide lists gigs that are in the planning stages but not finalized."

Lucy looked in awe at all the dates and locations listed. Josh leaned over to her and whispered, "Don't worry, I'll get a printout for you, and we'll set everything up in the calendar I want you to install on your phone."

Michael continued, "This last slide shows some of the goals Josh and I discussed, but I wanted to get everyone's feedback on them."

The meeting continued for another hour before everyone was satisfied with the schedule.

"So, Lucy, it looks like the next thing on your agenda is to work with Elizabeth next week while Toby scouts out a few locations. You have worked non-stop since you got to town – how about a few days off? Let's all meet back here next Thursday afternoon, OK? One more thing - are you on social media?"

"No, not really," Lucy answered. "I wasn't sure what was best but kept forgetting to ask."

"Well, we have been keeping you busy. Don't post anything this next week and I'll invite Vicki Jo to our next meeting. She's our social media guru and will walk you through everything. Any idea what to do with your time off?"

"Wow, this is really sudden, but I think I should go to Florida for a few days to see my mom. She's in a cancer center and not doing well."

"Of course you should," Josh stated with concern in his voice. "We had no idea."

"I agree," Elizabeth agreed. "This just might be your last time to fly without being recognized! Or has anyone already noticed you?"

"I'm not sure. A few people have looked at me a little strangely at the grocery store, but I look very different now from how I did on the show, so no one has approached me."

The meeting broke up and Lucy walked slowly to her car. Five whole days off – she hadn't had that much free time since before the TV show. She thought about asking Sonya to come down, but suddenly felt very tired and a bit selfish. She would email her parents the good news about the album and the duet with Travis but tell them that she really needed some down time before everything got crazy with media and touring and photo shoots and….was this really her life now? She hoped her mom and dad would understand.

Chapter 7

At nine on Wednesday night, Lucy was stretched out on her sofa, a fire in the fireplace and soft music playing in the background. She had enjoyed her five days off; sleeping a lot, cleaning the condo, shopping, but mostly sleeping. She called her parents a few times and they were happy she had time to rest. Finishing her glass of wine, she stood up and stretched, feeling more relaxed than she had in months. But tomorrow was it! There were fittings with Elizabeth and other meetings about upcoming appearances. Josh had uploaded all her appointments into her calendar, which was quickly becoming very full. She was just about to head into her bedroom when her cell phone rang.

"Hope I'm not too late," Sonya said. "Enjoying the last of your vacation?"

"It's been great. I guess I didn't realize just how tired I really was."

"So, it all starts tomorrow, right? I saw a little blurb on one of the Nashville Facebook pages that hinted about some big news coming up – anything you can tell me?"

"Nope, I'm sworn to secrecy. But you will be pleased. How are things going with you? How many animals did you save this weekend?"

"Well, that's what I wanted to talk to you about. The shelter let me go today – there just wasn't enough funding to keep all of us, and since I was just part-time, I was the one they let go."

"Oh, no! What are you going to do?"

"Obviously I have a lot of free time now. Do you want to have company for a while until I figure something out?"

"Of course! This place really is too big for one person – come and stay as long as you want!"

"I promise I'll make myself useful – I'll cook your breakfast or run errands for you."

"I'm not expecting you to work! I just love your company, and I've missed you so much."

They talked a few minutes more and then Lucy said goodnight. Crawling into her comfy bed, she thought that Sonya had the right idea – wouldn't it be great to have her here all the time? She couldn't wait to get Josh's opinion tomorrow.

Chapter 8

Lucy stood in front of the dressing room mirror, shocked by the piles of clothes that Elizabeth had picked out for her to try on. And much to her relief, except for just a few things, the outfits were modest yet still trendy. Toby had scouted out a location that was rustic but urban, and many of the outfits reflected that relaxed feel.

"How does that last one look?" Elizabeth asked from the waiting area. "I confess, it's one of my favorites."

Lucy stepped out of the changing room with a big smile on her face. "I love this one, too."

Elizabeth's skilled eyes roamed up from Lucy's well-worn boots and snug jeans to a black and white pinstriped dress shirt that hugged her curves, but not too tightly. The shirt was mostly unbuttoned, and she had a black tank top underneath. The outfit was completed by a gorgeous white leather jacket she held in her hands.

"I wasn't sure if I should put this on?"

"Wow, you look perfect. Maybe you can have the jacket over one shoulder or sitting beside you . We'll use it however Toby wants. I say we want this outfit for sure and we can take along another top or two and that cute denim skirt. Now let's look at jewelry."

They opened Elizabeth's large jewelry case and selected several long dangly earrings and a few necklaces. She snapped a picture of Lucy in the outfit to send to Josh and Toby.

Once back in her own clothes, Lucy made her way to the conference room to discuss the schedule. Toby was already there, along with a 30-something girl Lucy guessed was the social media expert Vicki Jo. Michael came in right behind her and announced, "Josh will be a little late, but said we are to start without him."

He moved to the podium and plugged in his laptop. Once again, concert dates, media appearances and other commitments filled the calendar for the next few months. Lucy's eyes were wide with amazement as she scanned the calendar looking for more than three consecutive days off.

Michael stopped to look at his cell phone that was vibrating on the desk. "OK, everyone, Josh wanted me to tell you that his surprise is ready."

He made a few clicks on his laptop and soon Lucy's wistful voice filled the room. "*If only……*"

She looked nervously around the room but saw everyone smiling and nodding. Darren's updated arrangement and the addition of background vocals made such a difference!

Once the song was over, the room erupted into thunderous applause. Darren and Josh had arrived and were smiling widely. "That's a Top Ten hit if I ever heard one!" Josh said proudly.

"With some proper exposure and media attention, this has potential to be Number One!"

"Lucy, the first thing for us to focus on is finishing your album cover so we can promote it during your first event in about ten days. Toby and Nathan, can you get that done?"

"We plan to shoot tomorrow. Is that enough time for you Nathan?"

"I think so. I've been playing around with cover design and layout already, so it can be tweaked and finished once we get the photos."

"Great. Michael, please show that photo I sent to you."

Michael clicked his computer, and the calendar of appearances was replaced by the picture Elizabeth took of Lucy in the dressing room.

"Wow, Lucy," Darren said. "Even in a dressing room you look great! Fresh and young, with a vulnerability but also strength. Elizabeth, I love it."

"We do, too. Lucy. Please meet me here tomorrow at eight and I'll do your hair and makeup. We'll meet you at the shoot at ten, Toby?" Elizabeth asked.

"Sounds great. Anything else, Josh?"

"Not for you guys. I do want Vicki Jo to stay and meet with Lucy, but the rest of you are free to go."

After the group left, Vicki Jo moved to a chair next to Lucy. Josh made the formal introductions.

"Lucy, this is Vicki Jo Campbell, and she oversees the social media for all our newer artists. Since we have some big announcements coming up, I wanted her to meet with you."

"Thanks, Josh. Lucy, I'm thrilled to be working with you and want to go over a few things with you. Are you on social media now? I didn't really find much when I searched for you."

"No, I never was very big into it, and especially not since the TV show."

"Good. For now, all official posts to your fan page will come from me. They will be mostly informational and will stay away from things that are too personal or controversial. I suggest you wait to set up a personal account. We certainly don't want any weirdos getting too much information or finding out where you live."

"Um, that's scary."

"It sure is. That's why I need you to let me handle things for a while. You have enough to adjust to for now. Anything else, Josh?"

"No, not really. I just want you to focus on your music, Lucy, and let us handle the rest."

"I'm fine with that, as long as it continues to reinforce my conservative, religious beliefs and values. I would rather give this all up if I can't stay true to who I am."

"No one is asking you to, and honestly, that's a big part of your appeal. The country scene is overflowing with cookie-cutter girls in short skirts with average voices. You are a breath of fresh air, and your character and values just radiate through you. No one here wants to change that."

"OK, since that's settled," Josh continued, "Vicki Jo, you know what to do. Start writing some initial copy with teasers about upcoming events. Toby will get pics for you right away. Lucy, we also want to shoot a few intro videos to drive up the suspense a bit. We might as well do them during your photo shoot tomorrow. Are you ready for this?"

"I hope so! Josh, I do have one question. You remember my best friend, Sonya? I was wondering if it would be OK if I asked her to move in with me for a while. The condo is great but kind of big for just me. I've been a bit homesick, and she called last night to tell me she lost her job. Plus, she could stay there and keep watch on things when I'm on the road."

"Sounds alright with me. Whatever makes you feel more secure and at ease is fine. OK, I think we are done for today. We'll see you back in the morning for the shoot. Thanks, Vicki Jo." And with that, Josh left the conference room. Vicki Jo reached over and patted Lucy's hand.

"I know it's all very overwhelming. Like Josh said, just focus on the music and let us handle all the rest."

"Thanks for everything," Lucy said as she picked up her purse and walked toward the exit. She paused in front of the wall of signed photos from many of her favorite artists.

"You'll be there soon enough," Vicki Jo said softly. "Mark my word."

Chapter 9

Lucy glanced at her reflection in the mirror as Elizabeth drove them to an industrial district for the shoot. It was a warm sunny morning, and her hair and makeup looked amazing, but she worried about how fresh she would look after being outside in the heat. They stopped in front of an abandoned warehouse and found Toby and Josh already setting up equipment and adjusting the lights.

"Wow, Lucy, you look great," Toby said. "I know it's hard, but I need you to look as relaxed and comfortable as possible. You brought your guitar?"

"Yes, it's in the back. Are you sure this outfit is OK? My makeup isn't too much?"

"Nope, it's perfect. Elizabeth is a pro at this. I know you brought other outfits, but this one is perfect for what I'm wanting. I've got the first shot set up for you already. Let's start with you leaning against this door frame."

Toby guided her through numerous positions and angle changes. Eventually, she started to loosen up a bit and have a little fun. They moved around the corner of the building to an area with more shade and a slight breeze. She felt beads of sweat start pooling on the back of her neck, and they had to stop a few times for Elizabeth to freshen her makeup. Eventually they moved inside and took a dozen or so more shots of her beside broken windows or walls with peeling paint.

"I've got one last idea," Toby said. " What if we have you just walking alone down this empty street – head held high – walking boldly toward your new future?"

"I like it," Josh said. "Just you and your guitar heading off toward the unknown."

Lucy spent the next several minutes walking up and down the street, a few times looking directly at the camera, but mostly looking off to the horizon, a wistful look on her face.

"I love it!" Toby said. "I think I have more than enough for the album and promo shots. Now for a little video. Lucy, sit here on this broken wall and let's just talk a bit."

Elizabeth touched up her makeup one last time and then Josh started interviewing her. She was comfortable with him, so her answers were casual and did not appear forced.

"Perfect," Josh said once they had about fifteen minutes of video.

"You can head back to the office, and I'll meet you there in a while. I have a stop to make first at Radio Nashville to talk about your interview next week. Great job everyone. Lucy, I need to prep you for your first radio appearance."

Lucy climbed back into Elizabeth's car and leaned back to close her eyes. "You really did great for your first-ever photo shoot. I'm starving, what about you? We're close to the Bluebird Diner. Have you ever been there?"

"No, I haven't," Lucy said. "But yes, I'm suddenly very hungry."

"OK! Let me text Josh and then we can go and enjoy a fabulous celebration lunch."

During the short drive to the café, Elizabeth explained what would happen over the next couple of weeks.

"We will have lots of meetings to finalize the album cover and other promotional items. You have several radio interviews lined up, and there will be rehearsals with your band. We will continue to fine-tune your wardrobe, and I'll keep searching for things that I think you will like. We need to get a nice selection set aside for you for when you start appearing on TV. I know Josh and Michael will be talking to you about merchandise. Do you have any ideas besides posters and T-shirts?"

"Wow, I haven't even thought about it. I know I love to collect keychains and coffee mugs. I'm not sure otherwise. Maybe a miniature guitar as a pin? Or guitar picks?"

"Good ideas. We will need to get started right away so we have some things available when the album is ready." Elizabeth asked her about her childhood and growing up in Missouri while they enjoyed a nice lunch in the busy café, and then they headed back to the office.

As they were pulling into the parking lot, Josh texted her to stop at the reception desk once they returned to the building. Curious, she went up front and found a huge bouquet of two dozen yellow and white roses and a box of chocolate-covered strawberries. The note tucked in the flowers said "Thanks again for making our duet so special. You truly are a star. Travis."

She carried the gifts into the closest conference room and shut the door. This was all moving so fast. Was this really happening to such a small-town girl? Roses and a gift from Travis Jones? A new album and a photo shoot? Her own merchandise?

She sat in the dark for several minutes until there was a soft knock on the door. Vicki Jo poked her head in and said, "Are you OK? What happened?"

Lucy showed her the flowers and the note. "It's all just a bit overwhelming," she said sadly.

"I'm sure it is. Do you want me to talk to Josh and see if you can go home early?"

"No, I'll be fine, I just needed a minute. We have lots of important things to do this afternoon."

Just then Lucy's cell phone beeped to alert her to a text message. It was a number she did not recognize, and she decided not to respond. She knew she needed to focus on her music and not let any distractions get in the way.

Chapter 10

The next week flew by in a whirl with rehearsals, wardrobe fittings, and then a meeting to discuss merchandise. Lucy suggested an enamel pin that was a replica of her guitar, and everyone loved the idea. They even agreed to incorporate it into her personal logo. Vicki Jo premiered Lucy's fan page, which had one of the photos from the shoot. Lucy stared at it in amazement – Toby was a photographic genius! It was then that Darren walked into the room with a huge grin on his face. In his hands was a record album-sized copy of her CD. The cover picture was one of Lucy walking down the street toward her new future, her guitar slung over her back. The inside liner notes contained more pictures and a place for her dedication. The back cover had the same picture as her fan page.

"Toby, Nathan – you guys did great with such a short turn-around time!" Josh said excitedly. "Lucy, what do you think?"

"It's amazing. I just don't know what to say. It's more than I ever imagined."

"Well, I love it!" Michael said. "If we all agree, I'll take the cover shot and plug it into the promo posters and on our studio website. Which ones do we want at the merch table? The cover for sure, but I think we need at least one more."

"Maybe one that's not on the CD?" Lucy asked. "As a fan, I would like to think I was getting something special."

"Great idea!" Josh said. They spent several minutes admiring the extra shots that Toby had taken, including one Lucy didn't realize he had done. It was while she was waiting for a shot to be set up and she was just casually leaning against a wall, not looking at anyone or anything in particular. She was totally relaxed and at ease.

"How about this one?" Josh asked as he pulled the picture from near the bottom of the stack. "Toby, what would this look like in black and white?"

"Well, let's see." He went to Michael's laptop and brought up the pictures on the large screen. He did a few manipulations and soon there she was, larger than life, in one of the most artistic pictures she had ever seen.

"Wow," Vicki Jo whispered. "That's the one!"

"I can soften the edges a little if you want, but I think it's pretty perfect the way it is."

"I would buy it," Michael said. "This is gonna be a huge seller – even poster-worthy if we wanted to do posters."

Josh chimed in, "OK, Nathan, get as much done as you can before Lucy's upcoming radio interview. Vicki Jo, start dropping those social media teasers we have ready and promote the interview. Toby, I want you there to snap a few pictures of the interview. Everyone ready? This project is about to launch!"

Lucy's head was spinning – this was really happening!'

Later, she arrived home to find Sonya's car parked in the shade a few doors down from the condo. "I can't believe you are finally here!" she squealed. "This is going to be so much fun!"

The two of them carried Sonya's suitcases and boxes inside and piled them in the living room.

"This is about one half of my stuff, and I left the rest with my parents. I can go back later and get it, but I wanted to wait to see if I really needed anything."

"How about we just order a pizza and then unpack later?" Lucy asked. "I have SO MUCH to tell you!"

An hour later, they were relaxing on the patio, a Two Boots supreme pizza between them along with a bottle of Sonya's favorite red wine.

"Here's to the start of our grand adventure together! This place has been so big and empty, but now it's perfect!"

"I'll start looking for a job right away, I promise," Sonya stated. "But as much as I loved my job at the rescue, I'm open to trying something different."

"Well, there's tons of jobs here, especially in the music industry. Have you thought about that at all? Maybe a receptionist or administrative assistant at a studio? You always were great with people – much better than I am!"

"We'll see. I do want to be as much help to you as I can for my best friend the Super Star!"

They talked and laughed well into the night, with Lucy finally looking at the clock and realizing how late it was. "Oh, crap – I need to be at the studio at nine to go over some tour details and talk about the radio interview. Want to come with me?"

"Would that be OK? I'll drive my own car so I can leave if you need me to. Plus, I've got errands to run."

"Sure, that would be great. We can ask Josh if he has any job leads for you."

At nine the next morning, after a light breakfast fixed by Sonya, the two drove their separate cars to the studio. Lucy parked in the employee lot in the back and Sonya luckily found a spot only a block away. Lucy introduced her to Lois who was manning the front desk. She looked back and forth between the two ladies. "You two really aren't sisters? The resemblance is uncanny."

After a quick tour, they made their way to the conference room where most everyone was waiting. Michael was busy at his laptop and the first two weeks of appearances loomed on the screen. Sonya's eyes grew wide with amazement as she studied her friend's schedule.

"How will you keep track of all of this?" she whispered to Lucy.

"I have no idea!" she whispered back.

"Well, we do," Josh said slyly as he came up behind them. "Good to see you again Sonya."

"Hello again Josh. Thanks for letting me hang out a bit. I promise not to get in the way."

"No problem. I'll do anything to keep our star happy."

"OK, everyone," Josh continued as he walked to the front of the room. "Our main focus today is the radio interview tomorrow at KRLQ. While not the biggest station here in town, we have a good relationship with their morning DJs, and it will be good practice for Lucy. Elizabeth, I need you to go over the wardrobe with her because I'm sending Toby along for pictures. Vicki Jo, how's the website look?

"Everything is ready and waiting for you to pull the trigger. Michael?"

Michael made a few clicks and Lucy's updated web page appeared. Scrolling through the pages, they saw a photo of the album along with pictures from the photo shoot. There was even a short audio clip of the title track and a countdown clock to when the album would be released.

Sonya's eyes were open wide as she leaned over to Lucy.

"So, THIS is your big news - amazing! And all done so quickly. You look gorgeous by the way!"

"Thanks. It's all pretty surreal."

"And here are the social media links," Vicki Jo continued. "I'll make all the official posts for you Lucy. You are free to read the comments, of course, but I want to warn you here. Many of your fans will LOVE you, but there will always be a few haters and even a crazy one here and there. I will delete anything inappropriate and will block the sender, hopefully before you even see them. I know the tendency is to take these things personally, but you just can't. Josh, are we ready to go?"

"I believe so. Anyone else have comments? Lucy?"

"It looks really great I can't tell you how much I appreciate everyone's hard work on this, on everything."

"You just keep making that beautiful music and we'll do the rest. OK, Vicki Jo, launch it!"

Vicki Jo went to Michael's laptop, entered a password and activated the website and then the social media accounts.

"I'm going to go ahead and 'follow' a few entertainers and groups, and a few places like the Opry and The Stage. Everyone here will 'follow' your account in the next day or two. My first post will be about the radio interview tomorrow. The trick is to find the balance between too little content and digital overload that will make you look desperate."

"OK, everything looks good so far," she continued. "I'm heading back to my office to monitor things. Lucy, if you ever have any questions, don't hesitate to call me."

"Elizabeth, I'll send Lucy down to you in a bit." Josh said as everyone started to leave. "I just need one more minute with her."

"I'll start laying a few things out. See 'ya in a bit."

"Ok, now that they are gone," Josh said seriously, "I wanted to talk to you about tomorrow. Here is a list of questions the DJ is likely to ask you. I want you to go over these and practice your answers – not so they sound memorized or too rehearsed, but comfortable, you know? Of course, they might spring something else on you, but these are the most common."

"Thanks, I'll look these over today."

"I have a meeting tomorrow that I can't get out of," he continued, "but Toby will be with you. Sonya, are you available to go along as moral support?"

"Sure, I'm happy to go. I'll start my job search a little later in the day."

"I can make some calls for you if you want," Josh stated. "Why don't you leave me your resume and I'll see what I can do."

"Thanks, I really appreciate that."

After meeting with Elizabeth and picking out a pretty blouse for the next day, Lucy confirmed the address of the radio station and then she and Sonya left to have lunch. They stopped at a nearby chicken restaurant and chatted for quite a while. Afterward, Lucy headed home while Sonya went job hunting.

Lucy spent her afternoon reviewing the questions from Josh, then decided to fix a nice dinner for Sonya including chicken fried steak, mashed potatoes and sweet corn.

Sonya got home around six, hot and exhausted but with no real job leads. They enjoyed a nice evening, but Sonya wanted to go to bed early. Lucy cleaned the kitchen and went to take a hot bath. Just as she was about to undress, her phone *pinged* with a text from an unknown number. Annoyed with the frequency of these random texts, she ignored it, but then sensed a movement outside her bedroom window. "Probably just the wind," she thought, "or maybe a raccoon?"

She made sure all the doors were locked and the curtains completely closed, but she still felt unsettled.

Chapter 11

Lucy tried to sound at ease and calm during her radio interview the next morning, but her nerves were on edge. She had slept poorly last night, constantly feeling like she was being watched.

Eventually, though, she relaxed a bit, and her answers came more naturally. Near the end of the interview the DJ told her he had a surprise for her. On the phone to say hello was Travis Jones! He mentioned their duet that would be included on his upcoming CD, and was hoping they could get together soon to perform it. Lucy was surprised at the time and attention he was investing into her.

After the interview, Toby and Lucy went to the studio and Sonya left for a job interview at a small record label on the west side of town. Josh caught Lucy in the hallway to tell her the radio response had lit up the phone and she had been invited back to The Stage that night. They planned to have dinner at Jeff Ruby's before heading over. Lucy was able to reach Sonya just as she was going into her interview. She said she needed to stop by the condo when she was done but would meet them at The Stage later.

The evening was dark and stormy, and the air was filled with uneasiness. Sonya pulled her car into Lucy's spot and jogged up the front steps. Just as she turned the key in the lock, she felt a person behind her who whispered, "Hello again, Lucy!" and he shoved her into the condo.

"There's been a mistake!" Sonya cried nervously to a tall man whose features were mostly hidden by a hooded sweatshirt. She could not see much of his face as he had a beard and long hair. "I don't know who you are. I'm not Lucy!"

"Oh, I know exactly who you are, you ungrateful witch!" he growled at her. "How dare you ignore me, and all the nice things I have done for you. Why don't you respond to my texts or answer my calls?" He grabbed her arm menacingly and forced her into the living room.

"Let go of me! What texts? I don't know what you are talking about!" Sonya yelled as she struggled to get free. Reaching up to scratch his face, she inadvertently pulled the hood of his sweatshirt away. Standing before her was none other than Lucy's idol, Travis Jones!

"Travis Jones? What are you doing here? Why are you talking this way?"

"I don't appreciate being ignored," he repeated. "Don't you realize what I can do for your career? You need to learn how the game is played here in Nashville, and you especially need to learn to be nicer to the people who try to help you."

"Please, there is a misunderstanding," Sonya begged as she tried to find a light switch. "I'm not Lucy – I'm her friend Sonya!"

"Don't play games with me. You need to be more polite to your benefactor!" He grabbed her arms again and pulled her into a sudden kiss. Sonya struggled against him, but he was deceptively strong. She did manage to get one good kick in his shin, but that only served to anger him further. Slapping her firmly across the cheek with the back of his hand, he laughed as she fell onto the floor, hitting the coffee table with her shoulder on the way down and breaking a vase. Dazed, she lay there while he towered over her, hurling obscenities at her and kicking her in the ribs and face with his steel-toed boots. Kneeling beside her, he ripped open her shirt and started to kiss her bleeding lips, his hands groping her while his body pressed against hers. Sonya closed her eyes in fear.

"It wouldn't have to be this way if you had just been nicer to me," he whispered menacingly as he continued to tear off her clothes.

Just then the lightning flashed, and Travis got a good look at Sonya's bruised and bleeding face. Recognition dawned in his eyes, and he realized the girl he had just beaten and almost raped was NOT Lucy, but someone who could almost be her twin.

"What have I done? You really aren't Lucy!" he groaned as he stood up and ran toward the door, pulling his hood back over his head. He gave one last glance back toward Sonya's half-naked body and then disappeared into the storm.

Unsure how long she had laid there, Sonya finally crawled across the room to her purse, which Travis had flung into the corner. Shaking badly, she had difficulty dialing Lucy's number.

"Hey girlfriend – where are you?" Lucy answered excitedly. "I'm about ready to go on."

"I'm so sorry – I should have been more careful……" came a whisper on the other end.

"What are you talking about? I can barely hear you."

"Please come home – he hurt me……."

"What? Who hurt you? OK, I'm calling the police and I'll be home as soon as I can!"

Lucy whispered to Josh to tell him what had happened, who then relayed the message to Joey. Darren called the police as they all ran towards their cars.

The rain was coming down in sheets and driving was almost impossible, but they were relieved to see police cars and an ambulance in front of the condo when they finally arrived. Lucy dashed up the steps and in the door to find her best friend lying on a stretcher and being tended to by EMT's. An officer was taking Sonya's statement, but her face was so swollen that it was hard to talk.

"Oh, Honey – what happened? Who did this to you?" Sonya tried to answer but winced in pain.

An officer stopped her and asked for ID. Shaking, she told him who she was and that Sonya was her best friend who was living with her.

"I really need to get her to the hospital," the EMT said. "I think her jaw is broken, along with a few ribs. She's having a bit of trouble breathing, so I'm worried about a collapsed lung as well."

"I'll let you all go to the hospital now, but will want to talk to you later," the officer stated as they prepared Sonya for transport.

Lucy followed the stretcher out to the ambulance but was not allowed inside. Darren offered to drive her to the hospital and Toby followed. Driving was difficult in the pouring rain. Josh said he needed to go home but would stay in contact with them and wished Sonya well. When they arrived at the Emergency Room, Sonya was already in an exam room. Eventually a nurse came out and told Lucy she could go in and see her. Darren and Toby remained in the waiting area.

"Only stay a few minutes," the nurse cautioned. "She's in pretty rough shape and needs to rest."

Lucy pulled back the curtain of Sonya's exam room and was shocked to see her best friend covered in bruises and her lips swollen. A tear slid down her cheek as she reached for Sonya's hand.

Sonya winced as she tried to smile. The pain in her jaw was excruciating and it was difficult for her to talk. The officer who was at her bedside said he would step outside to give them privacy.

"Oh, Honey, I'm so sorry. Do you know who did this to you? Did you tell the police?"

"No, I didn't tell," Sonya whispered. "I was so scared."

"I'm sure you were, and still are, but why didn't you tell the police who it was? Did you know him?"

"Not at first, it was dark and stormy, and he had on a hooded sweatshirt. But then I saw him. It was… it was… Oh, Lucy, it was Travis!"

"Travis? Travis Jones did this to you? Why would he do that?"

"Because he thought I was you!"

Lucy fell back into her chair as the reality of Sonya's words washed over her. Sonya was beaten and assaulted because she looked like her? Her supposed friend and idol Travis did this – thinking he was doing it to HER? This unbelievable situation was more than she could stand.

Lucy began shaking and sobbing as she held her friend's hand. "I'm so sorry, I'm so sorry," is all she could say, over and over.

"I didn't tell the police yet," Sonya whispered again, the pain was getting worse with each word. "I needed to let you know first that Travis was stalking you. What are you going to do?"

"Well, I need to get ahold of Josh and have him here when you talk to the police again. Oh, the media is going to have a field day with this! I just don't understand – did Travis give you a reason? Was he mad at me or something?"

"Just something about you being nicer to people who help you, that you need to understand how the game is played here."

Just then a nurse returned to the room and said Lucy would need to go back to the waiting area while they took Sonya for some tests. Lucy gently squeezed Sonya's hand and then made her way to Darren and Toby.

Before she could tell them about her conversation with Sonya and to ask for advice, Darren stopped her and showed her his phone. "This just showed up online. A few minutes ago, a car was pulled from the Cumberland River. They think maybe it ran off the road due to the storm. Anyway, they just ID'd the driver – Lucy, I'm sorry, but the driver was Travis Jones!"

Chapter 12

Lucy sat in the waiting area, totally stunned. The man who had just beat her best friend and attempted to rape her while believing he was doing that to HER was just dragged from the river, dead. How was she going to deal with this? She knew she needed to talk to Sonya again before speaking to Josh or Darren or even the police. Travis was dead! Who was going to believe Sonya's story now? There was no proof that it was Travis who assaulted her. And the media circus would surely be harmful for her career since Travis was so well-loved in the music community and such accusations would be scandalous. Her head was spinning, trying to understand all that had happened in just the past few hours.

"I'm so sorry, Lucy," Darren said gently. "I know that he had taken a real interest in you, and the duet album would have been an amazing boost to your career. The news is reporting that they think he lost control of his car during the storm. The entire country music world is tweeting their condolences."

"A real tragedy," Lucy said softly. "But I just can't get my mind off Sonya. Darren, he, um, whoever the guy was, really hurt her. And was going to rape her. I just don't know how to handle this. I think I need some fresh air."

Lucy made her way through the double doors and stood under an awning to watch the rain and to breathe the clean air. She felt so responsible for what had happened to Sonya and was hugely disillusioned by the music industry right now. Was Travis correct? Was this the way the music business really worked? Did she need to show more 'appreciation' when someone did something nice for her? Was he behind the random texts she had been receiving? Maybe what she needed was just to pack up her things and head back home.

Shortly after returning to the waiting area, Sonya's nurse called Lucy into a conference room. "We are going to take her upstairs and admit her. She has multiple fractured ribs and will likely need surgery for her broken jaw. Have you been able to reach her parents yet?"

"Her parents? No, not yet. But I will try again." Lucy remembered that she had been asked to contact Sonya's parents but had neglected to try once she heard the news about Travis. "Can I see her before she goes to her room?"

"Just for one quick minute. Then it's probably best if you go home and get some sleep. She's going to be here for several days."

Lucy walked slowly toward Sonya's examination room, worried about how she was going to tell her about Travis and fearing her reaction. She gently pulled the curtain to one side and glanced in toward her friend who seemed to be resting, finally.

"Hey, it's me," Lucy said softly. "I just wanted to stop by and tell you that I'm heading home while they get you upstairs and settled. Are you feeling any better?"

"Oh, hi," Sonya said groggily. "They gave me some medicine that is making me sleepy. At least I don't hurt as much."

"I'm glad. Get some rest and I'll come by tomorrow."

Lucy went back to the lobby, so thankful that Darren was still there. "Toby just left as he needed to get home to his wife and kids. I talked with Josh, and he said to take off as much time as you feel you need. But he does want to talk to you sometime tomorrow. Ready for me to take you home?"

"Yes, they are taking her to her room now. Darren, I hope you know how much I appreciate you being here with me tonight. It's been awful, all of it."

"Of course! This is more than any of us can bear alone."

"So much more," she said sadly.

Chapter 13

Lucy and Darren drove in silence back to the condo. The thunderstorm had passed, and the rain was just a light drizzle now. But thoughts and feelings were raging inside her, and she had no idea how they were going to get through the next few days.

"Do you want me to come in with you?" Darren asked gently once they pulled in front of the condo.

"Would you, please?"

"Of course. I'll stay as long as you need me to." He took the door keys from Lucy and slowly pushed open the door. Flipping on a light switch, they were overwhelmed by the violence that was evident in the rooms – broken glass, tipped over furniture, even some blood on the carpet. "You can't stay here tonight. Go pack a bag and I'll take you to the closest hotel. I'll have Josh get in touch with the cleaning service and have them come over first thing in the morning."

"OK," Lucy said numbly, almost frozen, as she stared at the places where her friend had fought for her life. As if in a trance, Lucy tossed a few things into a duffle bag and then Darren escorted her back to the car. He drove her to a nearby Marriott and helped her check in and find her room.

"Are you sure you will be OK here?" he asked. "I'm pretty worried about you."

"I think so. I just need to be alone for a while, to try to figure out what to do next."

"Next? You need some sleep and then let us handle as many details as possible for you. I suggest you turn off your phone. It's possible that some media folks will try to reach out to you for a statement."

"A statement? Why?"

"Because of your duet with Travis, and his obvious interest in you and your career."

Lucy cringed at the thought of having to make a public statement about Travis' tragic death. Darren had no idea how much 'interest' Travis really had.

Darren said goodnight and closed the hotel door behind him, and Lucy instantly jumped up to make sure it was double-locked. She thought back to last night – was it really just last night? – when she was getting ready to take a bath and felt like she was being watched. Was Travis already there then, peaking in at her, watching her? Was he behind the random texts? The thoughts made her nauseous and she dashed to the bathroom to put cold water on her face. She looked at herself in the mirror and hardly recognized her reflection. She certainly was not the same girl who had been at The Stage just a few hours earlier, ready to go on and sing a few songs for her new fans.

Once back in the bedroom, she glanced at the clock and saw that it was almost midnight. She felt it was too late to call

Sonya's parents, but knew she had to do it anyway. She dialed their number, and it rang multiple times before Mr. Vasquez groggily answered the phone.

"I'm sorry to call so late, Mr. V, but I needed to let you know that Sonya is in the hospital. They have decided to admit her – she has broken ribs and jaw, and there is maybe something wrong with one of her lungs."

"The hospital? What happened – a car accident?"

"No, I'm sorry, but she was attacked in our condo. I wasn't home when it happened, but she fought back, and he ran away. That's about all I can say right now."

Lucy gave him the address of the hospital and he said they would start out once the sun came up in a few hours. Lucy agreed that was probably best, since Sonya was finally resting after being given some strong pain medicines. Lucy apologized again to which Mr. Vasquez replied, "It's not your fault Lucy. We'll see you soon."

Lucy hung up the phone and turned off the lights. She stared out the window toward the Nashville skyline, sparkling like jewels in the dark. "Oh, Mr. V, it's more my fault than you will ever know."

Somewhere past three she finally fell asleep and was able to rest a couple of hours before she was jolted awake by her phone. Instantly worried about Sonya, she grabbed it and hurriedly answered before seeing who was calling.

"Lucy? Lucy Armando? This is Shawn Delaney from *Inside Nashville*. I hope I'm not calling you too early, but I was wondering if you care to make a statement about the tragic death of Travis Jones. I understand you recently recorded a duet with him for his new album?"

"*Oh crap!*" Lucy thought. This is why Darren warned her to turn her phone off last night.

"Lucy?" Shawn asked. "Are you there?"

"Yes, sorry. I'm not sure what to say – the events of last night seem so unreal. Do they know for sure what happened?"

"No, not that I'm aware of, just that somehow his car went off the road and into the river. It was quite a storm."

"Yes, it was. I was out in it, too."

"I heard that you were supposed to sing at The Stage but had to cancel at the last minute?"

"Yes, just before I was to go on, I got a call that my best friend had been taken to the hospital."

"Oh, I'm sorry to hear that. Do you have a comment you want me to publish?"

"I guess just that I was shocked to hear the news, and that I enjoyed our time together working on the duet."

"That's all?"

"Oh, and that I had always admired his work and that I will never forget how he impacted me."

"Thanks. Do you have any scoop you can give me about your new album or touring?"

"No, sorry – but it will be soon I promise!"

After they hung up, Lucy sank back into her bed, replaying in her head what she had just told Shawn. All of it was true, as she had enjoyed their time together and she was shocked to hear about his passing. But mostly, she would never forget his impact on her life.

Chapter 14

Lucy took a long hot shower then went down to the hotel dining room for breakfast. Although she wasn't very hungry, she did manage to nibble on a bit of scrambled eggs and a slice of bacon, along with a small cup of yogurt and a few grapes. She had just gotten back to her room when Josh called.

"How are you doing? I still can't believe what happened last night. Are you OK?"

"I don't know… I guess. I did manage to sleep a little until a reporter called me for a statement. Darren had told me to turn off my phone, but I guess I forgot."

"Figures. I just wanted to let you know that I called in a favor at the maid service, and they are sending a crew over right away to get things cleaned up. They should be done in an hour or so. But I really need you to come in for a few minutes today."

"Thanks Josh. I want to stop by the hospital on my way home. What time were you needing me?"

"We have a few things to work on. Most can wait until tomorrow, but I do need to review the schedule again. Your team is working hard behind the scenes, and Vicki Jo is going to make an 'official' post for you on social media. You are free to make statements to the press, of course, but I would keep

78

them short and sweet. It's not like you had a close connection with him or anything."

Lucy winced at his words. It turned out there was more of a connection than anyone would have dreamed of. How had she not noticed?

After checking out of the hotel, she took an UBER home and picked up her car, not even going into the condo. She drove to the hospital and stopped in the gift shop for some flowers and the celebrity gossip magazine that was Sonya's favorite. She got directions to her room from the information desk and was soon walking down a long corridor on the orthopedic floor. Tapping lightly on the door, she took a deep breath and poked her head into the room.

"Hey, girl, ready for some company?" she asked with more enthusiasm than she felt.

Sonya was lying in the bed with her face toward the window. Turning slightly and in obvious pain, she tried to smile in Lucy's direction. Her face was even more bruised than it was last night, with her eyes almost swollen shut. She did manage to raise her hand a bit and motion Lucy to come closer.

Lucy put the flowers on a stand beside the bed and sat in the only chair in the room. She gently held Sonya's hand and tried not to let the shock of her friend's appearance show on her face.

After taking a few seconds to compose herself, she knew it was time to tell Sonya about Travis.

"Sonya, Honey, there is something I need to tell you. I wish I could wait a while, but before the police come back to interview you again, I need to tell you what else happened last night. Just before they admitted you to this room, I found out that Travis was in some sort of car accident and ended up in the Cumberland River. He didn't make it. Do you understand? Travis is gone and can never hurt you again."

"Gone? Dead?" Sonya managed to whisper. "Really gone, for good?"

"Yes, they confirmed it was him after pulling his car from the river. I hardly slept last night; I was so worried about you. But I think maybe it would be best if you didn't tell anyone that it was Travis who hurt you. I mean, there's no proof, right? And the media gossip would be horrible, dragging you through the mud. But it's your call, what do you want to do?"

Sonya thought for a minute, and Lucy could see she was wrestling to find the best decision. Finally, she said with difficulty, "I think it would do harm to BOTH of us if I said it was Travis. He's gone, and already in hell paying for what he did. What good would further investigation do?"

"I'm so very sorry you got caught up in this. I just wish I had not been so star-struck that I could not see that his overly attentive behavior was inappropriate."

"It's not your fault, Lucy, he was the one with the problem. I'm just glad it's over and we can move forward with our lives and your career."

"I don't even care about my career right now. All I can think about is you and your recovery. I called your parents last night and they should be here before long. That's the other reason I wanted to talk to you early."

"PLEASE promise me that you won't let this derail your career," Sonya pleaded. "I could never forgive myself or HIM if that happened."

"I need a few days to think about things – you are my first priority right now, and I hope you will let me take care of you."

They visited for a few more minutes and then there was a knock on the door. Standing there were Sonya's parents with looks of concern and exhaustion on their faces. It was obvious they had been driving for several hours. After a few pleasantries, Lucy excused herself so the family could be alone. Sonya gave her hand one last squeeze and whispered, "promise me?" Lucy nodded and walked toward the door. Behind her she could hear Mrs. Vasquez say, "Oh, my poor baby girl!" while Mr. V said, "I hope the police are looking for the beast who did this to you."

Lucy was about to leave the hospital when she was stopped by a young girl about her age. "I'm sorry to bother you, but are you Lucy Armando?"

"Yes," Lucy said politely. "Can I help you?"

"No, I'm just excited to meet you. I've followed you since *Rising Star* and am anxious to get your new album when it drops. Soon I hope?"

"Yes, very soon. I hope you like it. It's a mix of original songs and a few covers."

"Whatever you do will be great, I'm sure. Can I have a picture with you?"

"Of course," Lucy said as the young girl got out her camera. "What's your name?"

"I'm Kendra," the girl answered. "I can't wait for my friends to find out I met you!"

"Well, it's my pleasure. I hope you don't mind, but I'm due at the studio in a few minutes."

"Of course. Terrible news about Travis Jones – such a loss to the music community. And just when he recorded that new duets CD. I imagine his record label will release it anyway, right?"

"I imagine so, but I really have no idea," Lucy said crisply. "I'm sorry, but I truly need to go…."

"Of course, thanks for talking with me and for the picture. I'm going to post it right away."

Lucy drove to the studio and parked her car in the back. She sat there for several minutes before getting the courage to go in. She knew there would be tons of questions about both Sonya and Travis. She slipped in the front door quietly, hoping to get past the reception desk unnoticed.

"Lucy?" the receptionist asked. "Can you stop by for a minute? There's something here for you."

Lucy cringed – the last time this happened was when she got the flowers and chocolates from Travis. You don't suppose he had something already ordered to be delivered today?

Taking a deep breath, Lucy returned to the desk and was handed a letter addressed to her, postmarked in Cincinnati. She nervously stepped into the nearest conference room and opened the letter.

"Hi Lucy – I've never done this before, but I wanted to drop you a line and let you know how much your music means to me.

I've followed you since Rising Star, of course, and can't wait for your album. I'm hoping your tour schedule brings you near Cincinnati sometime – I would love to hear you LIVE and to maybe meet you. Your fan, Dustin Pierce."

Her first fan mail, but after the events of last night, she dropped the letter like it was scalding her fingers. The sights and sounds flooded her memory, and her whole body trembled. After several minutes, she was finally able to shove the letter into her purse and head for Josh's office.

Vicki Jo stopped her in the hallway and congratulated her on her first fan picture tagging. Kendra had kept her word and posted the picture right away. Vicki Jo directed her toward the main conference room outside of Josh's office for a big meeting with all the team and a few media as well.

Lucy stopped in the ladies' room to try to freshen up a bit – when she left the hotel this morning, she had no idea she would be meeting media later. At least her top was clean and not too wrinkled. She applied a little bit of makeup and brushed her long hair before pulling it back into a ponytail. This would teach her to always leave home a bit more prepared.

Most of her team was gathered into the conference room by the time she arrived. The media representatives were talking about Travis, and she felt herself cringing inside.

Josh stood at the front of the room to start the meeting. "Welcome, everyone. Obviously, the events of the past 24 hours have shaken everyone and disrupted things quite a bit for most of us. Lucy, how is Sonya doing this morning?"

"I just came from the hospital. Her parents are with her now. She has a long recovery ahead of her I'm afraid. She appreciates everyone's concern."

"Of course! She's almost part of the family. Ok, well, I'd like to introduce you to Bobby and Jimmy from *Nashville News* – they wanted to talk to you a bit about the album, the upcoming tour, and of course the news about Travis. You probably don't know, but we have partnered with them for several years now, giving them early access to our new stars. They are the first media to see your tour schedule and album release date."

"Hi Lucy," Bobby said. "Happy to meet you. Like Josh said, we have worked with Star Records for many years and enjoyed lots of success. I'm sorry about your friend and hope she recovers soon. Before we go further, though, I'm curious if you have a comment for our readers about Travis?"

Lucy knew this was coming, and had been mentally rehearsing a reply that would sound both appropriately respectful but honest. "It's very sad what happened last night," Lucy said without a lot of emotion. "I grew up listening to his records and he had a great influence on my musical choices. Today more than ever I realize the impact he had on my life, and how it will always be with me. I enjoyed our time together recording our duet and appreciate the faith he had in me." Lucy was relieved that this answer seemed to satisfy the reporters and that they quickly moved on to other topics.

Once again, her tour schedule flashed on the monitor. Was it just two days ago that Sonya had sat here beside her, marveling at the schedule and all that went into making Lucy a star? And now she was in the hospital, fighting to recover from an assault that had been targeted towards her.

The meeting covered the same information as the one from before, and Lucy found her mind wandering. Her ears did perk a bit when Josh mentioned Cincinnati. She wondered if her new fan Dustin would be at the concert. And should she be afraid?

As if reading her mind, Josh brought up the topic of security. After the attack last night, he wanted Lucy to feel safe. "We have no idea if this was a random act, or somehow directed toward you or Sonya, but we need to make sure this never happens again. I think it's time we talked about beefing up security for you Lucy. We have a security firm we use, of course, but I was thinking of something a bit more personal for you. Do you happen to know of anyone you trust – a personal friend perhaps? I want someone who can blend in with the team but be another set of eyes and ears for you."

"Actually, I just might," Lucy said. "I have a friend from school, Ramone Torres, who has worked as a bouncer and is thinking about becoming a police officer. Do you want me to contact him?"

"No, just get me his contact information. I want to explain the situation to him and talk about what all would be required, the compensation, etc. OK, thanks everyone, I think we're done for now. Lucy, you need to be back tomorrow at ten to meet with your band and we will go over set design and lighting. Great job everyone."

Lucy went back to her car and then drove slowly home. She sat in her parking spot, holding her door keys in her hand.

Finally gathering her courage, she walked up the steps and put her key in the lock. She opened the door slowly and found everything looking like the day she moved in. Gone was the broken glass, tossed furniture and the blood stain near the patio door. After locking the front door behind her, she walked into Sonya's room and sat on her bed. Grief and pain washed over her, and she cried for her friend who was suffering only because of their resemblance to each other. Lucy curled up into a ball and cried herself to sleep.

Chapter 15

Lucy kept busy the next several days with rehearsals for the tour and visits to Sonya in the hospital, whose parents stayed for three days before heading back to Chesterfield. On the fifth day after the assault, Sonya's doctor felt she had healed enough to be released. The surgery on her jaw was less involved than they had feared, and her broken and cracked ribs were starting to heal. Lucy hated leaving Sonya alone when she went to rehearsals and fittings, but Sonya insisted she go, and said she would use that time to rest, anyway. Her bruises were starting to heal but it was still hard for her to talk or eat with her jaw wired shut.

Ramone accepted the job as Lucy's personal bodyguard and was able to rent a condo in the same complex. He planned to move to Nashville in the next week or so. She was thankful to have him join the team as she had known him most of her life. They had both been in the high school band and loved playing guitar. In fact, he had more natural talent than she did, and she always felt he would go far with his music.

Two weeks went by and soon it was time for Lucy's first three-city tour: Lexington, Kentucky; Cincinnati Ohio; and Indianapolis, Indiana. The venues were fairly small, but ticket sales had been brisk with a few hundred sold at each location.

A limit of five VIP tickets were available for each show which entitled the fan to a meet-and-greet session along with an individual picture and a signed poster. Lucy was exceedingly nervous, knowing that the profitability of the tour and the livelihood of those with her was riding on the success of these concerts. Josh had rented a small bus for them to use for the tour and a trailer to pull behind with their lighting and sound equipment. Lucy insisted that Sonya be allowed to travel with them, which Josh had agreed to. He knew Lucy would be more relaxed knowing Sonya was safe and being taken care of.

The day before they were to leave, Josh had the bus brought to the office so Lucy and Sonya could get a look around and supplies could be loaded inside. Lucy marveled at the amount of technology jammed into such a tiny space – a TV, mobile Wi-Fi and a gaming system. The sleeping bunks were small, and the ONE bathroom was even smaller. Lucy wondered how they were going to make it all work and if they would hate each other by the end of the week!

The next morning, Lucy and Sonya arrived with their suitcases and met with Elizabeth to pick up performance outfits for the trip. They were keeping things casual but with a conservative flair that satisfied Lucy's need for modesty. Soon the other members of the band and crew arrived, and everyone started loading the bus. Lucy made sure that Sonya was comfortably seated and doing NO lifting at all. Before long everything was loaded, and they started the fairly short drive to Lexington. Lucy looked around the bus and tried to wrap her head around the fact that she was on tour – her first tour! Also on the bus with her were Blake and Adam, along with a guy named Nick who was in charge of the lights and sound, and a young man named Randy who oversaw the merchandise and would also serve as emcee. They were in deep conversation with Ramone, who had slipped into his role of personal security quite easily. Sitting up front next to the bus driver was a long-legged blond named Marion who was the tour manager. She was the boss of everything it seemed, and Lucy was to bring any questions or concerns to her. This was only her fifth tour as manager, but Josh chose her specifically to provide a bit of female influence for the group. Even though she considered herself 'one of the guys,' Marion knew things could get a bit rowdy sometimes and Josh wanted to protect Lucy and Sonya from that, especially in the light of the recent attack.

Lucy's phone buzzed, signaling a text from Vicki Jo, reminding her to take a group photo on the bus along with others throughout the day. Ramone offered to take the picture, but Marion wanted him included in the shot so it would look like he was part of the team and not draw suspicions later if anyone was studying the photos. Everyone gathered around Lucy who was sitting at the table, and Blake was able to get a few good group selfies. Lucy forwarded them to Vicki Jo who promised to post them right away.

Shortly after crossing into Kentucky, they stopped in Bowling Green for a late lunch. Marion reminded them that they would not likely have time for a full dinner before the show, but Lucy didn't imagine she would be able to eat much anyway.

Lucy and Ramone gently helped Sonya down the bus steps and into a little café. Lucy looked around the diner and wondered if this was what her life was going to be now – endless bus rides and a string of nameless cafés..

Back on the bus after lunch, Lucy tried to close her eyes and rest but was just too excited. Adam sensed her uneasiness and sat down beside her to run through the set list one more time, even though he knew she had it memorized. She told Adam that it wasn't so much the music that made her nervous, but making small talk between songs and stretching the show long enough so the fans felt they got their money's worth. Adam and Blake would be helping her, of course, and they had practiced a few things for her to say.

Before long they reached Lexington, and the bus pulled in front of the Kentucky Theater. Lucy's name was on the Marquee! Excitedly, she hopped down the steps to pose at the front door. This was really happening!

Marion had arranged for a wheelchair for Sonya, and Ramone pushed her through some back hallways and into the green room. Lucy had a small bag with her toiletries and makeup along with her guitar, and her concert clothes were on a hanger. There was a large table in the middle of the room with sandwiches, drinks and snacks. Lucy went into a partitioned area where she could change and then sat near Sonya who insisted on helping with her hair. She heard Andy tuning his guitar and Blake was humming one of the songs they were to perform in just a few minutes.

Lucy looked at her watch – 6:45 P.M. Only fifteen more minutes until the VIP session. Five fans had paid extra to have a special meet and greet and to get a private photo. Lucy shook her head in amazement that even though they had not heard her sing live yet, they were willing to spend the extra money.

Marion announced that everything was ready, and it was time to head to the stage. Ramone pushed Sonya's wheelchair to a safe spot on the side of the stage where she would be able to see everything, and where he could keep an extra eye on the crowd.

Randy walked onto the stage and talked quietly to the five people who had special front-row seats. Then in a slightly louder voice he said, "Here she is – the one you've been waiting for! Our Rising Star – Lucy Armando!"

Lucy walked boldly onto the stage amid the applause of the small group, with Blake and Adam close behind. Three of the fans were young women about her age, and there was an older lady with a young teenaged girl. Lucy sat on a bar stool in front of them and said, "I hope y'all know how special you are to me."

She looked out into the eager faces of her fans and was almost brought to tears. To know that they were so invested in her career, so excited to meet her, that they would pay an extra $50 for their tickets - wow.

"You are aware, I am sure, that this is my first concert and first tour. You are part of a very special group to be my first VIP's. Randy gave you your gifts, right? We'll have time in a few minutes for me to sign whatever you want and to take some pictures, if that is something you are interested in. But first, do you have any questions for me?"

A young girl about 12 years old raised her hand. Lucy pointed toward her and said, "Hi! You have a question?"

"Yes, thanks. My name is Cassandra and I'm in the 6th grade. I wanted to know how long you have been singing and when you knew you wanted to have a career in music?"

"Thank you, Cassandra. I've been singing for a very long time. Do you like music?"

"Yes, I sing in our choir at school and am also in the band."

"Oh, what do you play?"

"I play the flute."

"Oh, so pretty. I was in band for a while – I played clarinet, but not very well. Guitar was more my interest. It seems like a long time ago. I started singing when I was a very small girl, mostly in church but also at my aunt's wedding when I was 15. I have always loved music and the way I feel when I sing a particularly moving song. Thanks for the question – anyone else?"

An older woman who reminded Lucy of her mother was next. "I loved watching you on *Rising Star*. Was it as exciting in person as what was shown on TV?"

"Yes, very exciting! And a lot of hard work and LONG hours. But I would not be here except for the show, and all of you who voted for me."

Lucy answered a few other questions and then it was time for autographs and pictures. Each one of the fans had an individual chance to talk with her and have their picture taken together. Lucy then excused herself and Randy told the group that the main doors were opening soon as the concert would be starting in fifteen minutes.

Lucy, Adam and Blake retreated to the green room for a last-minute warm-up and relaxation. They could hear Randy talking to the crowd, letting them know the show would begin shortly. Lucy looked at her bandmates and had a sudden rush of stage fright. What in the world was she doing here? She felt like a fraud – an imposter. She started to tremble, and Blake reached over to her and patted her shoulder.

"Hey, it's OK. Nerves are part of this business. Just remember to breathe and smile. You will be great! And Adam and I have your back. This is going to be an amazing first show!"

The next thing Lucy heard was Randy's voice booming across the concert hall, "OK, folks – it's time - the time you have been waiting for! Fresh off her win on *Rising Star* and here for her VERY FIRST solo concert, is Star Record's own Lucy Armando!"

The trio held hands for a brief second, then Lucy walked confidently toward the stage. The instrumental music playing in the background was from the new album. Sonya was nearby in her wheelchair, and she gave Lucy a big "thumbs up" as the group walked past. Taking a deep breath, Lucy walked onto the stage with a huge smile and wave. The crowd jumped to their feet and were clapping wildly. Blake and Adam were close behind her and took their places nearby. Lucy sat on the bar stool and picked up her guitar. Strumming the first few chords of her title track from the album '*If Only*', the crowd instantly fell silent as Lucy sang the first few words. "*If only you would listen, If only you could see. You would understand this message, you would know the real me.*" As she started the next phrase, she noticed that many of the audience were mouthing the words, singing along. They had listened to that song enough already to know the words? How was that possible?

As the final notes faded, the applause began and everyone was again on their feet. Lucy glanced offstage to see Sonya applauding from her chair. Once things quieted down a bit, Blake said, "I love that song, and love it more each time we play it together. How about you guys – wasn't that great? Did you know that Lucy wrote it?" The crowd cheered, and Blake continued, "And I love the way you were all singing along. Let's keep that going as we play another song from the album. My name is Blake, and this other lucky guy is Adam. Ready? Let's Go!" and the three of them quickly started in on a fast-paced honkytonk song.

The crowd grew even more enthusiastic as the trio easily transitioned from one song to another. After about 45 minutes Lucy said, "Wow, that was fun! I could sit here and sing for you all night!"

Of course, the crowd loved that comment too, and one young girl from the back yelled, "You do it, and I'll stay!" Soon the entire crowd was chanting "I'll stay – I'll stay!" Lucy smiled and replied, "Well, let us take a short break and then we'll be back to talk about it, OK? Get up, stretch your legs and we'll be back in a bit."

Once back in the green room, Lucy sank exhaustedly into the first chair she came to. The guys followed her, along with Sonya and Ramone. Marion came rushing in and gushed, "Well, as far as first concerts go, that was amazing. Lucy, you're just a natural out there charming the crowd, and the three of you are magic together - it really looks like you have been working together forever. The merch table was pretty busy before the show, and I imagine it is a nuthouse now. We've set up a place for you to do the 'meet and greet' after the show, so come back in here after the next set and an encore if they want one, and then I'll escort you to the area we have for you. Sonya, how are you feeling? Are you up to staying for the second half, or should I find someone to take you to the bus?"

"Oh, I'm staying for the second half – I wouldn't miss this for the world!"

"Are you sure?" Lucy asked. "If you're tired or in pain, I totally want you to go and rest!"

"No, really, I'm fine. And you can just sit me by the merch table after the show so Ramone can do his real duties, not just babysit me."

"I beg your pardon, ma'am," Ramone said in his most courteous tone. "I'll let you know that I am perfectly capable of keeping an eye on both you and Lucy's adoring crowd. I consider it an honor to hang out so close to you." He smiled slightly and Sonya blushed. Lucy wondered if maybe sparks were flying between them, and nothing would make her happier if she was right.

The second half of the show flew by quickly, and way too soon Lucy announced that it was time for the final song. Loud groans could be heard from the crowd, and Lucy smiled. Recording the album had been fun, but THIS – singing live in front of an excited cheering audience – this was pure heaven to her. How could she ever want to do anything different again?

Once the song was over, Lucy and the guys waved goodbye and stepped offstage. Almost immediately they hear the audience chanting, "I'll stay! I'll stay!" Sonya and Ramone were grinning wildly, and within 30 seconds or so Marion came rushing by. "They love you! Ready to go back out?"

Lucy, Adam and Blake returned to the stage to find the crowd on their feet, clapping and chanting. "Y'all are so amazing," Lucy said. "You sure know how to make a girl feel loved. Ready for one more?" She grabbed her guitar and the three of them launched into a rowdy version of *Boot Skootin' Boogie.*

The cheering was deafening as they waved goodbye again and headed back to the green room. Randy announced to the crowd that a signing line was forming out in the lobby to the left of the concert hall, and everyone would be able to get one item signed but would have just a *brief* few seconds with Lucy and the band in order to keep the line moving. No pictures would be taken at that time.

Marion rushed into the room with a giant smile on her face. "Well, someone from the show has already posted pictures online, and we are getting tons of hits. I would definitely say tonight was a huge success." The group then made their way to the signing line while Ramone pushed Sonya to the lobby and gently placed her chair near the merchandise table and out of the way of the crowd. He then stationed himself near the front of the signing line where he could keep an eye on everyone. The crowd was excited but polite, and the whole process went quite smoothly. Soon the last of the fans were through the line and everyone headed back to the green room to gather their things and then exited out through the back door to the bus. Lucy went out of her way to thank all the venue employees she saw, and then climbed the steps to the bus. Ramone and Blake had already gotten Sonya on board and situated comfortably. Everyone was talking excitedly but Marion hushed them so she could be heard.

"Lucy, you and the guys did an amazing job tonight, and I'm not just saying that. No one who didn't know would think that was your first concert ever! Social media is loving you, and in celebration of what was the first of MANY more concerts to come, I propose a toast to Lucy and her bright future ahead!" Ramone appeared with a bottle of champagne and a stack of red solo cups. Popping the cork, he poured about an inch into each cup.

"To Lucy!" Everyone shouted and raised their glasses.

Chapter 16

Lucy feared that she would have a hard time sleeping on the bus, but after a few hours of talking and drinking a bit of champagne, she was quickly lulled into a peaceful rest by the movement of the bus and the soft voices in the background. Sonya had gone to bed early and seemed comfortable after taking some pain medicine. Lucy had enjoyed a long chat with Marion about the schedule for tomorrow and was confident that everything was in good hands. Marion certainly knew her stuff.

After an hour or so, she awoke to hear a sound she had learned to dread in the past few weeks: Sonya crying while having a bad dream. She continued to suffer from PTSD-type memories of the attack, and often had nightmares where she relived her assault. Travis was long gone and buried but continued to haunt them both.

Lucy climbed down from her bunk and went to sit beside Sonya. She stroked her arm softly and said over and over, "It's OK, Honey, I'm here. No one can hurt you now." Eventually Sonya shifted a bit in her bed and seemed to settle into a more pleasant rest. "I'll never forgive you, Travis," Lucy said under her breath as she climbed back into her bed.

Sometime after midnight, the bus arrived in Cincinnati and parked behind the theater. Lucy woke up and noticed that they were no longer moving, but she rolled over and slipped back into her pleasant dream of songs and fans and applause.

It was late morning before most of the group awoke, and Marion started making coffee and pulling breakfast out of the fridge. Lucy had a slight headache from the champagne and vowed not to make drinking on the bus a habit. Sonya was a bit stiff but seemed to be in good spirits as well. Ramone hovered over her a bit, making sure she had coffee and a donut. "The schedule is different in every town we visit," Marion explained. "It really depends on how far we have to drive the night before. We decided for this tour to eat breakfast on the bus and then find a local diner for a late lunch. Dinner is whatever the venue provides for us – sometimes it's a nice spread, and sometimes not so much. That's why we try to stock the bus as much as we can in case y'all get hungry after a show. And of course, we rented this bus for this tour only, so each time will be a bit different as well."

Lucy realized that she was starving, so she microwaved a breakfast sandwich and grabbed a yogurt cup and some fruit from the fridge. She sat at the table with a steaming cup of coffee brought to her by Ramone. "Mind if I join you?" he asked.

"Of course not. What do you think about tour life so far?"

"I wasn't really sure what to expect, to be honest," he replied. "I'm fine with keeping an eye on the crowd, of course, but am not sure what I'm supposed to do when you are not on stage."

"You are making both me and Sonya more comfortable, just being here. I'm still so angry about what happened to her. Did you hear her crying last night?"

"I did, but then I heard you helping her, so I stayed away. I wonder if they will ever catch the guy who did this to her?"

Lucy grimaced, hating to keep the secret about Travis from him. "I hope so, too, but even if they don't, my main concern is Sonya and getting her back to health, both physically and emotionally."

"I'll do all I can, of course," Ramone said softly as he gazed across the bus to where Sonya was wrapped in a blanket and reading a book. "Don't take this personally, but although you two look remarkably alike, you are very different people. I always wanted to date her when we were in high school, but never got the courage to ask her. For some reason, I guess I thought of you more as my kid sister."

"I don't know for sure, but I would bet that she would have said 'yes' if you had asked her out. It's never too late, you know."

"The timing couldn't be worse right now, with her getting over her injuries and still so afraid of trusting anyone."

"But she trusts you already," Lucy said gently. "Don't push her, but I think she will be receptive when the right time arrives."

Lucy had just finished her second cup of coffee when her cell phone rang. It was Darren, wanting to know how she felt the night went. He saw great comments online but wanted her honest opinion.

"Darren, it was amazing. I was nervous at first, but the guys were great at helping me relax, and the audience was so supportive and excited. I loved it!"

"I knew you would," Darren replied. "I talked to Marion earlier, and she gave me the specifics. Merch sales were great, especially for your first show. All the comments we saw posted online were positive. Vicki Jo made an official post for you last night – have you seen it?"

"Yes, earlier this morning. It's still weird to have someone else posting as me, but I do understand. And I only read a few of the responses, I promise!"

"Great! Well, enjoy the rest of your day and knock them dead tonight. It's officially a sell-out!"

After a late lunch at a restaurant named Izzy's, the group entered the venue and settled into the large green room. The girls were given a different area to shower and dress for the show. Feeling better after a shower, Lucy returned to the green room and sat in one of the comfortable lounge chairs. Strumming her guitar, she found herself again playing a haunting melody, much more serious than her current mood. She set the guitar aside to do a sound check on stage, and then around 5:30 P.M. a caterer arrived with a selection of Italian pastas and salads, along with tons of bfread sticks. Lucy ate heartily this time and then went into the dressing area to get ready for the show. It wasn't long before she again heard Randy greeting the VIPs and it was time for her to greet her fans.

Lucy and the guys walked out onto the stage where she saw five people waiting for them. This time there was a middle-aged couple, a mother and daughter, and a young man who seemed to be by himself. He looked to be quite tall – at least 6 feet – with dark brown hair and a neatly–trimmed beard. He was nicely dressed in jeans with a plaid shirt and jean jacket. There was just something about him that caught her attention immediately, and she felt a bit of flutter inside.

Lucy sat on a barstool and again opened the discussion to questions. After a few minutes, the young man raised his hand. Lucy called on him and he said, "Hi Lucy, it's good to meet you. My question is about your songwriting – do you usually write the music first and then the lyrics, or do the lyrics come to you first and then you add a melody?"

"That's a good question, but there's not an easy answer. Sometimes I hear a word or a phrase that sticks with me until I try to do something with it. Other times, the music comes first. Right now, I'm kind of tinkering around with a melody, but have no idea what to do with it."

"Do you feel that your songs are really personal for you, that they represent true events in your life?"

"Not always. Sometimes it's just a cute idea I hear. But a lot of my songs have come from a place of honesty for me."

"Thanks for the answers. Oh, my name is Dustin Pierce, but everyone calls me Dusty."

Verse 2
The Romance

Chapter 1

Dustin Pierce – the guy who had written the fan letter? Instantly Lucy felt herself tense and she tried hard not to panic. Another of the VIPs asked a question, and she tried to focus on that, but Adam quickly noticed that something was wrong and covered for her until she gained her balance. Lucy shot a quick glance at Ramone who was standing beside the stage and saw that he noticed her demeanor change as well. He had been watching the small crowd but had not noticed anything unusual. The guy named Dusty had been the one talking when Lucy got nervous, so Ramone decided to keep a closer eye on him throughout the concert.

The Q&A session ended, and the VIPs were invited to the stage for pictures and a chance to chat privately. Lucy talked first with the older couple who reminded her of her parents. Feeling a bit homesick, she made a mental note to take a few days off as soon as possible to go to Florida to visit her mom. She had been so wrapped up with her own new life - recording the album, Sonya's attack and the news about Travis, and now the tour - how had she gone so long without seeing her mom? Yes, they talked on the phone regularly, but it wasn't the same.

Next in line to chat with her was Dustin, or Dusty as he said his friends called him. Lucy tried not to show any concern as she shook his hand, and he introduced himself again.

"Hi, Lucy, it's great to meet you in person. I really enjoy listening to your music and am so glad you came here so early in your tour. Sorry if I'm babbling, but I'm a bit nervous…"

"No need to be nervous Dusty. I'm new to this, too. And thanks for the letter – it was very sweet of you to write to me."

"I've never written to anyone famous before. Makes me feel like a star-struck kid."

"Don't worry. And I'm not so famous. So, what kinds of music do you usually listen to? Just country, or other things?"

"Oh, I'm pretty eclectic," Dusty said. "My play lists include everything from show tunes to 70's music like John Denver and Bread. Jim Croce is one of my favorites. But I also love current music, both pop and country. What about you?"

"Oh, I love 70's music, too! I feel like they were true story tellers, not just making up words to go with a crazy beat. Jim Croce was amazing! '*Time in a Bottle*' and '*I Got a Name*' are two of my favorites. Maybe I need to think about covering one of them someday."

"That would be cool. Well, I don't want to take up too much time since there are others waiting. Can you sign my poster and then take a picture?"

"Sure," she said, as she looked into his brown eyes. Standing beside him, she felt so tiny next to his six-foot frame. He had made her feel quite at ease, and her fears of another stalker had vanished. It was unfair to judge him harshly based on her experience with Travis. Leaning against him slightly, she inhaled a masculine scent that made her heart race a little. She smiled broadly as Randy took their picture.

"Thanks again for coming," Lucy said, "and for being one of my first VIPs. It means a lot to me."

"Thank you, Lucy. I wish you only the best on this tour, and all the tours to come."

Ramone had been watching intently and had noticed how she looked more relaxed now. This guy seemed harmless, but you never know. He vowed to keep an eye on him for the duration of the evening.

The rest of the VIP session went quickly, and soon the band was back on stage and singing before another enthusiastic crowd. Lucy glanced at Dusty several times during the first set, and he was relaxed and smiling the whole time. Once backstage during the intermission, Ramone approached Lucy and asked if she was ok.

"You looked a bit un-nerved earlier during VIP talking with that guy. What happened?"

Lucy told him about the fan letter she received the day after Sonya's attack, and how it had freaked her out a bit. But after talking with Dusty for a while, she realized she was just over-reacting and that he seemed like a regular guy. It wasn't his fault that his letter arrived that particular day.

The second set went just as well as the night before, and after the encore the band made their way to the lobby for the meet and greet. Once again, Lucy was in awe of the number of enthusiastic fans who wanted a chance to get their poster or CD signed, or to just say a quick hello. Sonya was again in a wheelchair near the merchandise table, and Ramone was watching from across the lobby. The line was nearing the end when Lucy noticed Dusty standing near the door, looking like he wanted another chance to talk to her. Once the line was done, Lucy nodded toward him, and he came to her with a small piece of paper folded in the palm of his hand.

"I hope you don't mind me waiting to talk to you," he said timidly. "I wanted to congratulate you on a great show – one of the best I've seen in ages. You have such a unique style and, well, I really enjoyed it." He reached his hand out shyly toward her and pressed the paper into her hand. "I'll let you go – I hope I get the chance to see you again soon."

"Thanks," Lucy said as he disappeared into the crowd and out the door. She unfolded the paper to see a note that said *"Hi – loved our chat. If you ever want to talk, here is my number. No pressure."*

Lucy's heart skipped a beat or two. He seemed very genuine, and she had found herself attracted to him. But then the fears came back – what if his nice guy façade was hiding another creep like Travis? She had been so flattered by the attention he had shown toward her and look what happened She really needed to think a while before texting or calling him.

Ramone had been watching their interaction and rushed to her side. "What was all that about? Do I need to follow him or anything?"

"No, it's fine. He just wrote me a short note. Nothing to get worried about," Lucy said quickly as she shoved the paper into her pocket but wondered why she was not totally honest.

How was Ramone supposed to protect her if she didn't tell him everything?

Once back on the bus and on the road again, Lucy retreated to a corner of the living area in the back and pulled the paper out of her jeans pocket. She stared at his number, and wondered if she would ever have the nerve to contact him. Or if she should? He certainly was handsome, and she had felt a sort of connection with him, but to call a total stranger? She needed to focus on the rest of the tour and deal with this in a few days.

Sonya eased herself down onto the sofa next to her. "What's that?" she asked.

"A note I got from one of the VIPs. Just thanking me for a great show."

"Oh, I remember him. What a cutie! What did he say his name was?"

"Dustin, but everyone calls him Dusty."

"Oh, that's right. Wow! Your second show and already getting fan mail and love notes! Is he going to hang your poster on his bedroom wall?" Sonya teased.

"Very funny. No, I doubt it. I don't know – there just seemed something intriguing about him. We had a nice chat during VIP, and we like the same music for the same reasons. But I doubt I will ever see him again."

"Would you want to? See him again, I mean."

"Maybe under different circumstances. If I had met him at school or at a party, sure! But I'm trying to make a career that takes me all over the country, and well, after what happened to you…"

"I told you I would not let HIM ruin things for you: not just your career but your social life as well. Please don't let one creep take all your happiness away."

"OK, only if you promise to do the same. I know it's only been a few weeks, but it breaks my heart to see how it is still impacting you."

"I know, I'm trying. And I'm doing better, I really am, it's just..."

Suddenly there was the loud crash of breaking glass, and Sonya began to tremble. She clinched her eyes shut and a tear ran down her cheek.

"I'm sorry," Adam called from the front of the bus. "Just a broken glass. I'll get it cleaned up right away."

Lucy grabbed Sonya's hand but before she could even say anything, Ramone was by her side. He put his arm around Sonya, and she buried her head in his chest. Ramone cursed under his breath, calling Adam a few choice names, then focused on comforting Sonya. Lucy went to the front of the bus to see Adam sweeping up the last of the broken glass.

"What happened?" Lucy asked.

"Not really sure. Guess I left the wine bottle too close to the edge of the table and I bumped it."

"Ok, I understand. It just freaked Sonya out a bit."

"Oh, I'm sorry. I would never want to make her upset."

"I know, we just need to be extra careful for a little while longer."

Adam followed Lucy back to the rear of the bus and got down on his knees next to Sonya.

"I'm so sorry. It was stupid on my part. Please forgive me?"

"Of course, I know you didn't mean it. I'm just still a bit jumpy I guess."

Marion joined them and asked how Sonya was doing. After confirming that she was going to be OK, Marion shared the latest news from the venue. "I just got off the phone with the manager. The concert was a sellout again, and merch sales were even better than last night. We will need to discuss final numbers once we get home, but it looks like the posters are the biggest sellers, along with the guitar pins you designed. And I just saw online that you are getting rave reviews from local media."

"Thanks to all of you and your hard work," Lucy said softly. "I feel like all I do is show up and sing."

"Well, you do more than that. If it was just your singing they wanted, they would buy a CD or stream your songs online. It's *YOU* they want, and you certainly have a way of making everyone feel at ease and have a good time. I don't know about you guys, but I'm tired and heading to bed soon. Breakfast is on the bus again in the morning, and then we'll find lunch somewhere, just like we did today. I heard from the venue that they are catering in fried chicken with all the fixins tomorrow for dinner."

"Good night, Marion," Sonya said. "I think I'll turn in as well. Lucy?"

"No, I want to sit up a while longer. You guys get some rest, and I'll talk to you tomorrow."

Lucy picked up her guitar and was softly strumming a few chords before she realized she was playing '*Time in a Bottle*'. Adam was seated nearby and started humming along. Soon Blake wandered in and the three of them finished the song together. Looking at each other in awe at how easily their voices blended, Blake said, "Wow, that was nice. Maybe something to consider for the future? Lucy, your voice is perfect for this song. What made you think about it tonight?"

"Just something one of the VIPs said during our chat. And yes, it's been one of my favorites for years."

"Well, we definitely need to run it by Darren. I bet he would come up with a killer arrangement for us. Although what we just did was special, too."

Adam and Blake headed to their bunks as Lucy put her guitar in the case. Just as she was finished, her phone rang. It was awfully late for Josh to call, so Lucy worried that something might be wrong.

"Sorry I'm calling so late," he said apologetically, "but I needed to run something past you. You're still up, right?"

"Yes. What's going on?"

"We have been approached by a radio station in Indianapolis who wants to interview you as soon as you get to town tomorrow – between eight and ten if possible. It would be great promotion for your show tomorrow night, and their station is fairly close to the venue. Marion will make the arrangements to get you there, but can you be ready by 7:30? This is not a station I have dealt with before, so I'm not familiar with their style. I wanted to ask you first. How does that sound?"

"Sure, I can be ready. Anything else I need to know?"

"No, I'll text all the contact info to Marion. She will go with you to take some pictures for your social media. This really is a good sign that they want to interview you – your tour is making headlines!"

"Yes, very exciting. Well, I had better get some sleep. Oh, by the way. The guys and I were wondering if you could ask Darren to work up a cover of '*Time in a Bottle*' for us. We were playing around with it a bit tonight and it sounded pretty cool, maybe something we want to do in the future."

"Sure, I'll have him check into it tomorrow. I'm not sure if there are any special copyright snags to deal with. Some artists don't like their works to be covered, and his estate might be one of those. Call me after the interview and let me know how it goes, ok?"

"Of course. Good night, Josh."

"Good night, Lucy. You are doing great, and we are all very proud of you!"

Lucy brushed her teeth and crawled into her bunk. Just before drifting off to sleep, she checked her phone one last time and did what Josh and everyone had told her *NOT* to do – she checked her social media page. She saw that several of the fans had already posted pictures from the show tonight and were giving rave reviews. She didn't see anything from Dusty but would have been surprised to find him on social media. He just didn't seem the type to be on a fan page. She got caught up reading the comments but then one jumped out at her. *"What a waste of time and money. Another over-hyped reality show winner with mediocre talent and less sex appeal than my old Aunt Agnes. She barely qualifies as 'pretty.' My ears (and eyes) are still burning."*

Chapter Two

Lucy stared at her phone in disbelief, then threw it across her bed. How in the world could anyone post something so hateful? She was angry, hurt and sad at the same time. All her self-doubt and fears came rushing back. Mediocre talent? No sex appeal? She knew she wasn't the sexiest performer out there and had gone out of her way to downplay that aspect of her personality. She wanted to be respected for her music, not for what she looked like. The crack about her talent is what cut the deepest – mediocre?

A tear rolled down her cheek and she brushed it away. Who was this person to judge her, to make such horrible statements? She grabbed her phone and looked again. It was posted by a guy named *Music Pro 1,* and when she clicked on his profile, she saw that he had hundreds of followers. It made her feel a bit better to see many fans had jumped on him to defend her, but was there truth in his words? How many others felt the same way?

Tossing the phone aside a second time, Lucy tried to get comfortable and to sleep. It was nearly two A.M. and she needed to be up soon to get ready for the radio interview. And then there was her third concert tonight - she certainly didn't want to disappoint those fans. Eventually she fell asleep, but her dreams were filled with jeering faces and fingers pointed toward her with disapproval.

What seemed like only a few minutes later, Marion was gently shaking her shoulder. "Wake up, Lucy. You've got time to freshen up before we head to the radio station. I've arranged for a car to pick us up in an hour."

"Oh, OK," Lucy said sleepily. "Where are we?"

"Indianapolis, behind tonight's venue. We got in around three this morning. I hated to wake you, but Josh really wants this interview."

"I understand. I didn't sleep well last night and I'm kind of confused, I guess."

"Happens more than you think! Each day is a different town, a different schedule. Welcome to the life of a travelling country star!"

Lucy dug some clothes out of her suitcase and headed for the bathroom. She freshened up as best she could at the sink and put on a bit of makeup. Even though this was a radio interview, she knew Marion would be posting a picture or two, maybe even some video. She decided to leave her hair down but curled her bangs. As she pulled on a plaid peasant top, she looked at her reflection in the mirror. She never believed she was beautiful, but hoped her hair and dark eyes made her face at least pretty. Smoothing a few wrinkles out of her top, she wondered if maybe she needed to spice up her wardrobe a bit. Not to be sexy, but maybe a bit more stylish? The words from last night were still playing in her mind....*old Aunt Agnes?* Was that what her audience expected? Did she really want to be part of an industry that was so superficial?

Lucy joined Marion in the kitchen where coffee and a bagel were waiting for her. "The car will be here in about 20 minutes," Marion said softly, trying not to wake the others. "Are you OK? You look a bit worn around the edges."

"Gee, thanks," Lucy said softly under her breath. "No," she said more loudly to Marion, "I'm fine. Just a bit tired, I guess. I know this is only radio, but do you think I look OK? I mean, especially when I'm on stage….should I be more flashy?"

"Why do you ask? And no, I think you're fine."

"Oh, just wondering. Maybe everyone doesn't appreciate my simpler tastes and conservative values."

"Where is this coming from? You didn't go online, did you? You did!"

"I'm sorry," she said with remorse. "I just read a few comments. Are people always so awful?"

"Sadly, yes, there will always be a certain number of jerks who make it their life's work to tear others down. There was a reason we all told you *NOT* to go online, especially in these early days. Promise me you won't do it again!"

"I won't, I swear. But how do I get those words out of my brain? It was brutal."

"You just need to kick them out, now! Focus on your true fans, the ones you met at VIP, the ones who stood in line for a chance to talk to you, the ones coming to see you tonight. THOSE are the people whose opinion matters, not the haters."

"I'll try. Looks like the car just arrived. I left a note for Sonya in case she wakes up before we get back. I would hate for her to think I ran away or something!"

The drive to the radio station only took a few minutes, and the pair waited in a conference room until it was time to be escorted to the radio booth. Lucy found that she was only just slightly nervous, and marveled how far her speaking skills had come since first auditioning for the TV show. The questions were pretty typical and standard, until one of the DJs, a lady named Samantha B., asked her about dealing with hostile social media.

"I'm not sure how much exposure you have had, but I know that online forums can be brutal sometimes. Do you ever read what is written about you? If so, how do you react when there is negativity?"

Lucy looked over at Marion, then back at Samantha. "Funny you should ask that today. I have not ever looked until last night, and to be honest, I was shocked by some of what I read. I would guess that at least 95% of it was positive and very much appreciated, but I did find a few that were cruel. I don't know anyone who would not be affected by such vile speech, but I'm doing my best to not let it get to me or to change my perception of who I am. I am a conservative Christian woman who happens to sing country music. You won't find me in overly tight skirts or skimpy tops just to get attention. My focus is on my music, and how much leg or cleavage I show or don't show shouldn't matter. I know that may not be popular with everyone, but that's OK. I want to be the type of singer that a parent would be proud for their child to listen to and see in person. There are plenty of other singers out there who attract a different type of audience than I do, and that's fine. I need to be honest to me, to my values, and to my faith. The rest will fall into place."

"That's a great way to look at it," Samantha said slowly. "But don't you worry that it will affect record sales or concert tickets?"

"No, I don't. I truly believe that there are plenty of people who appreciate something different, something refreshing that they don't need to shield their children from. I absolutely do not want to be the Super Bowl halftime show that parents need to be afraid of."

"Well, that certainly is a different way to look at the music industry, and I hope you can continue to pursue this in the way you want. But you're right: this business is filled with girls in skimpy outfits and fake eyelashes. I appreciate your willingness to chart your own path."

The interview ended shortly afterward, and Lucy and Marion prepared to leave. Samantha caught up with them in the lobby to thank them for the interview and to encourage her to remain strong to her beliefs.

Once back on the bus, Lucy sat at the table next to Sonya and Ramone and told them about the radio show. They were proud of her stance against the online bullies, but both cautioned her not to read any more, at least for a while. Lucy was about to call Josh when he called her first.

"Hey, I just heard from the station manager about your interview," Josh said quickly. "I'm not totally sure what speech you gave, but their lines have been lit up ever since. The station's social media was also blasted with comments of support for you and what you stand for. What happened?"

Lucy relayed to him the comments she had read last night, and how much it had upset her. But she also told him of her conversation with Marion this morning, and how it reaffirmed to her that she needed to stay true to her values if she was going to stay in the music industry.

After gently scolding her for going online, Josh told her how proud he was of her for not bowing to the online pressure, and that they would work even harder to maintain the reputation that she wanted. Lucy thanked him again for being supportive and told him she would do her best to make the tour a success.

Chapter Three

Lucy wiped the last of the fried chicken crumbs from her lips and leaned back in her chair. The meal tonight was just what she needed – chicken, mashed potatoes and gravy, coleslaw and brownies. She had even found time for a short nap after their early lunch and was now ready to get dressed and hit the stage for the final concert of this first tour. Looking around the green room at the people who were now her close friends, she could see that they were starting to feel like a family, and she loved each of them. She smiled when she saw Sonya and Ramone sitting close together playing cards, and Randy was with Adam and Blake playing video games. Marion was on her laptop doing business, as usual, and Nick the lighting guy was running in and out reporting on an issue he was having with the spotlights. Lucy loved the hustle and bustle of life on the road and was already fiercely loyal to all her teammates.

VIP was again a huge success, as was the concert. In fact, they had given the audience a second encore as a special thank you. As the last few people were making their way through the signing line, Lucy marveled at all that had gone into making this mini tour such a success. Randy came over and said they had run out of both CD's and guitar lapel pins, and most of the posters were gone as well. "We'll really need to analyze the numbers to make sure we have enough for the next tour," he said with a big grin. "I think we underestimated your fans, Lucy!"

The mood on the bus was celebratory, and everyone decided it was time to let loose a bit and have some fun. The drive back to Nashville would take about 5 hours, but no one seemed sleepy. Another bottle of champagne was opened, and soon music was booming throughout the bus. Everyone was laughing and having a great time, and Lucy knew again that this was the life she wanted.

Suddenly the bus made a wild swerve to the left and the driver jammed on the brakes. Lucy went flying across the bus and her right shoulder slammed into the table. Sonya was thrown to the floor with Ramone almost landing on top of her. Marion raced to the driver's compartment to see what happened as the others helped the girls back to their seats. Sonya was shaking and said her ribs hurt again, and Lucy's arm felt like it might be broken. Ramone tended to Sonya while the other guys got ice for Lucy's arm and fixed a make-shift sling. Marion came back into the living area and said there was a massive pileup on the highway ahead of them, and they were probably going to be stuck for a while.

She looked closely at Lucy's arm and said they would have to get her to an ER as soon as possible. She then went to Sonya who was still shaking and said her side hurt, the same side where her ribs were broken during the attack. Before long there was a knock on the bus door and a police officer was outside asking if everyone was OK. Marion told them about the girls' injuries but said neither were life-threatening. The officer told them that there would probably be a wait of over an hour before the bus could move again and asked if they wanted the girls taken to an ER now or wait until they got to Nashville. Everyone agreed they could wait until later, and the officer went to check on other vehicles. Lucy went to sit beside Sonya and did her best to comfort her, but the pain in her own arm was excruciating. And of course, all she could think about was how would she play her guitar with a broken arm.

After about an hour and a half, there was another knock on the door and a different officer told them the road ahead was finally cleared and they would be able to leave soon. Once the bus was again moving, the guys went to their bunks and Sonya stayed on the sofa next to Ramone. Lucy found a comfortable spot in one of the reclining seats and Marion made sure her arm was packed in ice. This was certainly a far cry from the party of just a while ago.

Lucy managed to nod off a bit before the bus pulled into the parking lot of Star Records. Marion had called Josh to report the accident, and he said he wanted both girls checked out as soon as possible. Ramone managed to carefully get them into his truck and drove them to the nearest ER, which just happened to be the same one where Sonya was taken after she was assaulted. Memories of that night came flooding back to both of them, and Sonya cried uncontrollably for the trauma this was causing.

It was about five A.M. when they arrived, and fortunately the ER was not busy. Both girls were treated quickly and released to go home – Sonya's ribs were just bruised, but Lucy's shoulder was dislocated. The ER doctor was able to get her shoulder back in place, but she needed to wear a sling for six weeks! Ramone drove them home and helped them into their condo. Lucy had visions of coming home from her first tour victorious, but instead she arrived home in a sling and worried about being able to play her guitar for the next six weeks.

Ramone stayed until he was sure the girls were going to be OK, then went home to his own condo. Lucy and Sonya looked at each other, tired and weary and battered, and then burst into laughter, which made Sonya's ribs hurt again.

"Look at us!" Lucy smiled. "What a pair of conquering heroes we are! No one would believe this crazy story!"

Sonya said, "It's almost time for the morning news. I wonder if we will be on?"

"I doubt it, but let's check anyway," Lucy said. The girls settled onto the sofa and Lucy found the local CBS station they both liked. It wasn't long before pictures of last night's wreck were being shown.

"A massive pile up on southbound I-65 last night brought traffic to a standstill," the reporter said. "The cause is still under investigation, but over 30 cars and trucks were involved. Included in the mess was the tour bus for *Rising Star* winner Lucy Armando who was returning to Nashville from her first three-city tour. No serious injuries were reported; however, we have learned that both Armando and a female friend who was also on the bus were taken to a Nashville hospital for evaluation. No further details are available at this time."

"I always wonder where they get their information," Sonya asked. "Do you think they have spies at the hospitals? Or maybe the ambulance drivers?"

"Could be," Lucy answered. "All the craziness of the last 24 hours has made me hungry. Wonder what we have here in the house to eat?"

"You rest and I'll find us something. I may be slow, but at least I have 2 working arms!"

"Are you sure? I know that your ribs are really hurting you."

"It's not too terrible, I think I was more stressed than anything. I hated being back in that ER!"

"Oh, me too. Don't go to too much trouble – what do we have that is easy?"

"Not much in the fridge, but there's frozen waffles and bacon in the freezer. Sound OK?"

"Perfect. That with some coffee and I'll be fine. Let's make a list and call a delivery order for later. I'm sure glad our local grocery store delivers since neither one of us is in any shape to go shopping!"

Sonya quickly fixed their breakfast, and they sat across the table from each other, reliving the tour and sharing stories and ideas. Lucy made sure they ate on paper plates so there would be no dishes to wash, and that Sonya was not doing too much lifting or bending. Still feeling responsible for her initial injuries, Lucy hated that her friend was again in pain, and that it was due to being with her.

After breakfast, they were about to head to their bedrooms for a nap when Lucy's phone rang. Josh sounded concerned when he asked how they were doing, and if there was anything he could do for them.

"Actually, we just had a bite to eat and are heading to bed for a while," Lucy said sleepily. "I'm just worried about what this means to our schedule, and to my ability to play."

"That's another reason I called. I was hoping to have a meeting tomorrow with everyone to go over the numbers from the tour. How about we have it at your place? We can have a celebration and decide what comes next, while you two continue to rest and heal. Don't worry about anything – we'll bring extra chairs and some food, etc., sound good?"

"That sounds fine. Just let me know what time so we can be awake and dressed!"

"Let's aim for 11 unless I tell you otherwise. Take it easy today and get some rest. We'll see you tomorrow."

Lucy relayed the information to Sonya and then went into her bedroom. Unable to get comfortable in her bed, she moved back to the living room and propped herself into a corner of the sofa. She took a pain pill the ER doctor had given her and drifted off to sleep.

The next thing Lucy heard was a loud knocking on the front door. She jerked awake and felt a sharp pain in her shoulder. She moaned as she pulled herself toward the door. Peering through the keyhole, she saw Ramone standing on the steps holding several boxes and a shopping bag.

"I'm sorry to bother you," Ramone said as Lucy opened the door and let him in. "But Josh called me earlier and asked me to bring these to you. I guess word of the accident was all over the news and your fans sent tons of things to you already. Plus, there's a gift from the studio."

He handed her a box that was obviously from a florist, along with a stack of 'get well' cards. "People have been dropping by all day with things for you,"

"All day? What time is it?"

"Almost three thirty – why?"

"Three thirty? Wow. We both have been sleeping all day. I wonder how Sonya is doing?"

"I'm doing better," Sonya said as she slowly made her way from her bedroom to the kitchen. "Even better now that you are here," she whispered as she looked at Ramone. "Is anyone else starving?"

"I hope so," he answered, "since this big bag here is filled with goodies from your favorite BBQ place: ribs, brisket, potato salad, beans, and Texas Toast. I also got a cheesecake and some fresh strawberries. You ladies sit down, and I'll take care of everything. I'm curious who sent you those flowers."

"Oh, me too!" Sonya gushed. "Hurry up and open them!"

Ramone sat the box on the table and found a pair of scissors in a drawer. Lucy gently opened the box to find a lovely bouquet of daisies and pansies, along with a small vase. Tucked into the bouquet was a card.

"Oh, they are lovely!" Sonya said. "Who are they from?"

"I have no idea!" Lucy said as she nervously opened the card. *"I hope you are feeling better soon,"* she read. *"The world – and I – need your magical voice. Dusty."*

"Dusty? The guy you met the other night?" Ramone asked nervously.

"I guess so. That's very sweet of him."

"I'm glad he included a little vase, since we only have a big one. I'll put these in water," Sonya said.

"I'll get the food ready, if you want to eat now?" Ramone asked.

"Oh yes!" Lucy smiled at the containers of food. "It smells heavenly."

Lucy's phone rang and she saw the call was from her dad.

"Hi, Dad, sorry I didn't call you sooner. It's been a crazy few hours."

"Are you OK?" he asked frantically. "What in the world happened?"

Lucy filled her parents in on the accident and their injuries.

"What a way to end your first tour!" her mother said worriedly. "Are you sure you will be alright? Is there anything we can do?"

"Thanks, but the studio is taking great care of us. Ramone just brought us some BBQ for dinner, and the fans have been sending cards and flowers."

"OK, well, keep us posted. We love you!"

"Love you, too," she said as she ended the call. "I do hate that my parents are so worried."

Soon they were seated around the table and Ramone dished up Lucy's plate while she struggled to use her fork left-handed. "This is going to be a *LONG* six weeks I'm afraid," she said sadly.

They had just finished eating when Ramone's phone rang. "It's the office," he said as he answered.

Vickie Jo was on the other end, wanting to know how they were doing so she could post in social media. Ramone gave the update then listened intently for several minutes.

"OK, I'll get everything set up on this end. See you tomorrow," he said as he hung up.

"We really are meeting tomorrow?" Lucy asked.

"Yes, they will all be here around before noon and we'll have a working lunch. The other news is that they hired a home health aide for a few weeks to help both of you with showers and other things around the house until you feel like you can handle it."

"Wow, that's very generous of them," Lucy said as Sonya looked on, amazed.

"For me, too? That's crazy – I'm sure I can manage," Sonya said.

"Yes, for you too. You were hurt while on their bus, so they want to take care of you. Plus, they all love you and consider you part of the team. The aide will be here around eight in the morning. I hope to get here at ten thirty to start setting things up before everyone else arrives. You two are to do *NOTHING*, understand? No lifting, moving chairs – nothing. Got it?"

"Yes SIR!" they both said laughing.

Ramone cleared the rest of their dinner and put the leftovers in the fridge.

"That was so yummy, I can't thank you enough," Lucy said as she slowly made her way back to the recliner. Ramone brought her a glass of water and her pain pills, along with an ice pack for her shoulder.

"Anything else I can do to make you comfortable before I go?"

"No, you have been wonderful. I'm not sure what we would have done without you."

"It's been my pleasure. Sonya, how are you feeling? Anything I can do to help you?"

"I'm a bit sore, but better than 12 hours ago, that's for sure. Want to stay and watch a movie or something?"

"I can stay a little while, but you both need your rest."

"OK, how about continuing our cribbage challenge from the tour?"

"You're on! Where is the board and I'll go get it."

"In my black duffle bag at the foot of my bed. Obviously, I haven't unpacked yet."

"You sit tight, and I'll be right back."

Ramone left the room and Sonya turned to Lucy. "It's OK that he stays, right? Are we going to bother you?"

"Of course it's OK. He's one of my oldest and dearest friends, and I know he's special to you, too."

"Yes, he is," Sonya said softly. "You don't mind?"

"Mind? Of course not! Nothing would make me happier!"

Ramone came back with the cribbage board and said, "What makes you happy?"

Sonya blushed and Lucy smothered a smile. "Singing on stage is great, but spending time with my new family makes me happy."

"Me too, of course," he agreed. "I'm so glad you called me and asked for my help. You both are incredibly important to me."

"You guys go ahead and play – don't mind me if I fall asleep soon. My pain meds are starting to kick in."

"We'll try to be quiet, I promise," Sonya said as she adjusted Lucy's blanket. "Sleep well my friend. I love you."

"Love you, too…" Her words were slurred as she drifted off to sleep.

Ramone and Sonya had been playing cribbage for about an hour when he noticed her trying to stifle a yawn.

"OK, enough for today. You need to get some rest, too. Anything you need before I go?"

"Just this," Sonya replied as she reached out to put her hand in his. "I never could have gotten through all of this without you."

"It's been my pleasure, truly. I hope you know that this is more than just a job for me."

"I'm so glad," she said shyly and then placed a soft kiss on his cheek.

"This is hard for me," she continued. "I still have flashbacks to that night when…" Her voice trailed off into the silent room.

"I know, and I don't want you to feel like I am pushing you or rushing into anything."

"I don't, really. I'm just glad you are here." She yawned again, and he rose to leave.

"That's my signal to go. Rest well and I'll see you tomorrow. Be sure to lock the doors, OK?"

"Of course - goodnight."

After checking the door and turning off the kitchen lights, Sonya started toward her bedroom. She was startled to hear a soft voice coming from the living room. "You two are so cute. I love you both."

"I hope we didn't wake you!"

"No, I've been drifting in and out. Sleep well."

"I will – you too."

Lucy drifted back to sleep and slept well until around midnight. Was it just 24 hours since the bus crash? Suddenly full of energy, she eased herself out of the recliner and walked quietly to her bedroom. She managed to get her suitcase onto her bed using just her left hand, and once it was open, found her toiletry bag and took it into the bathroom. She was shocked by her reflection in the mirror: bags under her eyes, messy hair and smeared makeup. She sat down on the edge of the bathtub and started washing up as best she could. She eased out of the jeans and T-shirt she had been wearing since the crash and into a pair of sweatpants and a comfy top. It sure was hard work with just one arm! Feeling refreshed, she went back into her bedroom and unpacked her bag, putting most everything into her laundry basket. Suddenly she remembered the note from Dusty that she had put in her jeans pocket. Fishing them from the basket, she was relieved to find the note and set it on her dresser. "I'm so glad I found that before it got destroyed in the washer," she whispered.

Satisfied once her bags were unpacked, she picked up Dusty's note and moved back to the recliner in the living room. She thought back to their meeting and the instant connection and attraction she felt toward him. She really wanted to get to know him better, but Travis and his deception came to mind. Would she ever be able to trust her own judgment again?

Lucy closed her eyes, trying to figure out what to do, but no answer came. When she opened her eyes, she saw her Bible on the table beside her. Turning to one of her favorite verses she had learned as a teen, she read James 1:5 *"If any of you lacks wisdom, you should ask God, who gives generously to all without finding fault, and it will be given to you."*

Feeling a bit guilty that she had not thought about praying sooner, she closed her eyes again. She spent the next half hour in prayer, seeking God's guidance and direction, and asking for forgiveness for being lax with her Bible study and prayer time. Vowing to do better in the future, she shut her Bible, leaving Dusty's note inside as a bookmark. Closing her eyes again, she drifted into a peaceful sleep.

The tantalizing smell of coffee tickled her senses. Lucy opened one eye enough to see the sun streaming in the patio window. "You are too good to me," she said to Sonya who was busy in the kitchen fixing breakfast.

Still in her robe, Sonya replied, "When Ramone told us about the home health aide, I thought they were crazy. But I'm so sore today, and I really want a shower. You are in different clothes – how did you manage that?"

"I couldn't sleep in the middle of the night. It sure wasn't easy, though."

"Well, breakfast is almost ready. It's not fancy, just toast and fruit. We never got groceries ordered yesterday. Hopefully we can do that later today. There is leftover BBQ but didn't figure you wanted it again so soon. The home health aide will be here in about an hour."

Lucy eased herself into a kitchen chair to find her toast buttered and fruit cut into small pieces.

"How do you know just what I need?" she asked softly. "You moving here was the best decision!"

"Nowhere I would rather be. So, why were you up last night? Were you in pain?"

"No, not really. Just lots on my mind."

"Anything in particular?"

"Dusty."

"I'm not surprised. I could see how his flowers affected you."

"Yes, but not just the flowers. I've been wrestling with whether to contact him or not. I want to thank him for the flowers, of course. I prayed about it and now I feel a real peace about taking the next step – *VERY* slowly of course."

"I'm glad. From what I could tell he seems like an upstanding guy. I even saw him on your social media page this morning, posting his well wishes. Be careful, of course, but I'm behind you on this one."

They finished breakfast and were chatting when home health aide Suzy Hunter promptly arrived at eight.

"Good morning, ladies," Suzy said. "As you know, Josh hired me to help for a few weeks while you recover from your injury. I'm an RN and work nights at University Hospital. What can I help you with this morning?" Sonya wanted help with a shower, and then she went to Lucy's bedroom.

"Hi, Lucy. It's your turn – how can I best help you?

Lucy looked at Suzy's eager smile and felt instantly at ease. "I managed to change clothes last night, but it was tough. I really would love a long hot bath, but I need to wash my hair, too, so I guess it will have to be a shower."

"Let's figure out a way to do both. I should be able to wash your hair while you are in the tub. I know I always feel better with clean hair."

"Oh, me too!" Lucy said as they moved into the bathroom. Suzy started the bath water and helped Lucy from her sling.

"Still pretty sore, isn't it?" Suzy asked.

"Yes, but not as bad as yesterday." They chatted about music and the tour, and soon Lucy was clean and wrapped in a towel while Suzy combed her long black hair.

"Do you want me to dry it for you?"

"No, it's fine. Whatever Josh is paying you is not nearly enough. I feel wonderful."

As Suzy helped her dress, she noticed Lucy's guitar in the corner of the room. "Have you tried to play?" she asked gently.

"No, I've been scared to."

"Want me to help you? I used to play a little when I was younger."

"Sure," Lucy said softly, nervous about using her hand and arm, and the pain it might cause.

Suzy opened the case and stroked the guitar lovingly. "Wow, this is beautiful – much nicer than the cheap one my parents got for me when I was in school." She took it from the case and handed it to Lucy.

"Let me know if this hurts at all," she said as she gently lifted Lucy's arm from her chest. She slid the guitar under her arm and placed the strap over her shoulder. Lucy's fingers gently strummed the strings, and she smiled.

"No pain yet!" she said as she played a few lines from '*If Only*'.

Suzy smiled and said, "I love that song. It has such a powerful message."

"Is that music I hear?" Sonya asked from the bedroom door. "Oh, how I've missed that!"

"Well, if you two ladies are feeling ready for the day, I'll go ahead and leave. Did you want me to start some laundry for you?"

"Yes, that would be wonderful," Lucy said. "Sonya, can you show her where everything is?"

"Sure, follow me."

"I put my schedule on the table," Suzy said. "Just let me know if we need to make changes, since I'm sure you will have doctor appointments and other meetings."

"Thank you so very much," Lucy said. Suzy carried Lucy's laundry basket and then left once the load was started.

"Since we have about half an hour until Ramone gets here, do you want to rest?" Sonya asked.

"No, I'm fine – better than fine actually. I'm not sure I ever enjoyed a bath more!"

Lucy spent the next several minutes looking at the box of cards Ramone had brought over from the office yesterday. So many caring people – fans who were genuinely concerned about her. Promptly at ten thirty, he arrived with several folding chairs in the back of his truck and placed them around the living room. Others from the office started arriving a few minutes later: Josh, Vicki Jo and Toby in one car, Marion, Adam and Blake in another. Just before eleven, Darren and Michael were the last to arrive. Michael carried his laptop and a stack of papers. Lucy remained in her recliner and of course, everyone was concerned about her well-being. Sonya offered to stay in her room during the business part of the meeting, but Josh refused to allow it. "You are part of this team now, Sonya, whether you want it or not! How are you feeling today? Better I hope."

"Yes, much better. Thank you again for sending the home health aide – she was wonderful."

"OK, everyone is here so let's get started," Josh said to the rest of the group. "First off, I want to go on record as saying that Lucy, your first tour was amazing, and we met or exceeded all our goals for you. The three venues were very pleased, and our phones have been busy with requests for radio and TV interviews, along with potential special appearances. Of course, any performances are on hold until you have recovered, but I think interviews would be fine. Do you agree Lucy?"

"Of course, as my injured shoulder won't impact radio visits at all. And it will help keep me busy until I can play again."

"And it might actually gain you some sympathy," Vicki Jo said, "even though that is not why we would be doing it. But keeping positive social media and press coverage will be good while you heal. How about I take a picture and then post it later? Your fans have been clamoring for an update."

"That's fine," Lucy said, "although I don't look great. I've got messy hair and no makeup…"

"How about we just do your sling and maybe the side of your face? We really need to give them a little something."

"OK, I guess," Lucy answered, although she was not totally comfortable with it. Would this bring out the haters to comment about her looks again?

The meeting continued for about an hour while they discussed revenues, merchandise sales, and working on her next album. They were on this final topic when a catering van arrived with a wide array of sandwiches, salads and drinks, along with a selection of freshly baked cookies for dessert. Ramone filled a plate for Lucy and made sure she was comfortable and had everything she needed. The rest of the group ate and chatted, finally leaving around one thirty to head back to the office. Before leaving, Marion and Vicki Jo made sure all the leftovers were put away and the trash taken out. Josh instructed both Lucy and Sonya to rest until next week and hopefully they could meet again, but in the office this time. Ramone was the last to leave, squeezing Sonya's hand and reminding her to lock the door.

Once everyone left, Sonya went online and ordered groceries to be delivered in the morning. They decided to stock up on a lot of things since they knew they would be pretty much homebound for several weeks. Once the order was in, she asked Lucy if she should check social media for the latest updates.

"Sure, but if you see anything overly negative, don't tell me, OK? I'm not sure I can handle it."

Chapter Four

Sonya clicked on Lucy's webpage and was surprised to see the picture Vicki Jo had just taken, along with a brief description of her injuries and expected recovery. There were hundreds of responses already, all positive. Sonya added a comment of her own, then closed the laptop. "I think I'll go lay down for a while. Is it time for another pain pill for you? You should probably nap until dinner as well. We'll just have leftovers, if that's OK. We have quite a bit of BBQ from yesterday and then sandwiches from today. I won't have to cook for quite a while."

"Yes, a pain pill would be good. I'm getting a bit achy."

Sonya was headed to the kitchen when there was a knock on the door. Peering through the peephole, she saw a postal worker on the steps. She opened the door and said, "Hi – can I help you?"

"I have a registered letter for Lucy Armando. Is that you? Is she here?"

"I'm her friend Sonya. Lucy is unable to come to the door right now."

"Please sign here," the carrier replied, handing Sonya the letter.

"What is it?" Lucy called from the living room.

"A registered letter – I'll bring it to you."

Sonya handed her a letter with the return address of 'Law Office of James R. Bobbenhouse' in the corner. "I wonder what in the world this is?"

Lucy opened the letter and read the first few lines, then her hands started shaking. Sonya grabbed it from her and began reading.

"Dear Ms. Armando: We are assisting the family of Travis Jones in settling his estate, and they have come across a locked box with your name on it. It is in our possession at our office. Please call at your earliest convenience to make arrangements to pick it up or have it delivered to you. Sincerely, James R. Bobbenhouse, Attorney."

Sonya dropped the letter like it was on fire. "A box? What kind of box would he have with your name on it?"

"I have no idea, and I certainly don't want it in my house. I wonder if I can refuse it without anyone getting suspicious? Most people would jump at the chance to have a gift from him."

"I know we decided to keep this a secret, but maybe it's time to get Ramone involved. This is just so creepy," Sonya said with a whisper.

"I agree. Why don't you reach out to him and ask if he can stop by after a while? This is just getting to be more than I can deal with. Your attack, my guilt, and now our additional injuries. Add in hateful social media and the pressures of the music industry – maybe coming here was a bad idea."

Sonya texted Ramone, asking if he could come over later, and he replied that he was in a meeting with Josh and Marion, discussing duties for him when they were not on tour. He said he would come over after dinner, if that was OK. Lucy said that was fine, so Sonya replied, "*See you later.*" She made sure Lucy had a glass of water, a pain pill, and a fresh ice pack for her shoulder, and then headed to her bedroom for a nap.

Lucy was getting comfortable in her usual spot in the recliner when she saw her Bible beside her, with Dusty's note sticking out. She still had not contacted him, and knew she needed to at least thank him for the flowers. She typed, "*Hi, Dusty. This is Lucy. Thank you so much for the flowers – that was very kind of you,*" but hesitated to press 'send.' What was she waiting for? What was the worst that could happen? She could always block him later if needed. Whispering a simple prayer for safety, she sent the text on its way.

There was no immediate response, which calmed her fears a bit. It was a Monday afternoon at three – surely, he was at work or busy. She wondered what he did for a living and was curious if or when she would hear back from him.

Lucy closed her eyes and drifted into a restless sleep. She dreamed she was in the recording studio and turned around to see Travis watching her from the control booth. But this time he was glaring at her angrily, his fists clenched in rage. Just as he was about to grab her, she heard a *beep* that jolted her awake.

She picked up her phone to see that she had a text from Dusty. Suddenly very nervous, she opened the text to see just a few lines, "*I'm glad you are feeling better. Take it easy. I know you will be resting so won't bombard you with texts. Just let me know when it is a good time, if you want, that is. D"*

Lucy smiled at his kind and considerate tone. She quickly texted back, *"Thx. On orders to take it easy for the rest of the week. But perhaps we can chat later?"*

"Sounds good," he replied. *"TTYL."*

Lucy gingerly went into the kitchen and again saw the box of cards from her fans. So many people loved her, and the staff at the studio were counting on her both financially and personally. She received another text, this time from Josh, telling her that both she and Sonya had follow-up appointments set for Wednesday afternoon. Ramone would drive them to and from, so they didn't need to worry about calling UBER. He included contact information for the doctor, along with a reminder to keep taking it easy.

"Got it, Thx," Lucy replied. She was hoping for good results and being released to go back into the studio sooner than the six weeks originally anticipated.

Sonya came into the kitchen a short time later and filled their plates with leftover BBQ and potato salad. "This is even better the next day!" she said enthusiastically. "We are going to have to go in person, once you are feeling better. I'm sure it smells heavenly in there!"

They had just finished eating when Ramone texted, *"OK to come over now?"* to which Sonya answered *"Yes, now is fine."*

"Sure you are up for this?" Lucy asked. "It will mean reliving that night all over again."

"Not really, but I do know that we need to be honest with Ramone. We can trust him to keep this confidential, but…" her voice drifted off and Lucy could see the memories haunting her.

There was a tap on the door, and Sonya rose to let him in. "Let's move to the living room, OK?" Sonya said. "That way Lucy can be in her recliner, and we will all be more comfortable."

"Why do I get the feeling that this is not just a social call to watch a movie or play cards?"

"Ramone, my dear friend," Lucy began hesitantly. "I have not been completely honest with you about something really big, and I feel that it is time that I confess to you, as it ultimately affects you as well. And it all has to do with the night that Sonya was attacked."

Chapter Five

Ramone sat next to Sonya on the sofa, gently holding her hand. Her eyes were closed, and he could sense her trembling a bit. "The attack? What in the world are you talking about?"

Lucy took a deep breath and said, "Actually, it starts earlier than that, from the first time I met Travis Jones."

"Travis? I'm confused."

Lucy proceeded to tell Ramone everything, from the excitement of singing with Travis and the unexpected gifts and attention, but also mentioned the mysterious text messages. "And now the hard part, the night Sonya was hurt."

"I'm not sure I follow you. What does Travis's attention toward you have to do with Sonya? Wait, you're not telling me that Travis..."

Sonya started sobbing as Ramone's eyes opened wide. "Travis is the one who hurt Sonya? But why?"

"Because she looks so much like me, especially on a dark rainy night. He called her *MY* name as he was hurting her, then ran away when he realized his mistake."

Sonya began sobbing, and Ramone took her gently into his arms. "I had no idea – I'm so sorry. But why are you telling me this now, and not when I first came here?"

Lucy explained that after Travis's death, they weren't sure that anyone would believe Sonya's story, and they just wanted to put it all behind them. That is, until the letter came today.

She handed the registered letter to him, and he read it skeptically. "A box? What in the world would he have for you? Are you going to take it?"

"I think I need to, so it doesn't raise any suspicions. But we both would really appreciate it if you were here to help us deal with any fallout. Of course, all this needs to be kept totally confidential. It wouldn't do anyone any good if this were leaked to the public."

"Of course. When do you want to go pick it up?"

"I just got a text from Josh that we both have doctor appointments Wednesday afternoon. Maybe after that?"

"That's fine. He sent me a similar text with the information. Why don't you call the attorney in the morning and see if that time would be OK. I'm here for you both, no matter what you need from me."

Lucy called the attorney's office in the morning and asked if later Wednesday afternoon would be an acceptable time for her to retrieve the box. The receptionist said it would be fine, as Lucy did not need to speak to the lawyer, just sign a receipt.

Ramone picked the girls up shortly after lunch on Wednesday and took them to the doctor. Sonya's ribs were just bruised, and she was told to take it easy but had no official restrictions. Lucy, however, received the devastating news that her shoulder was not improving, and she was potentially looking at surgery in the future.

"How much pain have you been having?" Dr. Reynolds asked. "Are you taking your pain pills regularly?"

"The pain is bearable most of the time. I usually take one at night or when I know I will be napping. They tend to make me very sleepy."

"You need to take them more regularly, to stay ahead of the pain. I'll write you another prescription – be sure to follow the instructions exactly."

"If I must," Lucy replied. "I've never liked taking a lot of pills."

"Come back in two weeks and we'll check you again. Get lots of rest."

Ramone took her and Sonya to the attorney's office, which was about 30 minutes away. He escorted Lucy inside, opening doors for her and helping her get situated. Sonya decided to wait in the car as she was worried that her anxiety would give something away. They only had to wait a few minutes before a receptionist brought them a metal box about the size of a shoe box. On the top was taped a card that said 'Lucy Armando' followed by a red heart.

"We didn't find a key for it, so it has not been opened. Please sign this receipt – that's all I need today."

Lucy had difficulty signing her name with her left hand, but after verifying her ID, the receptionist handed the box to Ramone who carried it back to the car. As they were about to leave, the receptionist called to her, "Lucy, I heard you recorded a duet with Travis. I'm a huge fan. Do you know when it will be released?"

Lucy stiffened and looked pleadingly at Ramone. He turned to the receptionist and said, "I don't believe any information has been released yet. I'm sure his record label will let everyone know when the time comes," and they walked out the door.

Lucy set the box on the seat between her and Sonya. Neither of them wanted to touch it, much less hold it. Once back at the condo, Ramone retrieved some tools from his truck and the three sat around the kitchen table as he worked to pry open the lock. "He certainly didn't want anyone to see what's in here," Ramone said with exasperation. Finally, the lock broke and the lid flew open. "Do you want me to look first?" he asked.

"No," Lucy said nervously. "This is my mess, it's my responsibility." With shaking hands, she lifted some handwritten notes from the box and then saw a collection of pictures he must have downloaded from the internet and printed: her winning *"Rising Star"* and other snapshots of her found on the show's website. In another stack were actual pictures wrapped in a rubber band, and once she got a good look at them, she gasped. The top picture was of the front of her condo and her car, and others were of the side and the patio, including the windows to her bedroom. She remembered the night before the attack when she thought she heard a noise outside - no doubt, it had been him. Most of the pictures were taken in the daytime, but there were a few evening shots that showed her silhouette behind the lit windows.

There were also pictures of her coming and going from the studio and even one from the grocery store. Many had been enlarged to show just her face and eyes, or a hint of cleavage as she bent down to pick up her newspaper. It was obvious he had been following her for weeks. The bottom piece of paper in that stack was a map to her condo. Shaking, she put the pictures down and looked at news articles about their duet. Her name had been highlighted on each page, and there were hearts drawn in the margin.

Feeling ill, Lucy finally turned to the handwritten notes. There were three pages – the first was about how much he admired her and wanted to meet her. He had watched every episode of "*Rising Star*" and knew he wanted to be with her. A few paragraphs later he talked about recording the duet and how infatuated he was with her. He also mentioned the flowers he sent and how he was looking for excuses to see her again. This continued onto the second page as well, as he professed his love and desire for her. The final page, however, was much darker and filled with anger. She was shocked to read his frightening words, "*Why is she not returning my advances or answering my texts? Is she ignoring me? Does she not know how much I can do for her and her career? I love her more than anyone else ever will. How can she not see that? I guess I need to teach her how things are done around here.*"

Visibly shaken, Lucy started forcing everything back into the box. She was speechless - obviously Travis was not the man he pretended to be.

Sonya had closed her eyes, trying to force the memories away. It was then that Ramone noticed something taped inside the lid of the box. "What in the world…." he asked as he tried to pry it loose. It was a key, but there were no markings on it. "A key? To what?"

Sonya looked at it closely and started sobbing. "It looks like a key to our condo!" Ramone reached into his jeans pocket and pulled out his spare keys. As best as he could tell, this was an exact match to the condo key Lucy had given him.

"How in the world did he manage to get a key? What was he going to do with it?" Ramone instantly regretted those last words, as both Sonya and Lucy were imagining the worst.

Chapter Six

The next several minutes were spent in silence as each one grappled with what the items in the box meant. It was clear that Travis was severely disturbed and a danger to them and society. Lucy still felt guilty knowing that Sonya's attack and resulting PTSD were only because they looked so much alike. Ramone was struggling to take in so much information all at once. His two dear friends had been carrying this burden for weeks, and he hadn't known.

Finally, Ramone spoke, "Well, what we learned here today is something I would never in my wildest dreams have imagined. Lucy, if it's OK, I'm going to take this box to my condo and hide it away somewhere. You two certainly don't need it anywhere in this house. But I don't think we should throw it away. Just in case…"

"No, I'm fine with that. I just want this chapter of our lives to be behind us. Sonya?"

"I agree that this has been a nightmare, and I doubt I could sleep with that thing in our house. Thank you, Ramone, for being here for us."

"No where else I would rather be. Now, how about we get out of here and enjoy some fresh air? A change of scenery? How does that sound, Lucy?"

"You two go," she said softly. "It's time for another of my pain pills, and the doctor was so insistent that I take them on schedule. You enjoy while I take a much-needed nap."

"Are you sure?" Sonya asked. "We could do something here. I hate to leave you."

"No, please, get out and have some fun. I'll be here when you get back."

"Only if you insist," Sonya said as she gave her friend a gentle hug. "We won't be late, I promise."

"Stay out as late as you want. I'll be fine."

"At least let me set out some dinner for you. We have plenty of leftovers – what do you want?"

"Just a sandwich and chips. I'll probably sleep the whole time you are gone."

Sonya and Ramone fixed a plate for Lucy, then left to drive around a bit before deciding to grab dinner and a movie. Lucy made herself comfortable in the recliner, which seemed to be her best friend. She opened the small prescription bottle and removed just one of the pills. She really wanted to rest, to find a way to put all this horror behind her. "Well, if one pill is good, I'm sure a second is even better," and she swallowed both with a large drink of water. She turned the TV to a channel that showed old shows from the 60's and drifted off to sleep.

The next time Lucy opened her eyes, it was to see the first hints of a sunrise peaking in through the living room windows. She had slept all night, the first time since the accident. She noticed Sonya's sweater on the back of a dining room chair, so figured she must have gotten home, although she never heard a thing. The TV was off, and the condo was silent.

She eased herself out of the recliner and made her way to her bathroom. She was surprised to see that it was six fifteen A.M. Suzy would be arriving at eight to help with her shower again so she laid out some clean clothes and took the opportunity to straighten up her bedroom a bit. Her shoulder was feeling much better, although it was a bit stiff from being in the sling for so long. She decided to surprise Sonya with breakfast for a change, so went back into the kitchen to see what was available and what would be possible to fix with one arm. There was a bag of pre-cooked sausage crumbles in the fridge, along with a can of biscuit dough. Biscuits and gravy sounded wonderful, and easy to make since they had a packet of gravy mix she could use as well. Before long, the smell of fresh bread and sausage gravy filled the air. She also made a pot of coffee and set out some fresh fruit. She turned around to see Sonya standing in the doorway, rubbing sleep from her eyes.

"What in the world are you doing? I'm supposed to be taking care of you!"

"I know, but I wanted to surprise you. I had the best night of sleep in ages and woke with a burst of energy. How did you sleep? I didn't hear you come in last night."

"It was close to midnight, I guess," she said sleepily. "We had a nice dinner at a cool place called *Etch* and then saw the new Marvel movie. Afterward, we drove down by the river and just talked for the longest time. He is so easy for me to talk to."

"I'm glad you have that. You need someone besides me to rely on, and he really does care for you."

Suzy arrived promptly at eight. She said she got an update about their conditions and that Sonya had been released. After helping Lucy shower and dress, she started a load of laundry and then took out the trash as she left. Both girls expressed their sincere appreciation for all her help.

"So," Sonya said later, "what is on the agenda for today? I don't think there are any meetings or phone calls on the calendar. Maybe you and I can get out and go to the park nearby or to the river? It really did me good to get out last night."

"That sounds lovely," Lucy responded, "but it's time for another pain pill. I wish they didn't make me so sleepy. But I do feel the pain starting to come back."

"I knew you did too much this morning!" Sonya scolded her. "Maybe we can at least sit out on the patio for a while? It's a beautiful morning."

"Yes, that would be nice."

Sonya carried their coffee cups outside and helped Lucy get situated. She went back inside to bring the pain pills and a big glass of orange juice. "I forgot to bring my phone," Lucy called to her. As Sonya was picking it up to bring outside, she noticed that there were two missed text messages and one missed call.

"Your phone must have been on silent?" Sonya asked as she handed it to Lucy. "I hope you didn't miss anything important."

Lucy saw that the missed call was from her mother. One text was from Josh, who wanted her to call when she got a chance, and the other was from Dusty. Lucy opened the text to read, "*Good morning – hope you are doing well. I have the day off from work, and would love to chat, if you feel up to it of course. D.*"

Lucy smiled and texted back, "*Good morning. Moving a bit slow – how about around 11?*"

"*Sounds good. TTYL,*" he texted back.

Next Lucy called Josh, who wanted to know if she felt up to doing a radio interview tomorrow. *Radio Nashville* wanted to chat about how she was doing and impressions of her first tour. Ramone would drive her, and Vicki Jo would meet her for a few photos for the website. "I don't want to push you too much," Josh said a bit sternly, "but it's imperative that we keep your name out there and your fanbase engaged. Attention spans are short, and you know there are plenty of young girls who are itching to take your place."

This was the first real pressure she had felt from Josh and could sense his frustration. "Of course," she answered. "What time?"

"Great! Ramone will pick you up at seven. I understand that's pretty early, but you know how morning radio is."

"That's fine, I'll be ready. Thanks, Josh – I won't let you down."

The call ended and Lucy sighed. Things were starting to get *real*, and she could feel the pressure to succeed increasing more each day. It didn't help that she missed some time after Sonya's attack, and then was sidelined due to her injury from the bus wreck. Neither were truly her fault, but she knew that this was not what Josh and the others had planned for her.

Reaching for a pain pill, she just wanted it all to be back to what it was those first few weeks, before the injuries and pain, before Travis.

Sonya hated to wake her but was worried about how much she was sleeping. Shortly before eleven she gently tapped Lucy's good shoulder and said, "Hey sleepy head! I think it's time we move back inside --- it looks like it might rain in a bit."

Lucy groggily opened one eye to see that the beautiful sunny morning was gone, and storm clouds filled the sky. "Thanks," she said. "How long have I been asleep?"

"A couple of hours," Sonya answered.

"Oh, Dusty is supposed to text, or I am. I don't remember which. But I don't want to miss him again."

"Well, I hate to leave you, but I just got word about a job interview as a receptionist at a small vet clinic not far from here. I need to leave in about an hour, if that's OK?"

"Of course – you would be perfect for that. Don't worry about me, I'll be fine."

At 11:03 Lucy's phone *pinged* with a text from Dusty. Prompt, but not pushy – qualities she admired.

"Come on inside and I'll leave you to your texting. I need to get ready anyway."

Lucy smiled and thanked Sonya again for all her help, but mostly for her friendship. Settled back in the recliner, she opened the text to see, "*I hope now is ok? I don't want to disturb you.*"

"*No, it's perfect. Was resting on the patio earlier but wide awake now.*"

"Cool. Don't want to push but may I call you? I'm not really a fan of long texts."

"Me either. That's fine."

After about 30 seconds, her phone rang, and she was thrilled to hear Dusty's voice again. Very deep and very southern, she wondered how he ended up in Ohio.

"Good morning, how are things today? Are you feeling better?"

"It's good to talk to you again. Yes, I'm better but it's going to be a long road. I have at least four weeks left in this sling, and then I will likely need some rehab. But it's certainly better than before."

"And your friend, Sonya, is it? How is she doing?"

"Much better, thanks. So, what type of work do you do that you get a day off in the middle of the week?"

"I work IT for a large insurance company here in Cincinnati. Remember that big data breech that was on the news a few weeks ago? Well, I ended up working tons of overtime, so they gave me today off as comp time. Those were some crazy long days."

"Oh, yes, I do remember. Did they ever figure out what happened?"

"Well, most of it is confidential, but I can say an employee opened an email that had a virus attached. It made a really huge mess for us."

"I can imagine. Have you been in IT long? Have you always lived in Ohio? Your voice sounds like Texas or Tennessee to me."

"Guilty. I grew up near San Antonio, Texas, and went to Texas A&M, majoring in computer science. I landed this job right out of college and have been here ever since."

"Do you like Ohio?"

"Most of the time, except in the winter. I *HATE* the snow!"

"Oh, I understand. We got enough in St. Louis, sometimes way more than we wanted! What about your family? Were they OK with you moving so far away?"

"It was just my dad and me. My mom passed away in a car accident when I was very young. My grandparents helped raise me, but they are gone now as well. Dad didn't want to stand in the way of my career and encouraged me to follow my dreams."

"I'm sorry about your mom. Do you have other family? Cousins, aunts and uncles?"

"Yes, I have a few. I'm especially close to my cousin Amanda, who is just a few months younger than me. Her mom was my mom's sister and reminds me a lot of her."

"It's good to have family. I'm an only child as well, and my parents are in Florida right now. My mom is getting specialized treatment for her cancer. We're not sure she is going to make it this time."

"This time?"

"This is not her first time with cancer. She bounced back before, but this one is really hard on her."

Sonya tiptoed into the living room with a smile on her face, waving to Lucy to signal that she was leaving for her interview. Lucy gave her a 'thumbs up' to wish her well.

"Is someone else there? Do you need to go?" Dusty asked.

"No, it was Sonya, but she just left for a job interview. I actually don't have anything on my calendar today. I do have a radio show to do in the morning, though, for *Nashville Today*."

"Wow, Impressive. Has the adjustment to all the fame and attention been difficult? I would think it would be challenging to know who to trust."

Lucy was quiet for a few seconds, then said softly, "For the most part, everyone has been lovely and supportive. But there are some awful people online, and even in person. There are times I have my doubts about continuing in this business."

"Oh, I hope it's not really that bad. I know it's been difficult with the bus accident and all, and the uncertainty of when you can play or tour again. But I truly hope those negative people are the exception and not the rule."

"Yes, very much so. But it does get discouraging at times."

"Oh, I can't even imagine the pressure you feel you are under. Look, it's been great talking with you, but I'll let you go back to resting. I'd love to call you again, if that's OK?"

"Yes, I would like that. I could text you my schedule each week, if that's something you are interested in?"

"Most of the important things are on your website, but yes, if it's not too much trouble."

"OK, well, it's about time for another pain pill and a nap. Please pray that my shoulder heals quickly. I really need to get back into the studio and on the road for a longer tour."

"Rest well, and I'll be praying. Talk to you soon." And with that, Dusty ended the call. Lucy closed her eyes and remembered everything about meeting him just a few weeks ago. She thought about his dark hair and eyes, and how his 6-foot frame towered over her. She looked forward to talking to him again soon.

She turned on the TV and found a country music channel. After a few commercials, an announcer came on and said they were doing a tribute to Travis Jones in honor of what would have been his 33rd birthday. Lucy felt paralyzed to change the channel, then turned around to see that Sonya had just come home from her interview and was watching the TV in horror. Lucy grabbed the remote and flipped to a cable news channel, but the damage had been done. Both of them were thrown back into the horrors of that night, and all the repercussions that followed.

"I'm so sorry," Lucy stammered. "I had no idea…"

"Is it ever going to end? Will we ever feel safe again?"

"We just need to have faith that this will fade in time. I cringe at the thought of the duets album dropping, and all the extra media attention that is coming because of it. Oh, how I wish I had never met him."

"Me too, obviously. Oh, I got the job! Just part time for now, but really nice people. How about I order a pizza for dinner? I'm in the mood for something different. Sound OK? Lucy?"

"What? Oh, yeah, that would be fine. I really need a nap first, if there is time."

"Of course. You rest, and I'll do some reading in my room. I have paperwork to fill out for the new job. Rest well, Lucy."

Ramone picked them up at seven the next morning for their short drive to the radio station. The interview would be between seven thirty and eight, and then they wanted to have breakfast at Big Al's Deli, which the guys in the band said was one of the best places in Nashville to eat. This would be Lucy's first real outing since the accident, and while she was anxious to get out of the house, she was nervous about being in pain and not able to take a pain pill.

The station receptionist took them to the booth where she met Ricky and Roz. Vicki Jo was already there and chatting with the DJs.

"Good morning," Roz said. "I know it's early, but we are excited to have you here. Sit here between us. Here's your headphones."

"Thanks. I wanted to introduce you to Sonya and Ramone, two dear friends from high school who are helping me navigate all of this."

"Welcome," Ricky said. "OK, any questions? If not, here we go!"

"Alright everyone," Ricky said to his radio audience. "As promised, we have Lucy Armando here with us today to fill us in on all that has been going on since dropping her debut album. First off, tell us about the tour! How exciting!"

"It really was more than I could have ever imagined. The crowds were great, and my bandmates quickly became my family. To be honest, I was really nervous at first, but after a song or two, I felt right at home."

"We heard great things from the fans that were there," Roz added. "Did anything surprise you?"

"There were two things, actually. First was that so many people would pay extra for VIP without me ever doing a concert before. The second was the number of people singing along. My album had only been out a short while. It was fun that they enjoyed my new music as much as the covers."

"And then there was the accident…" Ricky paused. "It must have been so frightening for you, for all of you."

"It was so sudden. We were celebrating and having a good time when the bus suddenly swerved and then came to a grinding halt."

"I think I heard only two of you were badly injured? That must seem like a miracle."

"Yes, just me and my friend Sonya who was travelling with us that night. I was really worried because I thought I had broken my arm."

"How is the recovery going? How much longer before you are back in the studio?"

"My doctor says I'm progressing, but it will be several more weeks, I'm afraid."

"Well, we all wish you a speedy recovery," Roz said gently. "Any last words for your fans?"

"I just wanted to thank everyone for their kindness and support. The cards and messages on social media mean the world to me. Be patient a little longer – I'll be back soon."

"Thank you, Lucy. Come back and see us anytime."

"Well, everyone," Ricky concluded, "that's the latest from Lucy Armando. Keep it here on *Nashville Now* for all the news from around town. We'll be back after this message."

The DJs took off their headphones and thanked her again for coming by on such short notice. Vicki Jo took a few pictures and then they walked back to the lobby.

"Another great job, Lucy," Vicki Jo said. "I'm heading to the office. Hopefully we will see you there next week? I know Josh has a few ideas for you to think about while you are healing."

"Sounds good. Thanks again."

Ramone helped her into the car, and she winced in pain. It was way past time for a pain pill, but she didn't want to miss the chance for a nice breakfast and time out of the condo.

They had just taken their seats at the restaurant when a small group of teenaged girls approached their table. "You are Lucy Armando, right? This is so exciting! Can we get a picture with you?"

"Of course," Lucy answered. "Come stand behind me and my friend can take the picture."

The girls giggled and jockeyed for position behind her. The one on the right bumped into her shoulder, bringing tears to her eyes. "Oh, I'm sorry," she said apologetically. "Did I hurt you?"

Ramone saw the pain in Lucy's eyes and said sternly, "Girls! I know this is exciting, but Lucy is recovering from a serious injury. Be gentle with her or I'll have to ask you to leave."

"We are so sorry – please forgive us."

"Sure," Lucy said cautiously. "It looks like our breakfast is coming. Thanks for stopping by."

The fans left and Lucy thanked Ramone for the help. "Getting out of the condo was a nice idea, but I really need some rest and my ice pack."

"I'm sorry if this was too much for you," Sonya whispered sadly. "Maybe we should just get the food to go so we can get you home?"

"No, I'll be fine. You'll need to cut up my French toast, though."

"Anything you need, you know that."

The next several days were very quiet with Lucy mostly resting, and Sonya and Ramone enjoying being together. Dusty called several times, and Lucy found herself looking forward more and more to their long chats.

On Monday, Ramone stopped by to wish Sonya good luck at her new job and to take Lucy to the studio. Walking in the door, she realized just how long it had been since she was there. How she missed the people and the excitement! Josh had scheduled a meeting in the big conference room for ten, and Lucy was anxious to see everyone again.

"Oh, Lucy, it's so good to see you!" Darren said happily. "It just hasn't been the same here without you."

"I'm glad to be back, even though I'm not 100% yet."

"Well, what Josh wants to discuss today won't take either of your arms, at least not yet."

"What in the world…" Lucy started, but was interrupted as others joined the group.

"She's back!" Vicki Jo said. "I'm sure your fans will be excited to hear the news!"

Once the group was assembled, Josh took the podium to brief everyone on sales numbers and requests for appearances. "It's slacked off a bit this past week or so," he said while looking at Lucy. "We need a way to generate buzz until we can get you back into the studio or on the road."

"I'm excited for whatever you have in mind," Lucy tried to reassure him. "I feel badly for the inconvenience this has caused everyone."

"It's really a fine line to walk. We want you to recover and come back strong and healthy, but as I mentioned before, there is a long line of pretty singers more than ready to take your place on the charts. So, this is what I propose - it's time to think seriously about a music video for '*If Only*'. I've been toying around a bit with some ideas, but I'm open to all input. We have this room booked for two hours, and I hope to have something roughed out before we leave. It is imperative that we get moving on with this, ASAP Lucy, I know I just sprung this on you, but I wondered if you had any sort of storyline in your heart when you wrote it. Were you going through a particular situation you would feel comfortable sharing?"

"Wow, to be honest, it was not one singular situation, but rather feeling overlooked because I did not fit the cookie-cutter mold of all the popular girls. I just thought that if people would look past the outside and my lack of trendy fashion and excessive sexuality to see my heart, they would find that I am willing to be vulnerable and honest. Does that make sense?"

"Absolutely!" Josh said excitedly. "Toby?"

"Hi, Lucy – good to see you again. We haven't talked much since I did your photo shoot, but I have certainly been following your career, and the accident of course. I'm glad you are doing better. As for the video, I will be leading the team in terms of concept and direction. I will have a couple of videographers helping me get all the best shots. We have the full resources here at Star to make a top-notch video, and we don't need to cut corners. I like the premise here, so let's all brainstorm some more."

For the next hour, everyone tossed out ideas that would match the underlying theme of the song. Knowing that her music appealed most to young girls between 15 and 20 years old, they decided on setting the video at a high school where the girl was struggling to fit in. She would not be total 'ugly duckling' but more of just a 'plain Jane' who didn't fit in the popular crowd and was not asked to the prom.

"What if we hired someone to play Lucy in her younger days, but we have grown-up Lucy watching in the background? It could be mature Lucy looking back on her life and reflecting on the changes between then and now?" Vicki Jo proposed.

"Oh, I really like the idea," Lucy said, "except I worry about the ending. She is not going to have a makeover and then everyone is jealous. I want to keep this honest, with her realizing that while she is sad that she is not accepted, she is not going to change her values or ethics just to get a date for the prom. It's important to me that everyone learn to love themselves as they are."

"I like that," Josh said. "It's not about getting even with those who mistreat you, but to be comfortable in your own skin. Anyone else have a thought?"

"May I say something?" Ramone asked. "I know I'm not part of the creative team, but I have known Lucy longer than anyone else in this room. One of the reasons we have been friends for so many years is that she is truly authentic. She doesn't pretend to be something she is not, just to fit in."

"I think that shines through in her music, and also in interviews and personal interactions," Josh agreed. "Toby, I need you to start checking around to see what schools we could borrow for a few days of shooting, and we need lots of students for background. We also need to find our 'faux-Lucy.' There will be shots of you singing, of course, but the acting will be by someone a bit younger and relatively unknown. You are OK with that?"

"Of course. I'm not sure I would be any good acting in a music video!" she said with a smile.

The meeting broke up just before noon, and Ramone was quickly by Lucy's side, asking if she needed to go home. "I am getting a bit sore," she answered. The thought of a pain pill and an ice pack was very appealing.

"Josh, do you need Lucy more today, or can I take her home? She's needing a rest I think."

"Of course, you can head home. Thanks for all the hard work and ideas. I think we got a lot accomplished. Keep resting – we need you at 100%."

"I will, Josh," she answered with a sigh. How she wished she could speed this process up a bit.

Chapter Seven

The next two weeks were filled with teleconferences, doctor visits, and lots of time resting. She was given some easy range-of-motion exercises to do until she could officially start physical therapy. The plans for the music video were progressing at a rapid pace, with the location determined and even a 'faux-Lucy' hired, Sabrina Lopez. Lucy studied her pictures and watched a video she had been in. She hoped that Sabrina would be able to convey the essence they were going for: honesty, vulnerability, strength and self-confidence, but still mixed with a bit of sadness and loneliness.

The long conversations with Dusty were getting more frequent, occurring almost every evening now. The only things more frequent were the less-than-subtle hints from Josh that they needed to get her back in the studio and on tour as soon as possible.

Her doctor refilled her pain pill prescription again, despite Lucy's complaints that they made her too sleepy. "You may not know this," Dr. Reynolds said, "but Josh is an old friend of mine. In fact, I am the doctor he sends most of his talent to. He has expressed his concerns to me regarding the length of time this injury is taking to heal. I told him I would impress on you the importance of taking your medicine as prescribed and doing some light exercises. I value my relationship with him – both personal and professional. You do understand what I am trying to tell you, right?"

Lucy nodded but hated feeling so pressured to keep taking the opioids. She often felt she was becoming too reliant on them, even taking more than prescribed a time or two when the pain was particularly intense, or when she wanted a good night's sleep. Star Records had already invested so much money in her and she felt very obligated to prove their faith in her was not misguided.

The night before the video shoot, Lucy's sleep was haunted with dreams of Travis peering at her from the shadows, his fists clenched in rage. "You need to learn how the game is played," he said menacingly, over and over. She woke up with her shoulder throbbing in pain. Reaching for her pain pills, she took two and then eased into a restless sleep.

"Lucy, wake up! We need to hurry if we are going to make it to the video shoot on time," Ramone said as he tried to shake her awake.

"What? What time is it? Oh, *OW*! My shoulder is killing me."

"We only have about an hour before we need to leave for the shoot. Do you need help? Sonya is in the shower, but I can get her to help you."

"No, just give me a minute, I'll be OK. Oh, I'm so stiff and sore."

Lucy walked gingerly from the recliner into her bedroom and gently removed her sling. There wasn't time for a full shower, so she just did the best she could, freshening up at the sink. She painfully pulled her long hair into a ponytail and put on just a bit of makeup, noticing that her eyes were a bit bloodshot and puffy. Dressed in jeans and a Shania Twain T-shirt, she put her sling back on and went to the kitchen to look for something to eat. She had never been to a video shoot before and wasn't sure how long they would work before a lunch break.

Sonya got out of the shower and dressed to go to her part-time job. "I'm glad Ramone is here to help get you to the shoot," she said, "but I wish I could be there. How exciting! Are you OK, Lucy? You look really tired."

"Gee, thanks. It was a tough night with bad dreams," she said vaguely, not wanting to upset her friend again. "And I woke up pretty sore. Josh told us to be prepared for a long day. Maybe you can stop by after work? They are just filming the students and exteriors today. My part isn't for a few days. The whole process seems fascinating to me. But I'm glad all I do today is watch, as I'm in way too much pain to be on camera."

"Well, take it easy. I'll text you once I get off work and you can let me know if I should come over."

"Have a good day. I know you love working with the kittens and puppies again."

"Absolutely," she said with a smile, and after a quick kiss on the cheek from Ramone, she skipped out the door.

"It's good to see her so happy again," Lucy said softly. "I wasn't sure the old Sonya was ever coming back. You played a big part in that, you know."

Ramone smiled and said, "There is nothing I wouldn't do for her. It's taken a long time, but yes, the old Sonya is on her way back."

She quickly ate a bagel and some grapes, then picked up her purse, still feeling a bit unsteady on her feet. "Ready?" she asked Ramone, as she put on her sunglasses to hide her bloodshot eyes. "I guess it's time to leave."

"I'm so glad they let me tag along to events that are not necessarily in my job description," he said happily. "I'm loving learning so much about the music industry."

Ramone drove her to Parkview Elementary School, which was in the process of being transformed into Park High. It was a nice sunny day, and the exterior shots were being set up first before it got too hot later. Lights and cameras were everywhere, and the parking lot had several tents set up for makeup and hair, along with one that had tables filled with drinks and snacks. Toby was in his element, rushing around and giving directions. Ramone found a place where Lucy could see all that was happening but stay out of the sun, although he did think it was odd that she left her sunglasses on. Josh arrived soon, along with Vicki Jo and a few interns Lucy was not familiar with. Soon Toby stopped by to introduce Sabrina.

"It's so good to meet you," Sabrina said sweetly. "I've been a fan since the TV show. I just knew you were going to win. I'm honored to be in your video today. I hope I make you proud."

"It's good to meet you, too. I watched one of your videos and you seem to be a natural in front of the camera. Mostly, I just want you to have fun and let the words of the song shine through. That's all I can ask."

"Of course. Toby and his team came up with a great concept and many of the other actors are friends of mine, so it will be easy to play off each other. *'If Only'* is my favorite song, by the way."

Lucy was fascinated to watch the process unfold. Sabrina and a few other students had actual parts to play, and Toby went over each scene in depth with them. The others were there just to fill in the background, getting out of their cars and walking into the school. The interns seemed to be in charge of them. They did a few rehearsals and then it was time for the first take. The parking lot was filled with cars and students talking excitedly about the upcoming prom. Sabrina arrived alone and walked silently to the front door. It was almost as if she was invisible. No one talked to her or even acknowledged her presence. Lucy felt the pangs of her old loneliness and knew they were on the right track.

After several takes, they moved the group into a front hallway filled with lockers and a few vending machines. Toby found a place for Lucy to watch where she would be out of the shot but able to see the action. Sabrina walked to her locker and put her books away, still feeling very alone. She looked at the huge banners and posters on the wall spotlighting the upcoming prom. There was a small table set up for ticket sales, and several of the main actors were in line. Sabrina walked past them, and a few of the students finally noticed her, then rolled their eyes. They laughed a bit and joked that obviously SHE didn't need a ticket.

Toby yelled "CUT!" and the cameras stopped. Lucy was shaken by the memories of high school that came rushing back.

But she knew that this was a bit of an exaggeration, that she really did have a few friends in school, including Sonya and Ramone. But the video was clearly making its point.

"That was great!" Toby said excitedly. "Let's run it a few more times so the cameras can get different angles, and then we'll break for now. If all goes well, we can start the night scenes tonight. What do you think, Lucy?"

"It's very emotional for me. It truly captures much of what I was feeling when I wrote the song. Everyone did very well!"

"Perfect. Let's run it again."

Lucy watched as they filmed the scenes a few more times, then Toby told everyone to be back at six P.M. so they could film some early evening shots. Her arm was really hurting by this time, and she was eager to get home and rest for a while. As Ramone was walking her to the car, Toby approached them.

"I'm glad you are pleased, and if all goes as planned, we will be about a day ahead of schedule. We could do your exterior and hallway shots tomorrow, if you feel up to it?"

"Tomorrow? Oh wow. Sure, if that's what you need. I already have my wardrobe picked out but will need some help with my hair and makeup."

"You think you will be OK without your sling?"

"As long as you don't expect me to do a handstand or play on the jungle gym, I should be fine."

"Great. Are you planning to come back tonight?"

"Yes, I would love to watch the process for shooting in the evening. Toby – I wanted to thank you for sharing my vision for this song. I really think we are on the right track."

"Ramone, what is your opinion? Does this remind you of high school with Lucy?"

"A bit, yeah. I always noticed her, of course, for the special person she is inside. But most of the popular kids, the jocks and cheerleaders, never really saw her. I think it's perfect for the song."

"Great. OK, I'll see you both later. Get some rest Lucy,"

They got in the car and Ramone turned to Lucy. "Are you really OK?" he asked gently. "You seem to be moving rather stiffly this past hour or so."

"Honestly, no, I'm not. My arm is killing me. And I'm starving. That bagel I had earlier is long gone, and the snacks they had didn't help much. Can we drive through somewhere on the way home?"

"Sure. Anyplace in particular?"

"There's an Arby's not far from the condo. Does that sound OK?"

"Whatever you want. Once I get you home and settled, I need to head to the office for a few hours. Josh wants to talk to me again about other things I can do while you are not on tour. You will have several hours to rest before I pick you up again at five thirty. Sound good?"

"Of course. I can't thank you enough for all you have done for me – not only here in Nashville but also being my friend when we were growing up. Sabrina was so alone walking those halls, but I had you and Sonya, and for that I am eternally grateful."

After their late lunch, Ramone got her settled into the recliner and then left for the studio. Lucy took a pain pill and quickly drifted off to sleep. What seemed like just a few minutes later she was jolted awake by her cell phone. Groggily picking it up, she saw the call was from Dusty. Trying to sound alert, she answered the phone. "Hi Lucy," he said quickly. "I just have a minute before I go into a meeting, but you were on my mind, and I wanted to call. How did the video shoot go today?"

"The video?" she said sleepily, slurring her words. "It was good – in fact we are going back tonight for some evening shots."

"Are you OK? Did I wake you up? I'm sorry if I did."

"I'm fine. What time is it?"

"Almost five."

"Oh, wow – it's a good thing you called. Ramone will be here in just a few minutes to pick me up. I hate to rush you off, but…"

"No, it's fine. Hey Lucy, I'm getting a bit worried about you. Those pain pills you take seem to be awfully strong."

"I know, but I can't seem to function without them, and the doctor insists that I need to keep taking them for a few more weeks at least. It will be alright, I promise."

"Text me later when you get home. I have some good news to talk to you about."

"Sure. I've got to run. I'll talk to you later," she said with a yawn.

Lucy ended the call and struggled into the bathroom to brush her hair and freshen up a bit. She was hungry again, but there was no time for dinner. Ramone arrived promptly at five thirty and said he had a text from Sonya saying she would meet them at the school. He asked Lucy if she had rested well, but she was too embarrassed to tell him that she had literally passed out earlier and only Dusty's phone call had interrupted her drugged sleep. She knew she needed to stop taking the pills but didn't know how since she was always in so much pain.

Sonya was at the school waiting for them, and was thrilled to be able to watch the shoot. Once again, the extras were milling around the parking lot and hallway, getting ready to decorate the gym for prom. A few of the other main actors were strutting around like they owned the school. Of course, Sabrina would not have been included in this fun activity. They were done filming after just an hour or so, and Toby came to where Lucy was sitting.

"OK, this went well. I'll need you here at nine in the morning for your hair and makeup. First, we will shoot you arriving at school and getting out of the car – there will be a few other students around but none of the main actors. Then you will go inside and walk around the halls. Your song will be playing in the background for you to lip-sync to. Nothing too strenuous, just sitting on the bleachers or standing in front of a locker, that kind of thing. Vicki Jo will be here for a few photos so we can start hyping the video. We'll all come back after dark for the prom scenes. You need to be in the same outfit as you wear tomorrow morning, OK? We will shoot the crowd scenes first, and there will be a few with you watching and singing in the background. Then we'll do a few more of just you after everyone else leaves and you are alone in the gym. Bring your guitar, too. I don't think we'll have you playing, but it can be sitting beside you as a reminder of what your life has now become."

"Sounds good. Yes, I'll be here ready to go at nine. The only problem is that I am not allowed to drive yet."

"Oh, crap – forgot about that. Hey, I have an idea. Sonya, are you available to be here in the morning and be a stand-in for Lucy during the driving scene? We can shoot it from far away, but you two look so much alike, I doubt anyone will be able to tell. We'll just fix your hair the same way and you need the same kind of blouse. Can we make that work?"

"Oh, wow – how fun! Sure, we can work something out. We have a few things that would look alike from a distance. I can drive the car into the lot and park, and then Lucy can take it from there! We'll figure it out before tomorrow, Toby, don't worry."

Sonya drove Lucy home while Ramone stopped to pick up a couple of pizzas and cheesy breadsticks. They chatted about the shoot, then Ramone told them about his meeting with Josh earlier.

"I've had quite the day," he said, "first with the video shoot and then Josh offering me an internship with Toby. I always had an interest in cameras and videos, and Josh is giving me the chance to explore the field while getting paid! Can't beat that!"

"Oh, Honey - that's so exciting!" Sonya gushed as she gave his hand a squeeze. "When do you start?"

"Actually, I start in the morning, just shadowing the other interns for now to learn more about the process. But I really appreciate this opportunity they are giving me."

"That's amazing," Lucy agreed. "Ok, I'm beat. I need to call Dusty, then head to bed early. You will pick us up at eight thirty, Ramone?"

"Yup – get some rest and I'll see you both in the morning."

Sonya walked him to the door, and they shared a short, whispered conversation, then a quick kiss or two. Lucy smiled and walked stiffly into her bedroom, resisting the urge to take a pain pill until after her call with Dusty.

Chapter Eight

Lucy changed into her pj's and sent Dusty a text, telling him she was home and anxious to hear his news. He called within just a few minutes.

"Hey, how did it go today? How much longer before I get to see your first video?"

"It was fun, but there is still lots to film, and then there is editing, and I don't know what else. But there's a whole video team who will be working on it non-stop. They really want this out in a week or so. In fact, they are letting Ramone work as an intern, and Sonya will be a body double for me for a driving scene, so that's exciting, too. Enough about me – what is your news?"

"Things have been crazy here at work for a while, as I've told you. This week I was offered a supervisory position that comes with better hours and better pay. I will have a bit more flexibility with my schedule, so hopefully I will be able to come down and see you sometime soon. I love doing IT, but I'm not totally in love with financial services and have been looking to move to a different industry. But in the meantime, adding 'supervisor' to my resume will be a good thing."

"I'm very proud of you. Yes, I agree. More variety to your experiences will only help down the road."

They chatted a little more, but he could tell that she was suffering a bit and needing time to rest. "I'd love to talk longer, but I think you need your rest for your early shoot tomorrow. I can't wait to see what they post on your website!"

They said their goodnights and Dusty ended the call. Within a minute or so, he texted, *"Rest well and have fun tomorrow. You are the Shining Star in my life. D."*

Lucy smiled, then tried to make herself comfortable in the recliner. How many weeks had she been sleeping here? Would she ever be able to sleep in her own bed again? She didn't want to take a pain pill, but knew she needed to be in top form tomorrow for the video shoot. "Just this one time, then I'm done with them," she whispered into the night. "Just this one time."

Ramone arrived promptly at eight thirty to take the girls to the school. They were dressed in very similar peasant tops, and their hair was hanging loosely down their backs. Ramone was amazed yet again how identical they looked, especially since they were not related. The school parking lot was filled with students and cameras. In the middle were tents for Lucy and Sonya to work with hair and makeup artists. To anyone who was not familiar with the two, they looked almost identical. Toby was confused when he came to the tent.

"Lucy? Sonya? Oh, my goodness! You two dressing alike is the perfect solution to our problem. No one will know the difference. Did you play games on others when you were in school? Try to fool a boyfriend or teacher?"

Sonya stiffened, and Lucy knew exactly what she was thinking. Ramone jumped in and said, "It was crazy at times. Even I as a best friend got confused once or twice."

"I'm sure. OK, Sonya, let's start with you. We've got a plain car for you to drive – certainly nothing flashy like many of the others in the lot. I need you to come in from that side road, pull in here and park next to that blue Nissan. Open the door and start to get out. We'll film that several times from various angles and distances, then we will switch over to Lucy. I will need you, Lucy, to get out of the car, pick up your purse and guitar, along with a few books. Close the car door and head towards the school entrance. Stop just outside the door. The song will be playing over the speakers, so just mouth the words. Sonya, maybe you could be singing as you are driving the car? We won't be filming close to you, but I imagine we could at least see your mouth moving."

"Sure, I know all the words, of course," she said with a smile. "I'm ready! Wish me luck!"

She drove the car down the block from the school and turned around. Lucy's song was blasting over some speakers set up in the bushes beside the school entrance. She slowly drove the car down the side street and into the lot, parking in the spot Toby had designated. She turned off the car, opened the door, and stood up, softly singing the words she knew by heart. "CUT!" Toby called. "That was great, just what we wanted. Now we need to do that several more times and we'll film from different angles, choosing later which ones we want to use. Places everyone!"

Sonya repeated the drive over and over, trying to keep things exactly the same. One shot was from overhead on a big crane, and another was from a car following behind her. After seven times, Toby was confident he had what he needed.

"OK, Lucy, you're next. Sit inside the car with the door open and take over the scene from there. Ready?"

Sonya and Lucy traded places, and she waited for Toby's cue. "Action!" he called, and Lucy slowly stood up and reached for her things. She also picked up her guitar and shut the car door, feeling a twinge of pain in her shoulder. She then walked slowly toward the school. She sang along with the recording, "*If only you could see the real me,*" lip-syncing as she walked across the parking lot. Other background actors were walking toward the school, too, but of course they did not notice her. Again, a wave of nostalgia washed over her as she remembered her difficulties at school. Why did she never really fit in? Why did so few people ever seem to acknowledge her? She was unaware of the sadness on her face until Toby yelled "CUT!"

"That was perfect, but are you OK? Is your arm hurting? You look like you're about to cry."

"I'm fine," she lied, "just filled with emotion, I guess. This hits very close to home for me."

"I understand, but let's try again without the sadness. Yes, you can be sad about the situation, but we also want you to be strong and brave and confident."

"Yes of course, I understand." And with that Lucy walked to the car and they tried again.

"Much better!" Toby called once she reached the front of the school. "Just like that a few more times and then we can move inside."

Lucy went back to the car again and placed her things on the seat. "You can do this," she whispered to herself. "I don't care if your arm hurts - don't let everyone down."

Toby yelled, "Action!" and Lucy again walked to the steps of the school. This time, she forced herself to think about the good parts of high school: her friends, her love of music, and her family. The other students rushed past her, a few even bumped into her as if she was invisible. She finally reached the door and placed her hand confidently on the handle. "Cut!" Toby called. "Much better, Lucy. Let's reset the cameras and do this a few more times. The transition between you and Sonya will be perfect."

After just a few more shots, they moved inside into a hallway filled with students and lockers. Again, huge PROM posters were hanging on the walls, and the building was filled with excitement. How was it that after all these years, the smells and sounds were still so familiar? Toby set up a shot where Lucy was just standing beside her locker, watching the chaos around her. She looked wistfully at the other students talking and laughing and she was feeling so alone. She allowed her emotions to come to the surface, (along with the pain of her throbbing shoulder) and a small tear trickled down one cheek. "CUT!" Toby yelled. "Lucy, I know I told you to be strong and brave, but the emotions here are just perfect. It's obvious to me and anyone watching how personal this song is, and what you were feeling when you wrote it. Just a few more times, and we'll move to the gym."

Lucy knew that her part in this video was to be like a flashback with her current self returning to high school and revisiting her earlier life. She was told that they would intercut her scenes with those they shot yesterday with Sabrina. She totally understood Toby's vision, and hoped the final product would enhance the song and its message.

After a few more takes, they moved to the gym and Ramone helped Lucy climb the bleachers and sit on the top row. With her guitar beside her, she watched as the students hung streamers and started decorating for prom tonight. She had never been invited to a prom and hadn't been brave enough to go without a date. She had only seen a few pictures of what it had looked like. Again, Toby was doing a great job of capturing the mood. Lucy sang a few lines and watched wistfully as the teens talked excitedly. Josh had arrived unexpectedly and observed silently from a doorway. He was excited to watch Lucy filming and was pleased at how quickly and easily the video seemed to be coming together.

"CUT" Toby yelled. "This is great. Let's run it a few more times, then we can break until the prom scenes tonight. Everyone, go home and put on your best prom outfits. All but you, Lucy, of course. I have to say you all are doing such a great job. I'm anxious to wrap things up tonight, way ahead of schedule!"

Before long, Toby was pleased with the scene and dismissed everyone to go home to get ready for the prom. "I have an idea," he said softly to Lucy. "How would you feel if we included Sonya and Ramone in the prom scenes tonight? I always love to sneak a little something special into my videos, and this would be fun. Do you approve? Think they will agree? They would probably just be in background shots – maybe around the punch bowl or dancing on the far side of the gym."

"Oh, how fun! Yes, I totally agree, and I bet they will too! What a great way to thank them for all the support they have given me, not just now but also back then."

Sonya and Ramone quickly agreed, and wanted to stop at a thrift store on the way home to see what they could find to wear. Lucy was so excited for them to be a real part of the video.

"The only thing, Sonya," Toby said quickly, "is that I need you to *NOT* look like Lucy tonight. Put your hair up, maybe wear something a bit more flashy, so no one will get confused."

"Of course! Yes, I'll do my best."

The thrift store was full of options, but Sonya settled on a short red sequined dress with a low-cut back and found some matching 2-inch heels. Ramone found a black and red plaid suit jacket that perfectly matched her dress.

"We had better hurry home," Sonya said. "I have a prom to get ready for!"

They returned to the school promptly at seven P.M. prepared to shoot well into the night. Ramone had stopped to pick up a wrist corsage for Sonya of beautiful red roses and a bit of baby's breath. Her hair was piled high on her head with just a few tendrils hanging down to frame her face, and her makeup was more dramatic than usual. Gone was the overwhelming resemblance to Lucy. She was pure Sonya tonight, ready to have fun at the prom.

Toby assigned the pair to one of the interns for their instructions, while he visited with Lucy.

"Again, we'll do just a few shots of you watching from the bleachers, perhaps standing on the edge of the dance floor or near the punch bowl. Most of the shots tonight will be of the students. Then we'll move outside to watch everyone leave. You will come out then to see the empty parking lot and your car sitting alone off to one side. You will walk to it, climb in and get ready to leave. We don't have Sonya to body-double this for you, so we'll just finishd with you alone in your car. Sound good?"

"Sounds perfect," she said excitedly, even though her arm was still sore from the morning's activities. "I can't wait to see how you put this all together."

"Oh, I forgot to tell you. We won't be playing '*If Only*' all the time during the prom, obviously, since it's a slow song and not exactly prom music. I had Darren arrange some of your other music to play in the background while the students are dancing. There will be one last slow song to end the prom, and that's when we will switch back to your song and how the video will end. Didn't want to confuse you."

"Thanks. I hadn't really thought of that. I'm even more excited to see the finished product."

They did a few shots of Lucy first, then continued with the students. They all looked great and were having fun dancing and laughing. Was this what prom was really like? She had to fight back sadness and a bit of jealousy as she watched everyone have so much fun. But then she smiled at Sonya and Ramone dancing on the far side of the gym and was glad to be able to do this for them. Sonya looked amazing, and Lucy was sure no one would suspect her to be the body double from earlier in the video.

Soon they moved on to a slow song, which Lucy recognized as more of the background music from her album. Darren had done an amazing job taking her music and arranging it into something completely different. She watched as her friends slow danced to the music and wondered if they recognized it at all.

Around midnight, they filmed a few shots of the students leaving. Toby dismissed everyone but Lucy. He thanked them for their hard work and told them to drive safely. He asked one of the interns to move Lucy's car to the proper spot and ready, since they would soon be outside to shoot the final shots. Then he had most of the gym lights turned off.

"Lucy, for this shot, I need you to walk slowly across the gym, sweeping the balloons and streamers away with your feet. Just do what you feel best as you walk toward the exit and then down the hallway. Stop once you get to the front door. Sound good? We'll be using a steady-cam that will follow your movements to make it more personal."

"Sure," Lucy said sadly. Not only was this scene very emotional, but it also signaled that the video shoot was almost over. This had been so fun and educational, and she hated it to end.

Alone in the gym with just Toby and a camera operator, Lucy walked slowly across the gym floor, softly kicking at a balloon and then stopping to pick up a piece of confetti. Letting it slowly drift toward the floor, she continued singing her song. She pushed open the gym door and went into the almost-dark hallway, the camera following alongside her. She went to her locker and ran her hand across it lovingly. There were no sounds other than her song, almost pleading with others to really look at her. She reached the front door and turned around, looking wistfully at the now-empty school, then exited into the dark night.

Toby motioned for the camera operator to stop filming, then they just stood there in silence. "I don't think I've ever said this in my life before, but I don't want to shoot this again. This was just amazing. Did it look as good from the camera?" Toby asked the videographer, Greg.

"I am speechless," he said. "Lucy, I know professionally trained actors who could not do what you just did. You are a total natural."

"Thanks," she whispered. "I just let the song flow through me to show what those words mean to me."

"Greg, let me watch the playback and then we'll decide for sure."

Greg adjusted the camera so they were at the start of the scene, and the three of them huddled around the monitor to watch what they had just shot. He was an excellent videographer and seemed to have captured all her emotions. Once the scene was finished, they again stood in silence.

"I say let's go for it," Greg finally said. "The steady-cam was the perfect choice here. Toby?"

"I agree. We have other cameras set up outside, and for this final scene, all I need is for you to walk down the steps and over to your car. We have the music queued up to play just the last few phrases as I want the song to end with you in your car."

"No problem," Lucy said, still a bit shaken from the last scene.

They stepped outside and Lucy saw Ramone and Sonya off to one side, waiting for her. Sonya was huddled in Ramone's arms and wearing his jacket. Lucy gave them a silent 'thumbs up' as they started to film the final scene.

She walked slowly to her lonely car on the edge of the parking lot. She opened the back door and placed her guitar gently on the back seat, stroking it lovingly. Opening the front door, she sat inside, a mixture of sadness and relief on her face. They shot this a few times, with the last frames captured by a camera mounted on the hood of her car. One final "CUT" from Toby and the shoot was over.

She heard a round of applause and was surprised to see that many of the students had stayed to watch the ending scene. Sonya and Ramone rushed to her side, giving her gentle hugs and Ramone helped her back into her sling. It had been hours since she had worn it, and her arm was aching.

"That's a wrap," Toby said excitedly. "Again, thank you to everyone. Lucy, I am so proud of you, doing all this while in pain and recovering. Sonya, Ramone --- thanks for all that you do for Lucy every day. I hope you enjoyed your few minutes as extras in the video."

"Yes, it was fun," they both replied, "but it's time to get our star home and into bed."

"Toby, and everyone, I cannot thank you enough for all your hard work," Lucy said with a lump in her throat. "This has been so much more than I ever dreamed of."

"Go home and get some rest," Toby said proudly. "I'll get the video to the team in the morning, and they will start editing. I imagine we can have this done in just a few days."

Chapter Nine

Five days later, Lucy was sitting alone at her kitchen table, reading fan mail and sipping a glass of wine. Sonya and Ramone had fixed a picnic lunch and gone to a local park. They wanted Lucy to join them, but she refused, knowing they needed some time alone without her tagging along. There was a knock on the door and Lucy rose stiffly from her chair. Frustrated that her recovery was so slow and worried about her growing dependency on the pain pills, she walked slowly to the door. Peering through the peephole, she saw a postal worker. The last time that happened, she received the letter about Travis' box of pictures. Trembling a bit, Lucy opened the door.

"Lucy Armando?" the postal worker asked.

"Yes, that's me."

"I have a registered letter for you. Please sign here."

Lucy scribbled a few letters onto the receipt with her left hand and took the large envelope.

"Have a good day," he said as he turned to go back to his vehicle.

Lucy carried the letter back to the table and sat down gingerly. Her hands shaking, she studied the envelope in fear of another correspondence from the attorney. Instead, she saw that it was from Star Records. What in the world would they be sending her in a registered letter?

She opened the large outer envelope to see two smaller envelopes inside. One was for her and one for Sonya. What could it be?

She tore her envelope open excitedly and was shocked to see an invitation to a private screening of her video! In two weeks on Saturday night, a red carpet would be set up outside the Belcourt Theater where the media was invited to meet Lucy and the team and attend a screening of her video. Could this be real? What in the world was she going to wear? There would be a red carpet for her video? This had to be a joke.

Also in the larger envelope was a note from Josh asking her to call as soon as she received the package. He knew she was surprised and would have a ton of questions, but he wanted her to receive an invitation, just like the media and special guests would be receiving. Of course, she called him right away.

"Surprise!" Josh said as he answered the phone. "I bet you weren't expecting that in your mail today!"

"No, that's for sure!" she laughed. "Is this some sort of joke? A red carpet for my video?"

"You can blame Vicki Jo for this — it was all her idea to get maximum publicity for you. We want to have a quick meeting on Monday afternoon to go over all the details. Do you think you can make it, or do we need to do a video call?"

"No, I'm sure I can make it. I've been sticking close to home since the video shoot, so this will give me a chance to get out a bit. I see there is an invitation for Sonya as well?"

"Yes, Ramone has already received his, but I made him promise to keep it a secret. You will notice that your invitation includes a 'plus one' if you have someone you would like to invite."

"Oh, thanks. I'm not sure. I'll have to think a bit."

"No rush, we'll go over everything next week. I will have Elizabeth reach out to you about finding the right dress and arranging for hair and makeup and all that kind of stuff. But again, congratulations! We will show just a teaser of the video in our meeting, because we really want you to wait to see the entire video at the premiere. Are you OK with that?"

"I guess I have to be!" she said with a smile. "Thanks, Josh. You all are amazing."

She had just hung up the phone when Sonya and Ramone walked in.

"Hey, what's going on?" Sonya asked. "You look suspiciously happy."

"Some mail came for you today," Lucy said with a smile as she winked at Ramone.

"What is it?" Sonya asked, curious about the strange looks between her two friends.

"Open it up and see!"

Sonya opened the envelope, and her eyes widened in shock. "A red carpet? And they are inviting me?"

"And me," Ramone said with a smile. "I've known since yesterday, but they wouldn't let me say anything. I guess I need to go rent a tuxedo!"

"Oh, Lucy, this is so exciting, but I don't own anything that would be appropriate to wear to a red carpet. What are we going to do? I have no idea where to start!"

"I just got off the phone with Josh, and he is going to have Elizabeth help with all of that. I cannot believe this is real, but I'm sure it will be a blast!"

"I'll leave you two to talk dresses." Ramone said. "Josh has asked me to come to the office to talk about my internship. Sonya, walk me to the door?" he said with a twinkle in his eye.

"Of course," she said sweetly. "Thanks for the picnic, it was lovely." They cuddled a bit at the door, and Lucy smiled but looked away. She was so happy for her friends but could not help but feel a small pang of jealousy. Would she ever find someone special of her own?

As if she could read her mind, Sonya came to the table and placed her hand on Lucy's.

"I hope that wasn't too awkward for you. Making you uncomfortable is the last thing either of us would want."

"No, it's fine. I'm happy for you, truly."

"I have an idea. What about inviting Dusty to come as your 'plus one' to the premiere? Do you think he is ready for that kind of media scrutiny and attention?"

"I honestly don't know. No one knows anything about him or about us. I'm not even sure there is an 'us' just yet."

"It's a big step, for sure. Lots to think about. What do you think we should wear? This is so exciting!"

Lucy pulled out her iPad and they spent the next hour looking online at dresses from previous red-carpet events. Lucy was horrified at the plunging necklines and slits that went way up the thigh, the sheer fabrics. There were very few that were modest enough to satisfy her conservative tastes.

Then they came across a picture of an A-list actress from the most recent Daytime Emmy award show. She was wearing a gorgeous crimson velvet dress with a high neck and long sleeves. It hugged her curves without being overly tight and had a long train. The simplicity was stunning against the actresses' fair features.

"Here! Something like this!" Lucy said excitedly. "Look how gorgeous she is without everything hanging out for all to see!"

"It is very pretty," Sonya agreed, "and perfect for you. I hope you don't mind if I find something a bit flashier?"

"No, of course not. We may look alike, but you are certainly your own person, and free to dress as you please, within reason of course!"

Elizabeth called a bit later and they set up a time for the next evening for her to come by and talk. There was no reason for Lucy to come to the office, and they wanted Sonya to be there as well. She had years of experience with red carpets and was excited to help with the premiere. She also hoped Ramone could stop by to talk tuxedos.

After dinner, Lucy sent Dusty a text, asking if he was free to talk. He sent back a smiling-face emoji, which made her laugh a bit. She was a little nervous about asking him to be her date at the premiere. Would he think she was going too fast? Was he ready to be seen as the boyfriend of a rising music star?

She nervously dialed his number, and he answered on the second ring.

"Hey, it's good to hear from you. How was your day?" he asked in his deep voice. "All is OK, I hope?"

"Yes, better than OK. I just found out today that my video is ready, and there is going to be a red-carpet premiere at an historic theatre downtown. I am in shock! The studio's stylist will be helping me, and Sonya and Ramone will be there, too, along with most of the cast from the video, and of course Josh and everyone from the studio. I'm so overwhelmed, I don't know what to think!"

"That is simply amazing! I knew from the first time I heard you sing that you were going to be a star. The studio obviously has faith in you, too. There is no turning back now!"

"That's kind of what I wanted to talk to you about. I have the opportunity to bring a guest, and I was wondering if you would like to be my date? I totally understand if this is more than what you are ready for, since there will be tons of media attention not only on me but on you, too. You will be in all the pictures with me – what do you think?"

"Of course, I would be honored to escort you. It's certainly not a world I am familiar with, and you will need to tell me what to do."

"Me? I have no idea, either. This would be a first for both of us. We are having a meeting next week where I will get more details, but figured I wanted to give you a heads-up, if it is something you EVEN want to do. Of course, there is NO pressure, and I want you to decline if you are not 100% sure."

"Actually, I think I'm OK with it. It would be a chance for me to see you again, of course, which would be lovely. And it would let me see you in your world."

"Only if you are sure. I don't want you to feel like I pushed you into it."

"No, I would love to come. And I'll deal with the media as it comes. I mean, this was bound to happen eventually, right? At least, I feel like this is the direction we were heading?"

"Yes, I think so," Lucy said softly. "I'm glad you said yes. This is going to be a very special night, and I would love to have you with me."

They chatted a bit longer, then said goodnight. Lucy went to her room to get ready for bed and saw a movement outside her window. Instantly, she was afraid that Travis was back, but of course that was not possible. She peeked out the curtains to see a balloon that had gotten trapped in one of the branches of the oak tree outside. Relieved, she slipped into pj's and climbed into bed. At least she had progressed enough to move from the recliner to her bed. Reaching for her nightly pain pill, she once again promised herself to stop them soon, then drifted off to sleep.

Chapter Ten

Elizabeth arrived promptly at seven the next evening, her arms loaded with pictures and fabric swatches. Lucy and Sonya watched in awe as she showed them various styles and fabrics that work best on the red carpet. Lucy had never imagined that picking the perfect dress could be so complicated!

Elizabeth felt prepared to suggest things for Lucy, since they had been working together closely for a while. They narrowed the options down to a few gorgeous gowns, each conservative but flattering to her figure. Elizabeth said she would pick them up for Lucy to try on in a few days. They needed to decide quickly so they could continue planning accessories such as her shoes and handbag, along with jewelry and her hair and makeup.

She was starting from scratch with Sonya, however, since they had only met once or twice. Sonya was more outgoing in her personality and fashion, and they quickly settled on a tea-length ivory dress with ruffles and accented in red. She would wear a pair of lace-up red pumps and carry a red and black bag. Ramone stopped by later, and Elizabeth suggested he find a textured black tuxedo with a red accent. He needed to go to a tuxedo rental shop to be measured and to select something appropriate. She wanted him to coordinate with Sonya, but not be an exact match.

Elizabeth then proceeded to tell the group about normal procedures on premiere day. The girls would spend the morning at a local spa where they would get a massage before getting their hair styled, followed by a manicure and pedicure. The afternoon would be a flurry of double checking the gowns to be sure everything was perfect and then dressing. The studio would provide trays of sandwiches and fruit for them to nibble on throughout the day, Makeup would come last, just before they were to leave for the theater. This could all be done at the condo and a limo would later take them to the red carpet. Lucy would stay in the limo until most of the others had been introduced. Josh and his wife would be last, just before Lucy and her date, if she had one. The media would be stationed at various intervals along the carpet for pictures and interviews.

It all seemed a bit too much to comprehend, but Lucy was glad that she had Elizabeth to lean on. And she knew that more information would come in their meeting next week. She told Elizabeth that she had invited a friend to accompany her, but she was worried about giving him enough time to select an appropriate tuxedo.

"To be honest, we really want all the attention to be on you, realizing, of course, that he will be in the spotlight as well. My suggestion to you would be to tell him to get the nicest, best-fitting traditional tux he can afford. Whichever dress you select would look lovely next to a nice black tuxedo. He can add a tie and pocket square later, if he wants, that coordinates with your dress. Perhaps he can arrive in time to get ready with Ramone and I could have a chance to do a last-minute check? What is his name, so I can add him to the list?"

"Dustin Pierce – he lives in Ohio."

"Nice. Please ask him to come down on Friday evening if possible so he is here all-day Saturday to get ready. He needs to have a fresh haircut. Does he have a beard? If so, it needs to be neatly trimmed. We don't want anything that will distract from you. This is *your* night."

"I'll be sure to tell him, thanks. I know he is concerned about not looking out of place."

"This is the first I have heard of him. Have you been dating long? I don't mean to be too personal, but is he prepared for how his life is about to change?"

"We've talked about it some. I actually met him early in the tour. We've just chatted on the phone since then. This will be our first real date."

"Wow – baptism by fire for sure. Does he have any experience with situations like this? Dealing with the media?"

"Even less than I do, I think. I hope he doesn't regret this."

"Well, I think we are done for tonight. I'll pick up the dresses we are interested in and will see you in the office next week."

"Thanks, Elizabeth, for all your help. We were all feeling overwhelmed."

Chapter Eleven

Lucy, Sonya and Ramone arrived at the studio on Monday morning for the meeting to work out final details for the premiere. Lucy was amazed at how organized everyone was, but then admitted, of course they were. They had done this dozens of times for numerous big-named celebrities.

Once all the specifics were settled, Josh took his place at the front of the conference room. "Great work, everyone. Looks like we've got it all covered. Now for the moment most of you have been waiting for – a sneak peek at the video. This is the trailer that will start running online later today, and tomorrow on TV and radio. I think the team outdid themselves with this one. Ready? Toby, please turn down the lights."

The room was darkened, and Michael pressed a button on his laptop to project the video onto a large screen on the wall. The first chords of '*If Only*' played softly in the background, and soon they saw the school parking lot full of excited students walking inside while Sabrina walked alone up the steps. Others were already inside the school and in line to purchase prom tickets. The camera panned to a lonely Sabrina moving slowly past them and caught the teasing looks from the others. Faded in the background was the misty silhouette of Lucy leaning against her locker, watching with sadness. It appeared that

Toby had used some form of special effects magic that made her look almost transparent. The song continued as the scene shifted into the gym that was being decorated for the prom, and Lucy was sitting alone in the bleachers softly singing, asking the audience to really see her. There was one short scene of the prom itself, and then it faded to the final scene of Lucy slowly walking down the darkened hallway. A young male voice then announced when the new video would be available for viewing online.

The screen went dark, and Toby turned the lights back on. Lucy was stunned, but everyone else was applauding and talking excitedly.

"Toby," Lucy said shakingly, "that was simply amazing. I had an idea what it would look like but was in no way prepared for this. How you were able to meld the various takes together into one cohesive video was magical."

Sonya rushed to Lucy's side and gave her a big hug. "That was so cool!" she said enthusiastically. "I know I watched a lot of it being filmed, but to see it finished, I'm speechless!"

"I agree!" Ramone said happily. "I learned so much by just watching, I can't wait for my chance behind the camera and see what I can come up with. Lucy, you looked amazing, by the way."

The meeting adjourned, and Ramone took Lucy home while Sonya left for her job at the vet clinic. During the drive, Ramone asked, "So, now that you are away from the crowd, what is your honest opinion? This is a huge step in your career – how are you really feeling about it?"

"Honestly, I'm overwhelmed. I know that I entered the contest hoping to win and be a star, but I don't think I ever really thought about all that would be involved. The amount of work: the number of people required to make it work, the pressure to succeed and not let all those people down. I don't know if I'm ready. Can you come inside and stay a while? Or do you have someplace you need to be?"

"Sure, I can stay a bit. Let me fix us some lunch and we can chat. I just realized we don't get much time, just the two of us."

"I'm happy for you and Sonya, of course, but I do miss the old days when it was just you and me in the band room, messing around on our guitars. Do you think you will ever tell Josh and Darren that you play, and how good you are?"

"I haven't played in ages, and I'm so thankful for the other opportunities they have already given me. I don't want to act like I expect a music career as well."

"I understand," she said. "But maybe you could play backup on an album or something. I hate to have all your talent just sitting dormant."

"We'll see. But you didn't ask me to stay just to talk about my guitar playing."

"No, it's about Dusty. I've invited him to the premiere, as you know. Do you think I made the right decision? I'm worried that all of this might be too much for him, and I'll lose a relationship before it has a real chance to start."

"True, but none of us are really ready, you know? Maybe experiencing this at the same time will be good for you two, and will certainly make for great memories to tell the grandkids someday."

"Grandkids? Slow down, OK? We haven't even had our first date yet!"

After a lunch of grilled cheese sandwiches, Ramone left for his afternoon appointment at the tuxedo store. "I have my picture of Sonya's dress, so I'm sure they will find something that will be appropriate. I haven't worn a tux since my sister's wedding six years ago. At least they are not as complicated as the dresses you ladies wear. Hair – makeup – shoes – jewelry. Crazy. We have many fewer moving parts or decisions."

"But this is Nashville, and I've seen pictures of some wild tuxes. Be prepared!"

Lucy felt restless after Ramone left. She tried watching TV, but nothing was interesting. Her arm exercises did little but made her shoulder ache even more. She looked at the clock, but it was too early for a pain pill. Plus, she was determined not to take so many. Deciding to take a nap instead, she was just getting settled when her phone *pinged*. There was a message from Vicki Jo telling her that the video trailer would go live at the top of the hour, a few hours earlier than they anticipated, and for her to be prepared for an avalanche of texts and calls. They would try to filter as many as they could from the office, but she was sure some would get through. She included the link for the livestream on the studio's Facebook page but warned her to turn the comments off and not read the reactions. She then ended with '*Congratulations, Star.*'

Lucy looked at the clock – just 18 more minutes and the wrld would get their first glimpse at the video. Would they like it? Would the haters come after her again?

She looked longingly at the bottle of pills sitting next to her, wishing she had time to take one. Her hand was shaking as she picked up her glass of water and took a big drink but put the bottle back down unopened. What was happening to her?

Chapter Twelve

Lucy clicked on the link from the text message and was taken to Star Record's Facebook page. There was a post announcing the video along with a picture of Lucy and a countdown clock. Her hands continued to tremble as she watched the minutes then seconds tick down. Five – Four – Three – Two – One!

The screen went dark, and she heard the music start. She had done what Vicki Jo suggested and turned off the comments. Watching in awe as the video trailer played again, this time there were thousands of fans who were online to watch with her. She wasn't sure she breathed at all during the 30 seconds of the video, which seemed like the fastest yet slowest 30 seconds of her life. The video ended and she sat her phone beside her. Closing her eyes, she started counting. Twelve seconds later her phone rang, and she knew she had just started the next phase of her life and her career.

"Please God," she whispered. "You brought me to this place, and I am thankful. But please help me through all of this."

Verse 3
The Decision

Chapter 1

Lucy lost track of the number of phone calls she answered, texts she replied to, and emails she forwarded to Josh. The video was insanely popular and hit 100,000 views overnight. Within a week, they were climbing toward one million.

She found herself rushing between radio station interviews, and even visited the local CBS station for an appearance to talk about the upcoming premiere. Her name was on everyone's lips, it seemed, and soon there were fan pages popping up on social media, with her most ardent fans calling themselves *'Lucy's Army.'* They were fiercely loyal, and Lucy heard accounts of them ganging up on the haters, even blocking them where they could. Elizabeth stopped by with three dresses for Lucy to try on, and together they decided on a powder blue chiffon gown with diamond accents. The pale color looked stunning against her long dark hair, which she wanted to wear down. Silver flats and a matching purse completed the outfit, along with a massive diamond necklace that they would borrow from a local jeweler. The studio was certainly sparing no expense in their promotion of this video!

She sent a picture of the dress to Dusty, who said he had already rented his tux but could go back and pick a coordinating tie. He also said he had a special gift for her that he hoped she could incorporate into the evening. Intrigued, she begged for hints, but he said she would just have to wait.

And the wait was not long, as soon it was Friday, the day before the premiere. Dusty arranged to leave work early and landed in Nashville at nine thirty. Ramone picked him up to take him directly to Lucy's condo.

"You're sure you are ready for this?" Ramone asked as he helped put Dusty's bags in the back seat of his truck.

"I'm scared to death, but excited for her, if that makes sense," Dusty said with a nervous smile. "I've told a few of my closest friends and my dad about having met her, but no one knows about tomorrow night. I can't wait to see their reactions!"

"I hope you are OK staying with me tonight. My condo is just like Lucy's with two bedrooms on opposite ends and you will have your own bathroom. We just figured it would make getting ready easier tomorrow."

"That's fine. I got an email from the studio saying everything was being arranged and I was not to book a hotel. They certainly are organized!"

"You have no idea. Every minute of this weekend is accounted for."

Nashville traffic was messier than usual this Friday night, and it was close to midnight when they reached the condos.

"I know it's late, but Lucy wants me to stop by for just a minute to say hello. Is that OK?"

"Sure. I know she is excited to see you again after all this time. But it needs to be quick. She's still in a lot of pain from her shoulder dislocation and needs her rest. Tomorrow is the biggest day of her life since winning the TV show."

"Of course, I understand. And thank you for all you have done taking care of her. She told me they hired you as extra security after Sonya's attack, but I know it means much more to her than that."

"Lucy is like a sister to me, and I would do anything to protect her. I'm grateful to the studio for allowing me to be a part of her team. I knew there was a spark between you two the night of her concert, you know." Ramone made a mental note to remember that Lucy had not told Dusty the full story of the attack and about Travis. He wondered if this secret would take a toll on their relationship in the future.

"Yes, I felt like everyone could see it. She is truly special," Dusty replied, unaware of the concerned look on Ramone's face that was hidden by the darkness of the truck.

"Just don't ever hurt her, or you will have me to deal with, too. Understand?" Ramone said with a smile on his lips but seriousness in his eyes.

"No, I could never do that. She is too precious to me."

"Good to hear. Ok, here we are," Ramone said as he entered the gate code and drove to Lucy's condo. "Just a minute, remember?"

He had barely parked the truck when the condo door flew open, and Lucy stepped outside. Dusty jogged up the steps and stood before her, his six-foot frame towering above her. She had forgotten how much taller than her he was. She smiled up into his face and whispered, "Hi – it's been so long. I'm so happy you are here."

He found it hard to speak at first. She was more gorgeous than he remembered, even though he had seen tons of pictures, and they had face-timed at least once a week. But to have her here, in front of him, took his breath away.

"I know you need your rest, I just wanted to see you for a second. I can't wait to spend tomorrow night with you." And before he turned to go, he leaned down and placed a gentle kiss on her cheek.

His scent was the same as before – strong and masculine in a way that made her knees weak. She leaned against him, resting her head on his chest.

"Yes, tomorrow," she whispered. "Good night."

Chapter 2

Lucy awoke to the sound of voices in the kitchen and the scent of fresh coffee brewing. She recognized Sonya's voice and then Elizabeth's, but who were the others? Why were there so many people in her house at this early hour?

She put on her robe with difficulty, hating that she was still in so much pain. She often wondered if there was more wrong with her arm than just a dislocated shoulder. Why was it taking so long to heal? Resisting the urge to take a pain pill, she moved slowly toward the kitchen.

"There she is – the woman of the hour!" Vicki Jo said excitedly. "We were going to give you just a few more minutes before waking you up. We need to leave in about 30 minutes to go to the spa. Let me introduce you to Molly and Daisy. They are two interns who are here to help get you ready, running errands or doing whatever we night need.."

"Good morning, ladies. I've never had a massage before," Lucy said shyly. "Is it as wonderful as everyone says?"

"Never had a massage? Oh, Lucy, you are in for a real treat!" Elizabeth responded. "In fact, I think it's something you should schedule at least once a month, probably more. It's certainly in your budget to pamper yourself a bit."

"I want to get a few pictures throughout the day of you getting ready," Vicki Jo interrupted. "I'll be going with you to the spa and then come back here to help you get ready. We have a cosmetics expert named Veronika coming later to help you two with your makeup. Elizabeth and I are going to the premiere too, of course, but will be handling our own preparations. You and Sonya get the special treatment today."

"Well, I'm not sure how I got included in this special treat, but I'm very excited and thankful," Sonya replied. "Perks of being your body double, I guess!"

"Take a quick shower but don't worry about your hair," Elizabeth said. "They will be fixing it after your massage. Make sure to wear either a button shirt or something loose that you can change out of later and not mess up your hair."

Soon they were out the door and headed to the spa. Lucy was in sweatpants and a loose T-shirt. Her hair was messy, and she had on no makeup. She laughed when she saw her reflection in the mirror – a far cry from the glamorous music star she would be tonight. She sure hoped Vicki Jo wasn't going to post too many pictures of her looking like this!

Five hours later, the group returned to the condo. Lucy's head was still spinning from the pampering and attention she and Sonya had just received. The massage was more amazing than others had said, and her hair looked the best it ever had. She had decided to leave it down, and now a mass of long curls reached down her back almost to her waist. Sonya's hair was again piled on her head in a chaos of spirals. She loved the edgy and daring look over Lucy's more conservative style.

Veronika arrived at four and quickly did their makeup, transforming Lucy into a demure angel while giving Sonya a bit of a rocker edge. Then it was time for the dresses and finishing touches. Vicki Jo went with Sonya while Elizabeth tended to Lucy. Gently easing her into the chiffon dress, she took care not to injure Lucy's arm. "Are you going to be OK without your sling all evening?" she asked cautiously. "I know you don't want to wear it, but we're not just talking about an hour or two. It may be close to midnight before you can put it back on."

"I refuse to spend the evening in my sling," Lucy responded with determination. "I don't want there to be any speculation or additional questions about my injury."

"If you're sure, but I want you to know that Josh said it would be OK if you wore it."

Lucy stepped out of her bedroom and into the living room where Sonya, Ramone and Dusty were waiting for her. The men were dashing in their tuxedos, and Sonya was adorable in her tea-length dress. Dusty walked slowly toward her with a giant smile on his face and admiration in his eyes.

"You are stunning!" he said under his breath as he reached her side. "I can barely breathe standing next to you!"

"And you, my dear friend, are quite dashing in your tuxedo. It looks like it was made just for you."

"No one will even notice me. They will only see you and your beauty. I might as well be wearing old jeans and a ball cap."

Lucy blushed and then Vicki Jo took numerous pictures of them both in the condo and standing beside the limo. The group of four opened a bottle of champagne and toasted the evening. Soon they were on their way. Elizabeth and Vicki Jo followed behind in a separate car, giving the friends a bit of privacy during the short drive downtown to the theater.

"I hope I remember every second of this night," Lucy whispered softly. "Never could I have imagined a life like this, and to be here with my dearest friends."

"I could get used to wearing a tux," Ramone said with a smile, "especially if this lovely creature is on my arm. I have to say, you two don't look like twins tonight! You are stunning, my darling!" he said to Sonya as he placed a kiss on her cheek. "Red is certainly your color."

Lucy and Dusty watched in amusement from their seats on the other side of the limo. "They are a cute couple," she whispered. "I'm so happy for them."

"Are you feeling OK without your sling?" Dusty asked worriedly. "Have you taken any medicine?"

"No, and I don't plan to. I'll be careful and use my arm as little as possible. I'll be fine," she replied with more confidence than she felt.

The limo pulled up outside the theater where Sonya and Ramone got out and joined the group of studio executives and actors at the end of the red carpet. The sidewalk was lined with media and a group of fans was being held back by a temporary fence. Lucy and Dusty watched from the limo as Josh and his wife approached and then joined them inside.

"Oh, my goodness, Lucy, you are gorgeous!" Josh gushed. "And you must be Dusty," he said as he held out his hand. "I'm Josh, and this is my wife, Cindy."

"Yes, it's good to meet both of you. Thank you for the invitation to be here with Lucy tonight. She does look amazing, and I cannot wait to see the entire video. I'm sure many of the million views online are mine."

"It looks like the event has started," Josh said. "We'll go out and mingle with the crowd a bit, and when the line is about through, Cindy and I will be last except for you two. Be prepared for this to take a while, as everyone is anxious to see you and talk about the video. The team has done a great job driving interest. I know this is a bit intimidating but try to relax and enjoy. You only get one first premiere."

Josh and Cindy exited the limo and joined the crowd. Lucy watched in amazement as the cameras and reporters jockeyed for the best positions to get photos. Soon it was Sonya and Ramone's turn as they joined other background actors and made their way into the theater. Just before she went inside, Sonya turned and looked back at the limo, a big smile on her face.

Dusty took Lucy's hand and said softly, "I know we don't have much time, but I have a little something I wanted to give you before we meet the reporters. Here." He handed Lucy a small box wrapped with a silver bow.

"What in the world?" she asked with confusion.

"Open it."

Her hands trembled a little as she lifted the lid of the box. Tucked inside was a diamond tennis bracelet. "Oh, my goodness!" she whispered.

"Let me put it on you," he said tenderly.

She held out her left wrist and he easily slipped the bracelet on. "Perfect," he said, as he kissed her fingers. "Just like you."

"Oh, Dusty, I don't know what to say. This is too much!"

"Never too much for you," he said as he leaned in close and gently kissed her waiting lips.

Time seemed to stand still as they shared their first real kiss. Her emotions were soaring when there was a gentle tap on the door. Lucy giggled as she lowered the window to find one of the interns motioning that it was her turn on the red carpet. Dusty opened the door and exited first. Holding out his hand to help Lucy to stand, there was a buzz of excitement as the reporters realized that their star had arrived.

Chapter 3

Lucy and Dusty took their place at the start of the carpet, just behind Josh and Cindy. The clatter of the cameras was deafening, along with the cheers from the crowd and shouts from the reporters. Josh smiled broadly and told the reporters that each would get their chance. Lucy turned to the fans and waved her left hand in their direction. The first reporter was Nancy Cooper from *Nashville Now*.

"Lucy, let me be the first to tell you that you look amazing! That is a gorgeous color on you. How are you feeling tonight?"

"It truly is a dream come true, and so much more than I could ever imagine. The studio has been wonderful to me, and the video is stunning."

"How was it, filming your first video?"

"It was fun, and so educational. I can't wait to do it again. I know you have seen the trailer. I hope you enjoy the full version we have for you tonight."

"And who is this handsome gentleman who is escorting you?"

"This is Dustin Pierce – he is handsome, right?" she said more to the crowd than to the reporter. "I'm so glad he could be here with me."

"Well, you look fabulous and very happy. Have a wonderful evening." And with that, they moved along the carpet to the next reporter. This was repeated numerous times, and they posed for endless pictures along the way. Some were just of Lucy, but most were of the two of them. She started out the evening with her hand resting on his arm, but before long they ended up hand in hand. About halfway down the carpet, they met Ricky and Roz from the radio station she had visited a few weeks ago. "And who is this lucky fellow with you?" Roz asked with a twinkle in her eye. "Have you been keeping secrets from us?"

"This is Dustin," Lucy said as she looked up at him fondly.

"I'm the lucky one," he said proudly with his Texas drawl. "There is no way I would miss this special night with her."

"Oohh, a southern boy. You know how to pick them!" Roz said teasingly.

Lucy just smiled and they continued toward the theater. The questions seemed endless, and she could not imagine why so many people needed so many pictures of her. Eventually, they made it to the entrance of the theater and Dusty held the door open. The fans were screaming for her, and she turned back to wave one last time, accidentally using her right arm. Pain shot from her shoulder to her wrist like a bolt of lightning, and she tried not to gasp or cry.

Dusty knew immediately that something was wrong. "You OK?" he asked softly.

"Oh, wow, that hurt. I'll be alright in a minute; I just need to catch my breath."

They walked into the lobby of the theater where Josh and others from the studio were waiting. Sonya and Ramone were across the room chatting with some of the actors. Darren and members of her band were huddled in another corner, discussing music she imagined. Dusty positioned himself protectively in front of her right arm so no one could bump into her. She smiled up at him weakly while her eyes rimmed with tears.

The group mingled for a while, and everyone enjoyed glasses of wine and expensive hors d'oeuvres. Eventually Josh announced that it was time to go inside and enjoy the video. Lucy and Dusty were escorted to an area in the front where they could have the best view, and then they were surrounded by Josh, Darren, and the rest of the studio staff who had worked so hard on the project. Dusty helped Lucy into her seat, being careful not to touch her arm. He could tell it was still bothering her, and he was worried that she would not be able to enjoy the video and the rest of the evening.

The lights dimmed and the video started. As before, the screen was blank as the first notes of music filtered softly around the room. Then the video played out before them, and again Lucy marveled at the magic Toby was able to accomplish. She glanced around the room a bit to see everyone's eyes glued to the screen. She prayed that it would receive the praise and provide the financial boost that the studio was hoping for.

She found Sonya sitting with Ramone across the room just a few rows back. She waited for the scene of her driving the car to appear on the screen. It was obvious that no one realized that it was Sonya and not Lucy who was driving. She smiled at Sonya who was excited to see herself on screen, if only from a distance.

The audience was completely silent as the video continued to play. After the final shot of Lucy alone in her car, the room was quiet again. No one spoke, no one moved. Lucy had a momentary feeling of panic that everyone hated it and did not know how to let her down gently. Then from somewhere near the back she heard, "That was simply stunning!" The room then erupted with cheers and clapping. The house lights were turned back on, and Lucy could see a standing ovation. Josh stood at the front of the room and motioned for quiet. He asked Toby and Lucy to join him on the stage. Dusty went with her to help her up the steps, but then stood off to one side. The applause started again, and Josh put one arm gently around her shoulder.

"Thank you so much, everyone, for being here tonight. As you have just witnessed, our *Rising Star* Lucy Armando is well on her way to becoming *America's Star!* What an amazing video. Thank you to Toby and his team for their fine work, but most of all to Lucy and her amazing song. As we speak, the video is being made available on all streaming platforms and social media. Everyone, grab your favorite device and like, comment, and share. Enjoy the food and drink in the lobby. Thanks again for coming, and let's have one more round of applause for Lucy Armando!"

Dusty helped Lucy down the stairs and out into the lobby. People were talking and laughing and celebrating the success of the video. She was surrounded most of the evening by well-wishers and media who were congratulating her on the success. Her arm continued to throb, and eventually she was unable to stand the pain any longer. Excusing herself to go to the ladies' room, she made her way carefully through the crowd. Once inside a stall, she leaned against the wall and silently cried. There were still several hours left in the evening, and she could barely focus. Opening her purse, she found the bottle of pain pills and held it gingerly in her hands. She really didn't want to take one but knew that Josh and the others expected her to be the life of the party for at least another hour. She opened the bottle and counted the remaining pills – there were only six. The outer door opened, and she heard two of the background actresses talking and laughing excitedly while they fixed their makeup. Lucy stayed quiet and prayed they did not find her in this condition. They left after a minute or two, and Lucy was alone again. Holding the bottle in her right hand, Lucy carefully lifted one pill out and looked at it closely. She was trembling a bit as she admired the blue and white stripes. "Just one more," she whispered as she quickly swallowed it.

Chapter 4

Lucy made her way back to the lobby and found Dusty talking with Sonya and Ramone. She admired his good looks from across the room and smiled. There were many good-looking men at the party, but she only had eyes for him. As if he knew she was watching, he looked across the lobby at her and smiled. He mouthed the word "OK?" and she nodded yes. She would be fine now.

The evening wore on and Lucy enjoyed being the center of attention. But after about an hour, she found herself slurring her words a bit and she was unsteady on her feet. Dusty even caught her one time as she was about to slide from her chair.

"What's going on? How much have you had to drink? Do we need to leave?"

"Drink? Not much," she said slowly. "I guess I shouldn't have……" and her voice drifted off.

"Shouldn't have WHAT?" Dusty asked. "Lucy – look at me! What's wrong?"

Lucy looked at Dusty but there seemed to be two or three of him floating around. Dusty motioned for Sonya and Ramone to come over. "I think something is wrong with her. She can barely stand, and her eyes are all glassy."

"Lucy, Honey, are you OK?" Sonya asked softly. "Did something happen?"

"I guess I shouldn't have taken that pill after drinking champagne," she mumbled.

"Pill? Did you take a pain pill?"

"Just one, I promise."

Ramone looked at Dusty and said, "We need to find a way to get her out of here without arousing any suspicion. Any ideas how to do that?"

"I could go to Josh," Sonya said, "and tell him that she twisted her arm again and we needed to take her home."

"Do it quietly, please!" Dusty begged. "Is the limo waiting outside for us?"

"Sonya, you talk to Josh, and I'll check on the limo," Ramone instructed. "Dusty, I'll help you get her out the back door where you can wait for the car. Hurry everyone – we cannot let the press see her like this."

Sonya slipped quietly across the room and tapped on Josh's arm. She whispered in his ear that they needed to get Lucy home because of pain in her arm. He nodded and sent a text to the limo driver to meet them around the back of the theater. He thanked Sonya again for taking such good care of her for them.

Ramone and Dusty managed to get Lucy to her feet without too much difficulty and guided her toward a quiet hallway. Ramone flagged down the limo and soon all four of them were headed back to the condo.

"Are we going home?" Lucy slurred. "Is the party over?"

"Yes, Honey" Sonya said softly. "We'll get you home and in bed and you'll feel better in the morning."

Lucy slumped against Dusty's shoulder and was asleep within a minute. The rest of the group looked worriedly at each other.

"Has this ever happened before?" Dusty asked.

"No, never. I mean, there have been a few times when she overslept and then was hard to wake up, but I don't think she ever mixed the pills with alcohol before," Ramone answered.

"This is really serious and could ruin her career if the media found out. What are we going to do?"

The limo stopped in front of Lucy's condo, and the group managed to get her inside and into her bed without too much difficulty.

"Anyone need some coffee?" Sonya asked as they moved to the living room. "That was certainly not the way I thought our night would end."

Ramone sent Josh a text to let him know that they were home safely, and that Lucy was resting.

"I honestly had no idea the issue with the pills had gotten this bad," Sonya said.

Sonya and Ramone sat on the sofa and Dusty was in Lucy's recliner. He saw her Bible on the table next to the chair and noticed his original note to her was being used as a bookmark. He looked sadly around the room, trying to understand how they had all missed the warning signs of her opioid misuse.

"I don't feel right leaving her like this," he said with concern. "What if something happens during the night?"

"I'll be here, but you two are welcome to stay if you want."

"Do you mind?" Ramone asked. "Not only am I her friend, but I was hired to look out for her."

"Of course I don't mind. Let me get some pillows and blankets. Do you want to run home and change?"

"I'll come with you and get my bag," Dusty said. "My flight is not until after lunch, but I need to be here with her, if you understand?"

"Of course. Sonya, we'll be back in just a few minutes."

The men left and Sonya went to the bedroom to sit beside her friend. "Oh, Lucy, when did things get so bad? Why didn't you tell me you were having trouble with the pills? Or did you, and I just didn't listen?"

Lucy did not wake up when Sonya eased her out of her dress and into a T-shirt and sweatpants. She hung the dress in the closet and took off her expensive necklace and earrings. She noticed a tennis bracelet on her arm and wondered where it came from. She didn't remember it from when they were getting ready earlier.

She heard the door open and left the bedroom to meet the guys in the kitchen. They had changed into casual clothes and Dusty had brought his duffle bag. His tuxedo was in its own travel bag.

"I'm going to change," Sonya said. "Help yourselves to whatever you can find to eat or drink. I think we have a long night ahead of us."

"Ramone, I'm really worried," Dusty said sadly. "She has such a bright future ahead of her, and tonight was supposed to be a celebration of that. Do you think anyone suspected anything?"

"No, I doubt it. We got her out pretty quickly, but we absolutely need to have a serious talk with her tomorrow. How can we get help for her without the studio or the media finding out?"

Sonya returned wearing sweats and her hair was pulled into a ponytail. She had scrubbed the excessive makeup from her face and was looking like her old self.

"I'm not sure how to go about it, but it needs to be done," Sonya replied. "She's very lucky that we were able to handle this for her tonight. We're not always going to be able to do that. Do you think we need to talk to Josh?"

The group sat silently while they wrestled with the decisions ahead of them. They took turns checking on Lucy, making sure she was sleeping safely. Eventually Sonya and Ramone fell asleep while cuddled on the sofa. Dusty was in the recliner, watching for the first hints of sunrise on the horizon.

The silence was broken by the jolting sound of Ramone's cell phone. Jerking awake, he grabbed the phone and saw Josh's name on the caller ID. "Oh, man. This can't be good," he mumbled under his breath.

"Ramone, where are you?" Josh demanded. "I know it's early on the morning after a party, but I need answers, now!"

"Hi Josh. I'm at Lucy's condo. Sonya and Dusty are with me."

"Where is Lucy?"

"She's still asleep in her bedroom."

"What the hell happened last night? I just got a very disturbing text message from the limo driver. Talk to me, Ramone!"

"The limo driver? What did he say?" Ramone asked cautiously. Sonya and Dusty were watching in horror as Ramone struggled to make sense of the call.

"He said that Lucy was completely incapacitated and unable to walk, and that you three had to practically carry her into the house. Is that true? And if it is, were you going to tell me?"

"Lucy hurt her arm earlier in the evening, actually before the video even played, and was really struggling. I guess sometime during the party it got to be too much, and she took one of her pain pills, not realizing what would happen since she had been drinking a bit of champagne. We didn't have time to think, just knew we needed to get her out immediately and to let her sleep it off. We've kept an eye on her all night and were going to call you later."

"Is that all of it? Are you hiding anything else from me?"

"No, Josh, that's the whole story. Dusty knew that she had hurt her arm but seemed to be managing it well. None of us knew about the pills until later."

"Let me know once she wakes up and I'll be on my way over. This is totally unacceptable, and we need to get it stopped! Let's just pray that no one else noticed."

Josh hung up, and Ramone looked at his friends with despair. "He'll be over as soon as Lucy wakes up. What do you think is going to happen to her?"

Sonya went to the kitchen to make another pot of coffee and started fixing breakfast. "Dusty, can you check on her one more time? I'm worried that she is still asleep."

"Sure," he said as he walked quietly to her room and gently opened the door. He was startled to see that her bed was empty – where was she? He then heard her crying in her bathroom.

"Lucy, are you OK? May I come in?" He tried the doorknob but discovered that it was locked.

"Go away. I'm too embarrassed to talk to anyone."

"I'm not just anyone. It's me, and I want to help you."

"I look horrible," she said between sobs, "and I feel even worse. Just leave me alone."

"No, I won't. Please let me in."

After a few seconds, she opened the door, and he was shocked to see her disheveled appearance. Her makeup was smeared, and her eyes were puffy, swollen and bloodshot. "I'm so confused," she whispered. "What happened to me?"

"I know your arm was hurting you – when did you take the pain pill?"

"I'm not sure. After the video and a bunch of interviews, I remember that much. I went into the bathroom, and…."

"I wish you had told me earlier how badly you were feeling, and we could have gotten you out sooner. Mixing your pills with alcohol was a really bad decision."

"I wasn't thinking about that, I just needed the pain to go away."

"I'm going to have Sonya come in and help you take a shower. Josh will be coming over in a bit."

"Josh? Why is he coming? Does he know about this?" she asked fearfully.

"Actually, the limo driver told him. He is upset, of course, and very worried about you. We all are."

Lucy started sobbing again, and Dusty gently took her into his arms. He saw the bracelet still on her wrist and touched it gently.

"It's so beautiful," she said sadly. "And I ruined our beautiful evening."

"No, not ruined. Just a slight detour. We'll work with Josh to find an answer and get some help for you. Where are your pills? Do you have many left?"

"They are in my bag from last night. And no, there are just a few."

Dusty found the pills and took them with him to the living room. Sonya went in to help her get cleaned up, telling her that Josh would be there in about an hour.

They were still in the bedroom when there was a firm knock on the door. Ramone opened it to find Josh and Vicki Jo.

"How is she?" they asked with concern.

"She just had a shower, and Sonya is helping her dress. They should be out in a bit."

"How did things get this far out of control?" Vicki Jo asked with concern. "She never let on to me that she was having problems."

"None of us realized," Ramone said sadly. "I know she said many times she didn't like taking them so often, and I believe she was in more pain than she let on. I guess she tried to deal with this on her own, without telling any of us exactly how bad it was."

"Well, I'm glad you all were there to help her last night, but this *has* to be the last time for this type of thing to happen," Josh lectured. "We have way too much time. effort, and money invested in her to lose it all now. Of course, I'm worried about her as a person and a friend, but from a business perspective, this is a potential disaster. The media would have a field day if this got out! I hope she will realize that."

"Yes, Josh, I do," Lucy said softly from her bedroom doorway. "I'm so sorry about all of this."

"How are you feeling?" Josh asked. "You gave us all quite a scare."

"I know, I just wasn't thinking. Most of the evening is a blur."

"Lucy, I want you to know that we are all here for you," Vicki Jo said gently. "You can call me and talk anytime. And I have the number of an addiction specialist who wants to help. We are all on your side, Lucy, please believe me."

"Addiction? I wouldn't go that far….."

"Dependency perhaps? Misuse? The terminology doesn't really matter here. We all just want you healthy and strong again."

"Thank you, everyone," she said as she gently stroked the tennis bracelet on her arm. "I love you all."

Chapter 5

"On a much brighter note," Josh said with his first smile of the morning, "the rest of the evening was a huge success. Downloads of the video are already in the thousands, and the studio phones are going crazy with people wanting to book interviews and TV appearances. Did you know that a rep from Country Music TV was there last night? She came in a bit under the radar and did not tell anyone exactly who she was with. Obviously, she was impressed, as they are featuring your video this morning, and according to the texts I keep receiving, the audience loves it."

"Your fans have been busy this morning as well," Vicki Jo said. "I haven't seen this much excitement for a new video from a rising star in a long time."

"That's amazing," Lucy said with a wistful sigh. Normally she would be smiling and laughing, but her head hurt too much for that, and she was still feeling the sting of embarrassment and the scolding she had received from Josh. "This is all due to you and the video. And to think I almost ruined it."

"We can't keep focusing on what might have happened," Josh said firmly. "We were lucky this time, though. I've got to get back to the office. Please call the doctor as soon as possible and set up an appointment – she has an emergency number for weekends. I'll get back to you once we set up a schedule for next week."

After Josh and Vicki Jo left, the friends returned to the living room and Ramone turned the TV to CMT. The video had just ended, and the DJs were talking excitedly. Lucy couldn't help but smile as they praised not only the concept of the video but also her performance. Within a few minutes, they decided to show it again.

The group watched in awe as the video restarted with Sonja driving into the school parking lot. "You honestly cannot tell it's not you," Dusty said with amazement. "I would never have guessed had you not told me."

Once they got to the prom scene, Sonja jumped up excitedly and ran to the TV. "There we are!" she pointed. "I thought I saw us last night, but it was so fast I wasn't sure."

"Toby told me that they would include you two, even if just for a second or two."

The room got quiet again as they watched the end of the video. Dusty reached out for Lucy's hand and looked deeply into her eyes.

"Did you really feel that lonely? I'm very sad if this is true."

"The video is a bit of an exaggeration, but yes, I felt pretty invisible while in school. Other than these two special people here, I didn't have a lot of friends or fun. And no, I never went to the prom."

"I wish I had known you then," he said softly. "I would have noticed you."

Lucy blushed, and Ramone took this as his cue to take Sonya for a walk and leave the two alone for a while. Other than a few minutes in the limo, they had had no privacy.

Finally alone, Dusty took her into his arms and kissed her deeply. "I only have an hour before I need to leave for the airport, but I've wanted to do that since early last evening. Thank you so much for including me on your special night. It was amazing – the video was amazing - you are amazing. You are an incredible woman, and I hope after last night more people will see the real you."

"Thank you," she said softly, finding security and safety in his arms.

They chatted quietly for the next 30 minutes, then Ramone and Sonya returned to take Dusty to the airport. Lucy stood by the door of the truck as Dusty climbed in. He leaned down to kiss her gently one more time, then she watched them drive out the gates.

"Come back inside and rest," Sonya said gently. "I'm sure you will see him again, and from the look on his face, I would guess very soon."

Chapter 6

Lucy had her first counseling session on Tuesday. Her therapist Amber Todd listened with empathy and provided some coping mechanisms for her. She also agreed to talk to Dr. Reynolds about the need to find alternative medications so she could stop the opioids completely. Dr. Todd believed it was time for Lucy to be released to start driving again and to begin intensive physical therapy. She felt this would help Lucy's mood improve and not be so fearful about the future.

The schedule of media interviews was growing every day, and Lucy was in constant demand. By the end of the week, Josh called a meeting about planning the next tour.

"First off, Lucy, do you have an update on your physical therapy? How are you feeling?"

"I'm doing a lot better. I've been playing my guitar again, and the pain is manageable. I'm optimistic to be good as new very soon."

"Good," he said, looking at her with concern. "Any other issues or worries?"

"No, I'm feeling stronger every day."

"OK – we have had a huge number of requests for appearances and concerts. Bigger venues are interested, including

Kansas City and Charlotte. Toby is ready to start working on the next video, and Vicki Jo has had her hands full managing all the social media. I've blocked out this room for the rest of the day. Lunch will be brought in after a while, but we really need to take advantage of all the positive press we have right now and move ahead quickly."

Lucy was excited to be back among the team and planning the next events. It had been a week since her last pain pill, and she was amazed and how much clearer her thinking was now.

Toby wanted the next video to be an upbeat song to contrast with the last, and they all agreed on '*It's A Happy Day*', the second single from the album to be released. Michael had started filling out the calendar for the next two months, and once again Lucy was amazed with all that went into making her music a success.

"We have some other requests that I've held off mentioning," Josh said slyly. "How would you all feel about a trip to Hawaii next fall?"

"Hawaii? Seriously?" Lucy was shocked.

"Yes, it would be part of a music festival that they do each November. You would not be headlining, of course, but near the middle of the ranking. I know that I could use a long warm weekend in Hawaii in November."

"Let's certainly put that on the list for next year!" Lucy said enthusiastically. "But November is a long way off. KC and Charlotte sound fun. Is there any place we could stop in between?"

"St. Louis? Chicago? Maybe even DC?" Ramone asked.

"I'd rather keep it more southern, since we are going into the winter months," Josh replied. "Maybe Atlanta or Dallas.... let's work on that."

They broke for lunch, but the conversations continued.

"Lucy, I have to say you are looking well rested," Toby said. "Are you excited about the next video?"

"Yes, very much so. The concept of a fun day at a dog park is perfect for the song. I'm ready for something fun and light, after the heaviness of the last one."

The meeting concluded around three and Ramone started to take Lucy home. "Can we stop somewhere first?" she asked.

"Sure," he answered. "What do you need?"

"I'm wanting a new cell phone, well, an additional cell phone, that can just be for my closest contacts. My current one is being overrun with media and crazy fans and even reporters. I have no idea how they found my number, but I cannot block them fast enough. I thought a private line would be the best solution."

"I agree it's a good idea. There's a store not far from the condo. Sonya should be home by now. How about we take some BBQ home and celebrate tonight."

"Celebrate?"

"We are going to Hawaii!!"

Chapter 7

Time flew by as Lucy juggled video shoots, time in the recording studio, tour prep and her therapy sessions. Dr. Todd met with her two afternoons per week, and Josh maintained discretion about the reasons she was unavailable for interviews at those times.

They worked with a local animal shelter to film the video, and this time both Sonya and Ramone could be seen playing with the puppies or giving a bulldog a bath. There was also a plea at the end for pet adoption. The video was fun and upbeat, with humorous scenes running through a dog park and cats climbing trees. Although it looked crazy and hectic, they were able to complete it in just a few hours.

Lucy was faithful with her exercises, and her arm was getting stronger each day. Soon, the pain was a fading memory that only bothered her if she lifted something heavy or twisted into a strange position. Dr. Reynolds finally released her to drive again, and she relished the freedom it gave her.

It was a beautiful late fall day and most of the leaves were gone from the trees. Some stores had even started decorating for Christmas, which she thought was pushing the holiday just a bit. Realizing she had not bought anything new for herself in months, Lucy decided to do a bit of shopping. She found a good parking spot at a leather goods store and slipped inside. Several people looked at her, and this time she could tell they recognized her. Her video was up to almost one million views, so she should not be surprised, especially in a music town like Nashville.

A young salesclerk with stars in her eyes approached her. "You are Lucy Armando, right? It's exciting to have you in our store today. What can I help you with?"

"I'm needing a new winter coat, along with some boots and gloves. I'd also like to look at the purses."

"Of course. Is there any particular color you are attracted to?"

"I'm tired of black. Maybe a dark green or maroon?"

"Sure, the coats are back this way. I love your new video, by the way. '*If Only*' has been a favorite of mine since it first came out."

"Thanks – it holds a special place in my heart. But I hope you enjoy the rest of the album as well. It was a lot of fun to make."

"Oh, I love them all. I was wondering – has there been any news about the duets album with Travis Jones? It's been quite a while since his passing, but no one is talking about it."

Lucy took a deep breath and prepared to make her standard speech. Would she ever be able to hear his name without flashing back to that night?

"No, I have not heard anything. I do know that his parents are still settling his affairs, but his studio would oversee the album. Sorry I can't be of more help."

"No problem. OK, here are the coats. Anything look interesting?"

Lucy selected a hunter green trench coat along with coordinating gloves and scarf. She found a pair of black snow boots and then asked about purses.

"Sure, we have a special selection of top-brand purses here in this case," the clerk said. "Any particular size?"

"Oh, I don't want anything very large. It needs to be functional but also not in the way on our crowded tour bus."

"Oh, are you going out on tour again?'

"We are working on the final details, so be sure to watch my website. You will know almost as soon as I do!"

Lucy arrived home with her purchases just as Sonya was pulling into her parking spot.

"Someone has been shopping!" Sonya teased. "It's about time! You have been needing new things for ages!"

"I know. I needed a new coat, and then just kept shopping. It's a fun thing to do occasionally. Have you noticed that Christmas decorations are up already?"

"It's crazy, which reminds me. Are you going to put up a tree? It might be fun. I don't imagine you have one hiding in that giant closet of yours?"

"No, I don't, but I would love to decorate. Do you work on Saturday? I don't have anything on my calendar that day and we could make a day of it."

"I have to work until noon, but we could meet for lunch then head to that big Christmas store near the mall. Do you want a real tree or artificial?"

"I would love a real tree, but with our crazy schedules, I think it will have to be artificial. What about you? What kind of tree did you have as a child?"

"It just depended on the mood mom was in each year. Usually it was artificial, so I'm fine with that."

Saturday afternoon they went shopping, and within a few hours their tree was up and they even put a some lights on the patio. Lucy and Sonya relaxed in front of the fireplace with a glass of wine, Christmas music playing softly in the background. Lucy closed her eyes and relished the moment. It was a Saturday night, but she was glad to be home and relaxing. She missed Dusty terribly – for some reason they kept missing each other in the evenings and had not had a long conversation in over a week. There had been another huge data breech at his work, and he was working over 60 hours per week. When he did get a chance to call, he was so exhausted that he usually just went straight to bed instead.

On Sunday afternoon, Lucy got a text from Darren asking what her favorite Christmas song was. She replied, *'Oh Holy Night,'* and all Darren said was, *"good."*

"That's an odd question – even from you. What in the world is this about?" she asked.

"We just got a request for you to sing a Christmas song on the local ABC station next week. I already have an arrangement done for that song that another artist had used a few years back. Let me raise the key a few steps and I'll send it over to you. Come in tomorrow morning and we'll see how it sounds."

Lucy agreed, and then sent Dusty a text, "*Hi – hope your work is settling down and you are getting some rest. Any idea what you schedule will be over the holidays? Would love to see you.*"

Before he had a chance to reply, her phone *pinged* with an update to her calendar. She looked at the week ahead and saw she rarely had more than a few hours in a row without appointments.

It was several minutes before Dusty replied. "*Sorry, I really can't talk right now. I'm at work – again – with no idea how long I'll be here. Maybe tomorrow morning?*"

"*No,*" she replied. "*I have to go to the studio to work on some music. I miss you.*"

"*I miss you too. Sorry, gotta run.*"

Lucy stared at her phone sadly. What was happening to them? Why was it so difficult to even find time to talk on the phone? Was their budding romance going to survive their crazy schedules and different lifestyles?

She listened to the arrangement Darren sent over and knew it would be easy for her to sing for TV later in the week. Feeling restless and stressed, she tried to watch a movie but couldn't focus. Sonya suggested that they bake cookies, but nothing sounded interesting. "I guess I'll go take a nap," she told no one in particular. "It's not often I have much free time anymore."

She was walking toward her bed when she tripped over one of her new boots and stumbled into her closet door. She did not hit her shoulder directly but twisted her arm a bit and pain shot down toward her elbow. "*OW*" she yelled, and Sonya rushed to help her.

"What in the world happened?" she asked with concern.

"I tripped over my new boots and hurt my arm. Oh, no, I cannot go through all this again!"

"Lay down on your bed and I'll get you an ice pack. I'm sure it's OK."

"It had better be. Josh will never forgive me if I mess it up again. Sometimes I feel that his patience with me has already run out."

"Here's your ice," Sonya said when she returned to the room, "and I brought some Tylenol. You know your doctor doesn't want you to take anything stronger."

"I know, thanks. I just need to rest a bit and pray this goes away quickly."

"Do you need to call Dr. Todd? She wanted you to call if you ever wanted to talk."

"No, not yet. We'll see how I do in the next hour or so. Thank you so much for taking care of me. Where would I have been all these months without you?"

Sonya went to the living room and texted Ramone, asking him to come over for a bit. This was the first real test of Lucy's sobriety, and she wanted all the help she could get.

Chapter 8

Lucy rested for just a few minutes then cried out in pain. She instinctively reached onto her nightstand for her bottle of pain pills, but of course they were not there. In frustration, she knocked over her waterglass which then crashed onto the floor and broke. Sonya and Ramone rushed into the room.

"Lucy, what happened?" Ramone asked. "Are you alright?"

"No, I'm not!" she said, crying. "My arm hurts and I need a pain pill! Tylenol doesn't work, you know that. I might as well have eaten an M&M."

"Oh, Honey," Sonya said sympathetically. "I know it hurts, but you need to be tough. Do you want me to call the doctor?"

"No, I can't let anyone know I've hurt myself again. I'm just in such pain."

"I'm going to make you some tea and bring you a fresh ice pack. We are here with you, both of us….we'll get you through this. Ramone, can you help pick up the broken glass?"

Sonya went to the kitchen to fix a cup of tea, and then she texted Dusty. "*This is Sonya. Lucy hurt her arm again — we are giving her Tylenol but it's not helping. She's in terrible pain. Can you call her, or text? She really needs all her friends right now.*"

"*Of course,*" he replied. "*Give me just a few minutes to wrap up this project and I'll call her. I'm so sorry she is dealing with this again.*"

Sonya returned to the bedroom to find Lucy wrapped in Ramone's arms and they were doing the deep breathing techniques provided by Dr. Todd.

"Just focus on your breathing," Ramone said softly. "In, out, in, out. There you go."

"Here's some ice," Sonya said gently. "And I texted Dusty. He said he would call in a little while."

"Thanks, I think. I'm not sure I wanted him to know about this."

"He cares about you, and you need all your friends right now."

"I suppose. I just hurt so much, and the Tylenol is not working."

Her phone rang and she motioned to Sonya to answer it for her.

"Hi, Dusty" Sonya said. "Lucy is here but hurting pretty badly. I'll put you on speaker, if that's OK."

"Lucy, Honey, it's me. Talk to me….how can I help?"

"Dusty, it's so hard. I hurt so much and really want a pain pill," she sobbed.

"I know you are in pain, but the pain pills will not help you. Do you have ice? What about the other strategies the doctor gave you?"

"We've been working on her deep breathing," Ramone said, "and it seems to be helping a bit."

"There are no pills in the house, are there?" Dusty asked.

"No, we got rid of the few I had left," Lucy replied. "I know in my head that I cannot take one, but….."

"I know," Dusty answered. "But you can do this. Just try the relaxation techniques and call me later if you need me. Any time, day or night, OK?"

"OK, thanks for calling. I do miss you."

"I miss you too. We'll work something out to get together over Christmas, I promise."

Dusty ended the call, and a single tear slipped down Lucy's cheek.

"Just lean against me and close your eyes," Ramone said after a few seconds. "Rest a while. I'm here to take care of you."

Lucy closed her eyes, and to everyone's surprise, was able to drift off to sleep. Sonya climbed onto the bed as well, gently holding her friend's hand and stroking it softly. Eventually all three were asleep.

After about an hour, Lucy gently opened her eyes. Momentarily confused, she looked around her bedroom to see her two best friends holding her, keeping her comfortable and safe. She shifted her position a bit and was pleased to find that the pain had reduced to a dull ache instead of a stabbing pain. Sonya opened her eyes and whispered, "Hi. How are you feeling?"

"A bit better, actually. You all are the best, you know, sacrificing your Sunday afternoon to care for me."

The rest of the afternoon was quiet, and Ramone went home after they had a bit of dinner. He promised to return in the morning to go with her to the studio.

"Do you want to spend the night in the recliner again?" Sonya asked.

"No, I think I will be fine. Thanks again for everything."

"I need to go to work early, but I'll make sure there is an easy breakfast ready for you before I leave. Text me later and let me know how it goes."

Lucy was relieved to find that her arm was much better when she got up on Monday morning. She was able to dress without too much difficulty and was enjoying a light breakfast when Ramone arrived to drive her to the studio.

"How are you feeling? You look a lot better than when I left last night."

"Yes, so much better. You two are just the best friends I could ever ask for. Even though I've been released to drive myself, I love that you are looking out for me."

"Well, let's get you to work and I'm anxious to see what Josh has in mind for me next."

The time in the studio with Darren went well, and soon they were satisfied that the song would be perfect for TV on Friday. Looking at her calendar, she saw radio station interviews scheduled for almost every day, along with an appearance on a podcast. She ran into Josh in the hallway who asked her to come into his office.

"Lucy, first off, how are you doing? The issues from the red carpet all resolved now? You look well rested."

"Thanks," she said a bit guiltily. "It was nice to have several days at home with nothing really planned."

"Good, because it's going to be crazy all the way up to Christmas, I'm afraid. You worked on that song with Darren?"

"Yes, just finished. It sounds really good. His arrangement is very pretty."

"I agree. I can't imagine what this studio would be like without him, and I hope I never have to find out. Where are you off to now?"

"I have a meeting with Toby and a few others to discuss another video, then the band and I will get together to brainstorm songs for the next album. After that, Elizabeth wants me to pick an outfit for TV. So yes, a busy day."

"I'm glad you are staying active, and we are keeping your name in front of the public. We lost a bit of time with your accident, you know, but now that you are better and released to travel, I want to get serious about finalizing your tour for early in the spring. Once we settle on the set list, we need to start rehearsals and talk about an upgrade to your lighting. Each step up the ladder means we need to keep improving and finding ways to keep the audience engaged. They don't want to see the same concert over and over."

Lucy didn't miss his not-so-subtle comment about her injury. The bus accident was not her fault, of course, but she wondered how much it had cost the studio in lost time and revenues. She felt the familiar twinge of anxiety, but knew she needed to move past it and make the most of her time at the studio.

Her first two meetings went well, and after a late lunch, she went to Elizabeth's office to talk about what to wear on TV on Friday. They went through her closet and found a few suitable items, but none looked very festive for the holiday season.

"Are you busy the rest of the afternoon?" Elisabeth asked. "Perhaps we should get out of here and do some shopping!"

"I'm free the rest of the day. Shopping sounds fun."

Their first stop was a trendy shop not far from the studio. Lucy had never seen so much fringe or glitter or sequins since the TV competition.

"I doubt there is anything here for me," Lucy said reluctantly. "These are all the types of things that I want to stay away from."

"Let's not give up so easily. Surely there will be something you like, and it would be nice to get something more festive for the holiday season."

"I guess," she said reluctantly. "But I'm not forfeiting my conservative Christian values just because it's the holidays."

Elizabeth chose several outfits and escorted her to the dressing room. Lucy looked through the items and cringed a bit. Low cut necklines, short skirts, long fringe…how was she going to convince Elizabeth that this was not what she wanted? Lucy continued to scour the racks for something more appropriate.

Finally, she found a deep green velvet dress that had a bit of sparkle added. The neckline was rounded and not overly low, and the hemline was presentable. She hoped that Elizabeth would approve, because this was one she felt comfortable in.

"You look stunning, Lucy, you really do. They also have a deep maroon and a purple one just like this. Want to look at them? I really think this green looks perfect on you."

"I'm happy with the green," Lucy said, "but I know I can't wear it on TV in front of a green screen. The purple sounds nice as well. Do you think we should get more than one, so I have an option for other events before New Year's?"

"We could. I'm not sure anyone would notice they are the same dress, especially if we change accessories or your hairstyle. It is a very pretty dress – festive, yet conservative, which I know is important to you."

They found a few more things then Elizabeth drove her back to the studio. "Are you done for today?" she asked.

"I think so," Lucy replied. "I'll be back tomorrow to work with the band again. I'm going to go through my notebooks to see if I have any other songs for the next album. Do you have any favorite songs you would like us to cover? I'm open to all ideas."

"Hmm, let me think. With your voice and style, I would love to hear some upbeat songs like from the Judds or Reba."

"Nice ideas – I'll ask Darren if there are any issues with copyrights. Thanks for taking me shopping. I'll see you tomorrow."

Lucy drove home and sat on the sofa with her guitar. Almost immediately she found herself playing that same sad melody that had been haunting her for months. Frustrated, she put her guitar down and sent a text to Dusty.

"I know you are busy, just wanted to say Hi. Will you have a chance to call later? Miss you."

"Yes, I can call tonight. I have some good news for you, for a change. Miss you, too. D."

Sonya came home from work and Ramone arrived shortly after. They had fallen into the routine of spending their evenings together whenever they got the chance. Lucy didn't mind, of course, but did find herself feeling increasingly lonely and sad, especially as the holidays were approaching. They found "It's a Wonderful Life" on TV and settled down with popcorn and tissues, since Lucy and Sonya always cried at the end. About halfway through the movie, Dusty called, and Lucy excused herself to her bedroom so they could talk privately.

"I'm glad you called," Lucy said sweetly. "It seems like such a long time since we had a chance to say more than hello and goodbye."

"I know. Things have been crazy for both of us. But not for much longer, at least on my end. We have the data breech almost handled, and my boss is giving us all two weeks off, from just before Christmas until the New Year. Any chance we can spend some of that time together?"

"Oh, that is fantastic! Of course I want to see you. I have to stay here in town, though, but there is plenty we can do. Or we can just hang out close to home and enjoy the peace and quiet."

"I don't care, I just want to be with you. Do you have appearances over Christmas?"

"I'm not sure just yet. I heard a rumor the other day that things often happen at the last minute here --- either someone cancels suddenly, or an opening will pop up unexpectedly. But if I do, you are welcome to come, of course, and watch all the craziness behind the scenes."

"I honestly don't care what we do, I just really want to spend Christmas with you."

"That would be lovely. Once you know your dates for sure, send them to me and I'll try to clear my calendar as much as possible. I can't promise anything, of course."

"I understand." They chatted a while longer then said goodnight.

Chapter 9

Lucy arrived at the TV studio promptly at six A.M. on Friday morning. She was already dressed in the purple velvet dress and her hair hung in soft curls around her face. Elizabeth was there and offered to help with her makeup. The hosts Bob McCain and Rachel Suarez were excited to meet her and to have her sing for them. After a brief interview, she stood in front of a green screen to sing "Oh Holy Night" while Darren's beautiful arrangement played in the background. The screen was filled with famous artwork depicting the Nativity. Once the song was over, the station went to commercial, and Lucy was free to go. The hosts and station staff were pleased with the song and asked her to come back again soon.

With nothing left on her schedule for three days, she made a quick call to Josh to tell him she needed to fly to Florida to visit her mother. It had been several months since she had visited, and knew this would be her last chance until the new year. Josh approved, of course, and Lucy rushed home to pack a small bag and then took an UBER to the airport. Last-minute flights were quite expensive, especially this time of year, but she could easily afford it now and chastised herself for not visiting more often. The last text from her dad was that mom was really struggling with her chemo treatment.

She found a direct flight from Nashville to Tampa and was soon seated in first class. It was obvious that most of the passengers recognized her, including her seat mate.

"Lucy Armando?" the young man asked. "I just saw you on TV this morning. I sure never imagined sitting next to you this afternoon."

"I didn't know I would be here. This trip is rather spur-of-the-moment."

"Nice. I'm on my way to a convention. Not many places nicer than Florida in the winter."

"Agree," Lucy said without much emotion. She certainly did not want to explain the reason for this trip to a stranger and risk violating her mom's privacy. The last thing anyone needed was a bunch of tabloid media prowling the halls hunting for a story.

One of the best parts of first class was that she could exit the plane first, and was soon in a car and on her way to the hospital. It wasn't until she was inside the facility that she called her dad.

"Hi, Dad. How are things going today?"

"Hi, Honey. Things are about the same, I guess. They are giving her the strongest chemo they can but she's not handling it very well. She's resting now, but I know she would love to talk to you. How have you been?"

"I've been busy, of course, even on local TV this morning. Do you think she is up for a visit?"

"It's hard to say from day to day. When are you thinking of coming down?"

"I'm already here, Dad – I'm in the lobby. Surprise!"

"Oh, my goodness! She will be so happy! Come on up so you can be here when she wakes up! What a wonderful early Christmas gift!"

"I wanted to bring some flowers, is that OK? I wasn't sure if there were any new restrictions?"

"No, flowers are still fine. Something colorful would be nice. She has been here so long and is getting very discouraged."

"I'll be up in a bit," she said sadly, worried about when (or even if) her mom would ever be able to go home. She stepped into the gift shop and looked around at all the pretty trinkets and flowers. There were books, magazines, candy and stuffed animals. She found a pretty bouquet of red roses and a prayer book, but then a picture on a magazine cover caught her eye. It was of her and Elizabeth shopping earlier in the week! It was taken inside the store, either by a customer or store employee. The magazine was a gossip rag that was usually full of rumors or outright lies, and she never paid it much attention, but this time she couldn't resist. The article itself was pretty boring – Lucy and an unidentified woman were spotted shopping. No big deal. But then the story speculated as to why they were shopping…. Upcoming concert? A New Year's Eve special? A date with mystery-man Dustin from the red carpet? Did people actually spend good money on this rubbish? And why would anyone care that she was dress shopping?

The clerk smiled at her sweetly and wished her a good day. Celebrities and famous people were in Florida all the time, and the staff had learned not to make a big deal when one was in the facility, either as a patient or a visitor. Lucy smiled in return and headed for the elevator.

She found her mother's room and took a deep breath to compose herself. The last time she had facetimed with her parents, her mother looked quite thin and frail. Would she look even worse today?

She went into the room and realized she was nowhere near prepared for how much her mother had declined in such a short time. Her father rose to hug her and whispered quietly, "I'm so glad you are here. She's not getting better, and we even had a discussion last night about how much longer she was going to continue with the chemo. It just seems to be making things worse, not better. She's lost so much weight and all her hair. I'm not sure she has the strength to keep fighting."

Lucy sat beside the bed and gently placed her mother's hand in hers. "Oh, Mom," she whispered sadly. "This is so unfair."

Her mother's eyes fluttered open weakly. "Lucy?" she said softly. "Is that really you?"

"Yes, Mom. I came down to surprise you. I've missed you so much. Is there anything I can get for you? Some water? Another pillow?"

"No, just seeing you is enough. I mean, I love it when we facetime, but nothing can take the place of this! I imagine you are still keeping busy?"

"Yes, I was even on local TV this morning. But I want to talk about you. How are you feeling? I hate that I have not been here more often and am so far away. I'll do better, I promise."

"Your father and I understand, and we are so proud of you and all that you have accomplished so quickly. A few of my nurses know I'm your mom and are always asking for updates."

"I'm sorry if they are bothering you, mom. I hope they are being respectful of your privacy."

"I believe so. Everyone here is so nice and considerate."

They visited for a few more minutes and Lucy noticed that her mother was getting very fatigued.

"I'll let you rest Mom and go check into a hotel. I'll be back later, OK?"

Her father motioned her out into the hallway and then led her to a small waiting area. "I'm so glad you came today – I'm worried that she doesn't have much time left."

Lucy felt her eyes fill with tears but tried to be strong for her father. She could tell that he was exhausted after being her caretaker all these years. "I'm so sorry, Dad. I can tell this has been so hard on you, too. I wish there was something I could do for you."

"Being near your mom is all I want right now. Do you have someplace lined up to stay?"

"No, I figured I'd ask at the information desk – I imagine they have some good recommendations."

"And I'm sure your name will open a few doors, right?"

"I'm not that big of a deal Dad, at least not yet. Have you had dinner?"

"No, but this is the time I usually go to the cafeteria. It's really not bad. Want to join me?"

"Sure, but I know you don't want to be away from mom for too long."

"No, I really don't, especially on days like today."

They enjoyed a leisurely dinner, and Lucy could tell that her dad appreciated the break. Eventually, he let out a sigh and she knew he needed to go back.

"I'll go find a hotel and come back before visiting hours end. Is there anything I can bring back for you?"

"No, I'm OK. I'll see you in a bit." She watched as he walked down the hallway, his shoulders slumped with the responsibilities he felt. After talking to the front desk and getting a hotel recommendation, she called UBER and stepped outside for some fresh air while waiting for her ride. Her phone *pinged* and she saw a message from Sonya.

"Hope you are safely in Florida. How is your mom doing? Call when you get a chance – we have news!"

She texted back, *"On my way to hotel. Will call in a bit."* What in the world could the news be? She had said *"we"* – she and Ramone? She couldn't wait to call and find out!

Her UBER driver was a young lady about her age. Recognizing Lucy immediately, she tried to contain her excitement and Lucy had to smile.

"Yes, it's me," she said with a friendly tone. "Can you take me to the Fairmont Hotel please?"

"Of course," her driver said. "I know I should act all cool and calm, but you are my favorite singer right now. I'm one of your biggest fans! Would it be too much to ask for an autograph or a photo?"

"I have a signed photo in my bag – how would that be?"

"Perfect. My name is Angela Slater. This is very exciting for me."

"To Angela," Lucy scribbled onto one of her photos. "Thanks for the ride!"

"Oh, thank you, Lucy. My friends will just die of jealousy!"

They pulled up to the hotel and Angela opened Lucy's door.

"May I ask a favor?" Lucy asked quietly.

"Of course – anything for you."

"I would really appreciate it if you would wait a day or two before telling your friends or posting this on social media. I'm in town to visit someone who is very ill, and I don't want their privacy invaded. Can you do that for me? I would hate for my visit here to cause harm to my friend. I'll make it up to you, I promise. Maybe concert tickets or a signed copy of my next album. Please."

"Of course – and I would have done it without the promise of tickets. There is no way I want to do anything that will harm your friend."

"Thank you so much – I'm going home Sunday afternoon. And please don't mention that I was at the cancer center. I don't want anyone to know."

"Sure - maybe I'll even make something up like I picked you up at the airport and took you to an undisclosed location. It will be fun to keep your secret. On a serious note, I do hope that your friend is going to be OK."

"Me, too," Lucy said sadly as she walked into the hotel lobby.

Chapter 10

The hotel manager insisted on putting her in a suite, even though she was only going to be there for two nights. Waiting in her room was a plate of cookies and fruit, and several bottles of water were in the fridge. One entire wall was windows that looked out onto Tampa Bay. She unpacked her small bag and settled into a recliner to call her friends.

"Sonya – what in the world is going on? Your message has been driving me crazy!"

"Let me put you on speaker phone first. After you left today, Ramone and I took a drive to our favorite place along the river – you know, that place where you can see the reflection of the skyline. Anyway, Ramone was acting a bit strange, and I didn't understand what was going on, until he pulled out a small ring box and asked me to marry him! We're getting married!"

"Oh, My Goodness! I am so happy for you! When? Where? I need details!"

"No details yet, but probably late next year sometime. I was hoping you would be my Maid of Honor?"

"Of course, I would be thrilled! Wow - married! I'm so excited!"

"We know your schedule is expected to be really busy next year, but we want to include you as much as possible in the planning," Ramone said happily. "I'm not sure we ever would have reconnected after all these years if it wasn't for you."

"I'm just so excited. Who all else have you told?"

"Our parents, of course," Sonya replied. "But you are the only other one. We wanted you to be the first of our friends."

"Thanks. I really needed your good news tonight."

"How is your mom doing?" Ramone asked. "How long are you staying?"

"She's not doing well at all. It's really sad to see her just a shell of her former self. I plan to fly home Sunday afternoon. I don't mean to cut you short, but I promised my dad I'd go back over this evening before visiting hours end."

"Of course! Go back and please tell her hello from me," Sonya replied. "And give your dad a big hug. I'm sure this is hard on him."

"What time is your flight?" Ramone asked. "I'm happy to pick you up, you know. No sense hiring a car when I am available."

"You don't mind? It's getting a little weird with everyone recognizing me. I'm even on the cover of one of those gossip magazines now! Someone snapped a picture of me shopping the other day."

"Of course. We'll both come to pick you up. We can grab some dinner somewhere or come straight home, whatever you want."

"Home sounds wonderful right now. Unless you want to go out?"

"We can go out anytime. In fact, home sounds nice to us, too."

Lucy called for a car to take her back to the hospital. This time the driver was an elderly man who had no idea who she was. Or if he did, he didn't act like he cared. She spent an hour with her mother before the nurses announced that it was time for her to leave. After giving her mom a lingering hug and kiss, she again called for a ride to the hotel. Her driver was a Hispanic man around 50 years of age and he drove in silence, barely acknowledging her.

Back in her room, she decided to order room service of cheese and crackers along with a bottle of her favorite wine. Relaxing in the recliner in front of the windows, she watched as boats moved in and out of the Bay. The lights of the city were twinkling below her, and she felt at peace.

She was almost asleep in the chair when her phone rang. "Hi, Dusty," she said after the second ring. "I just got back to my hotel. How are things with you?"

"Things are fine. I finally got my vacation dates finalized with my boss. I'll add them to your calendar if that's alright."

"Of course. I'm excited that we get to spend some time together."

"How are you? How is your mom?"

"Not doing well, I'm afraid. Dad even said they have talked about stopping the chemo."

"I'm so sorry," he said gently. "Losing a mom is never easy."

"No, it's not. You were so young when your mom died. I cannot imagine losing my mom as a child."

"So, you are going home on Sunday?"

"Yes, I got a flight that lands around six. Ramone and Sonya will pick me up. OH! I have the most exciting news! They are getting married! Ramone proposed this afternoon!"

"Married? How wonderful for them! I don't know them all that well, but they have taken great care of you this past year or so, and they seem perfect for each other."

"They really are. Sonya asked me to be her Maid of Honor, of course. I can't wait to go dress shopping with her and help with all the planning!"

They talked a bit longer before Lucy said she needed some rest, as she had started her day way before dawn at the TV station.

She slept fairly well, and the next morning she again ordered room service, this time a full breakfast of French toast, scrambled eggs and sausage, along with a big glass of orange juice. There was a coffee pot in the room that she had already filled twice. She called for a car and was back at the hospital before ten. She spent the entire day there, even though her mom slept most of the time. Her dad was showing signs of exhaustion, so Lucy sent him to the room he had been staying in for the past several months and ordered him to rest. He thanked her, saying he wouldn't be gone for long. Lucy pulled her phone from her purse and looked at her calendar. Dusty had added his vacation days, and it made her happy to see how long he would be in town. She forwarded the dates to Ramone – would it be OK for Dusty to stay with him, or was he wanting more privacy since he and Sonya were engaged now? Ramone replied that Dusty was welcome to stay with him as many nights as he wanted. He and Sonya had the rest of their lives to be together.

Lucy looked at her mother, so gaunt and frail from the disease and the chemo. How much longer could she keep fighting? And would they know when the time was right for her to stop?

She spent the day texting with Josh and others and the studio, along with reviewing a long email from Darren about arrangements for songs for the upcoming tour. They had dates confirmed all the way into April, and her head was spinning. There was even a long stretch where she would be gone for almost two weeks. The venues were getting larger, and the expectations were climbing. Toby wanted to book another photo session for the new album and add a few new posters for the tour.

The nurses were in and out several times, checking her mom's vital signs and administering her medications. A chaplain stopped by and offered to pray with her. She accepted readily and found peace and comfort in his kind words.

Her father arrived later, and they again ate dinner together in the cafeteria. He looked to be well rested and in better spirits. She filled him in on the events of the day, which he agreed had been pretty similar to those of the past week or so. He suggested that they should go back to the room, but that she then go to the hotel early to rest.

"I'm fine, Dad, really. You are the one who has been sitting vigil for so long."

"No, it's OK. I missed her today, and want to spend the evening with her, alone. I hope you understand."

"Of course." They went back to the hospital room and Lucy said goodnight to her mother, promising to return in the morning for a few hours before flying back to Nashville. She then called a car for a ride to the hotel. Christmas music was playing in the hallways, and it broke her heart to know that this was probably her mom's last holiday season.

As she was waiting in the lobby for the car to arrive, she noticed a TV crew setting up for a live shot. It was a local Tampa FOX channel, and she was afraid that they had found out she was there visiting her dying mother. She pulled the collar of her coat up nearer to her face, and prayed the UBER driver would arrive soon. She was relieved when a group of doctors came into the lobby to give an update about a new cancer drug that had been in clinical trials. She got a text that her car was arriving, and she dashed out into the cool evening air and was soon safe in her hotel room.

"I need to leave for the airport around two," she told her father the next day. "I wish I could stay longer, but my schedule is crazy from now until the end of the year. I'm just happy that I was able to spend this weekend here with you and mom."

"I'm sorry she hasn't been more responsive to you. But this is our new normal, I'm afraid."

As the time got closer for her to leave, she pulled her chair up next to her mom. She took her hand gently and said, "Mom, it's me, Lucy. I need to leave for a little while, but I wanted to tell you again how much I love you, and what a great mom you have been all these years. I know I have made my share of mistakes, but you never lost faith in me."

She fought back tears as she struggled to say goodbye, perhaps for the last time.

"Always know how much I love you," she said again. "Always."

"Lucy?" her mom said faintly. "Is that you?"

"Yes, Mom, I'm here. I love you, Mom."

"And I love you, Honey. My baby girl, my pride and joy. I love you more." And with that she drifted back to sleep.

Lucy could barely catch her breath, but knew it was time to leave. She hugged her dad and made her way to the lobby.

It wasn't until she was back in a first-class seat that the tears started to flow. She leaned her head against the airplane window and prayed that no one would sit next to her. She was in no mood to make small talk to anyone.

Her prayer was answered, and soon the plane was taxiing from the gate. She sent a quick text to Ramone to let him know they were leaving on time, and then she closed her eyes. How was she going to survive without her mother? And her poor dad….

She felt a gentle hand on her shoulder and opened her eyes to see a flight attendant.

"I hate to disturb you, Lucy, but would you like a drink? You seem really upset. Is there anything I can do?"

"Some hot tea would be nice, but otherwise, I'll be ok. Life is just hard sometimes."

"I'll bring your tea and ask the others not to disturb you."

"Thank you," Lucy whispered. "I really appreciate it."

Before long, she was standing outside the baggage claim area, waiting for Ramone and Sonya to arrive. She had been left alone on the rest of her flight, and for that she was very appreciative. After just a short wait, Ramone's truck pulled up in front of her.

"Thanks so much for picking me up. I was dreading another UBER ride. It seems like that is all I did all weekend."

"Are you OK? I'm worried about you," Sonya asked.

"No, not really. That was probably the last time I will ever see her, to have a conversation with her. She has declined so much, and she and Dad have pretty much decided to end her treatment. My heart is breaking."

"Oh, Honey, I'm so sorry." Sonya put her hand on Lucy's and a flash of sparkle caught her eye.

"Your ring! Oh, how beautiful! Ramone, you did good! I'm sorry I've been so distracted. Give me all the details."

"There's time for details later. Let's get you home. I'm sure after a hot bath or long shower you will feel up to talking more about it. Ramone wants to grill out one last time this fall, and there is an early Christmas present that arrived for you today, from a certain Ohio man, if I'm not mistaken. But there's a note not to open until Christmas."

"Christmas presents.........geeze. I'm so far behind! I have done almost no shopping for anyone but myself lately. What kind of friend am I?"

"No one is blaming you! It's been a very busy time for you."

"But I really need to do something for all the people who have been so supportive this year. And not just order something generic, I want it to be personal."

"I know there isn't a lot of time. What if you find a cause you support and make donations in everyone's name? Do you have a cause you are passionate about?"

"Cancer detection and cure, of course," Lucy quickly answered. "Would it be too impersonal to do that? Would people at the studio be upset?"

"No, I doubt it. Especially since most everyone knows about your mom. I think that would be totally fine."

"Let me think about it. I'd still like to bake some cookies or something to take into the studio."

"Oh, I'm sure they would love that," Ramone stated. "Especially the guys. We all love a good Christmas cookie or two."

They were about to sit down to a dinner of steaks and baked potatoes when her cell phone rang. Lucy saw Vicki Jo's name on the caller ID, and wondered why she would call on a Sunday evening.

"Hey, Lucy, I hate to call you on a day off, but have you seen your social media lately?"

"No, not today. I've been pretty busy."

"Well, an UBER driver from Florida just posted a picture she said you gave her. Is that true?"

"Yes, it is. I went down to Tampa to visit my mom. I asked the driver – I think her name was Angela – to wait until tonight to post it. I didn't want anyone trying to track me down and risk disturbing my mom. I'm glad she kept her promise. What all did she say?"

"Just that she picked you up at the airport and took you to a secret location. She said that you signed the picture for her and were very gracious. Anything else happen I should know about?"

"No, she was sweet. I did, however, see my picture on the cover of a gossip magazine in a gift shop. I guess someone took a picture of Elizabeth and me shopping last week. Crazy."

"I'm sorry, but yes, it can get strange at times. And we are just at the beginning. OK, I won't keep you. Are you coming to the office tomorrow?"

"Yes, I need to meet with Darren and the band again. We are almost ready to start recording the next album. It's hard to believe we are doing album #2 already."

"OK, I'll probably see you around. I'm glad you are home safely."

Chapter 11

The rest of the week flew by as Lucy had several radio interviews in addition to working on the new album. On the 20th, she rushed to the grocery store after work to stock up for her extended holiday time with Dusty. As she went up and down the aisles, she realized she did not know much about his food preferences. What did he like? Not like? Did he have any allergies? They had eaten very few meals together, and she tried to remember if he had mentioned anything in particular. She was stunned to acknowledge that she was falling in love with someone she knew very little about. She decided to send him a quick text. "*Hey, at the grocery store. Anything I should know? Allergies?*"

"*Nope. Pretty flexible. No seafood, I guess.*"

"*Thx — see you soon!*"

Sonya helped her unload the numerous bags of groceries and put everything away. "I'm so glad he is able to come down for such a long time," she said. "You guys deserve some extra time together. It's nice to see the pantry so stocked again. With our crazy schedules, it just made it easier to order in or pick up fast food. I hope you don't mind if I take over cooking for you again?"

"No, that would be great, but I was hoping Dusty and I could cook at least one meal for you and Ramone as an engagement meal. I'm still so excited for you. Have you settled on a date yet?"

"It really depends on your tour schedule, but we are looking at October or early November. We want to keep it away from the holidays."

"I hate that my tour is impacting your wedding date."

"Well, you are the one who brought us back together after so many years, so I guess it's only fair. What time does Dusty's plane get in tomorrow?"

"Three P.M. And he doesn't go back until the 2nd. I hope we don't get sick of each other!"

"Are you planning anything special while he is here?"

"I wanted to keep it spontaneous, especially since Josh told me today that The Stage has asked about me performing one night, and we have been invited to attend the fireworks that FOX will be broadcasting on New Year's Eve. I also want to get to the Opry at least once. I haven't planned anything other than that. I'm hoping the weather stays nice so we can get out and explore the city. You and Ramone are included in all of this of course. But I'm hoping Dusty and I have plenty of alone time. I really think that things are taking a serious turn."

"Looks that way to me, and I'm so happy for you. He really seems like an upstanding guy."

Lucy had arranged for the housekeepers to come early the next morning so everything would be sparkling clean for Dusty's arrival. Ramone played taxi driver again and left for the airport shortly after lunch. Lucy put on a new velvet top and curled her hair. She wanted to look nice but still down-to-earth.

"*The eagle has landed*!" Dusty texted from the baggage claim area. "*See you soon*!" followed by a heart emoji. Lucy felt a flutter of excitement. Was she really falling in love with him? And did he feel the same?

Before long, she heard Ramone's truck pull into a parking spot near the door, and she rushed out to see Dusty climb out. He reached into the back seat and gently lifted out a bouquet of flowers. She threw her arms around him, lifting her face for a quick kiss.

"I'm so glad you are here – 12 whole days? Are you up for that?"

"I'm up for 12 or 112 – I have missed you so much."

Once inside, Sonya put the flowers in water while the others sat around the table.

"Are you hungry?" Sonya asked him. "Need something to drink? I know they don't feed you much on airplanes anymore --- unless you fly first class like our famous friend here."

"A warm drink would be nice. Coffee maybe?"

"Coffee is perfect. I heard a rumor that we might even get a bit of snow for Christmas. I know that's nothing new for you as a northerner, but it doesn't happen often down here."

"Don't forget that I'm a native Texan, so I'm not a huge fan of snow other than at Christmas. I'm sure whatever you get will be less than we have in Ohio."

"I just put lasagna in the oven," Sonya continued. "I've also made a big salad and there will be garlic bread."

"Sounds great! I don't cook much for myself, and certainly not something fancy like lasagna."

"Not fancy at all. I'm just a regular cook, but you won't go hungry this week."

"I can attest to that," Ramone added, patting his midsection. "I've put on a few pounds this year, and I give her most of the credit."

"We've got about an hour until we eat," Sonya concluded. "Why don't you two get settled in the living room while Ramone and I make ourselves scarce."

"Thanks," Dusty smiled. "I hope you don't mind?"

"Of course not," Ramone answered. "We have some Christmas gifts to wrap so we'll leave you for now."

Finally alone, Dusty took Lucy into his arms and kissed her deeply. "I'm so glad to be able to spend the holidays with you. And I appreciate Ramone letting me stay with him. I could have gotten a hotel."

"I know, but there is no sense spending a bunch of money when he has an empty room just across the parking lot. And I like the idea of you being here close."

They huddled together on the sofa, drinking coffee and sharing memories of Christmases long ago.

"I meant to ask – I drink my coffee black but maybe you don't? Do you need cream or sugar?" she asked.

"A little creamer would be nice if you have some. It's not a big deal if not."

"No, we have plenty. Sonya loves flavored coffee but refuses to pay the high prices at Starbucks."

Lucy brought back a small basket full of various flavorings, and Dusty chose Italian Cream. "I have to agree with Sonya on this one. The price some of those places charge is criminal. What I really want to know is how you are feeling – honestly. I don't want you to act brave on my behalf."

"I've had a few rough days here and there, but for the most part I'm doing pretty well. Thanks again for helping to talk me down from the ledge a few weeks ago. Now that was a horrible night."

"I'm sorry that this is still such a struggle for you. I wish they could figure out why you still have so much pain."

"I just have to be careful not to injure it again. I have no cravings for the opioids otherwise."

"I'm relieved to hear that. OK, next question: I want to take you out someplace special, just the two of us. We could get dressed up and hit the town. How does that sound? Will it be a problem, since you are recognized so easily now?"

"I would love that. Let me think about the perfect place. And the recognition is just part of my reality now. Does it bother you?"

"The attention has been a bit strange to get used to, but I'm fine with it now. A few people approached me after the premiere, but most everyone is just happy for me. One guy I work with made a joke about me being "Mr. Armando" now. I just told him that I would be the lucky one to be married to someone as special as you."

Lucy's heart skipped a beat, and she blushed. Did he really just say he would love it if they were married? She was unable to reply, and he quickly jumped back in. "I'm sorry. I hope that didn't sound pushy. But I was just being honest. I've fallen in love with you, Lucy."

"I love you too, Dusty. Things are just so crazy in my life right now. I don't know where I will be from week to week, or even day to day. But I do know that I want you in my life and pray that we can find a way to make it work. I cannot imagine my life without you in it."

The rest of the evening and the next few days were filled with long conversations and delicious meals prepared by Sonya. On Christmas Eve, Lucy and Dusty dressed up in their finest and went downtown to the exclusive restaurant The Catbird Seat. Most of the wait staff recognized her, of course, but were used to serving celebrities and treated them with respect. After dinner, they stopped at a local Methodist church that was having a late-night service. They sang "Silent Night" while holding candles, and Lucy marveled at Dusty's deep bass voice.

"I had no idea you sang so well," she said softly. "Another thing I am learning about you. Is there anything you cannot do, Mr. Pierce?"

"I enjoy singing but could never get up in front of a large crowd like you do or sing on TV. But no matter the situation, you always make me feel like you are singing just for me. Few performers can do that."

They arrived home just before midnight. Sonya and Ramone were waiting up for them, and they toasted to their friendship before heading to bed. Ramone promised to have

Dusty back in time for breakfast, which Sonya had already said would be epic.

Alone in their condo, the girls changed into their pajamas and then sat beside the tree.

"When I was young," Sonya said, "we used to have a race to see which of us kids would wake up first on Christmas morning. Whoever was earliest would come to the living room and turn on the lights on the tree. Then we would 'camp out' on the sofa or recliner to prove we were the winner. By the time mom or dad woke up, the floor was covered with pillows and blankets as all four of us would be up. We continued this for years, long after we stopped leaving cookies for Santa. I'm happy to be here, of course, but do miss those days with my family."

"You could have gone home, you know," Lucy said softly. "Or did you not want to? I'm sure they miss you."

"I know, and I probably will sometime soon. But my life is here, now, with you and Ramone and my job. I love Nashville – it feels like home to me."

They chatted a bit more then said goodnight. Once in bed, Lucy struggled a bit to fall asleep. So much had changed since she first arrived here, and so much would change in the year to come. Sonya and Ramone would be married, and her upcoming tour schedule promised to take her across the country. Would she and Dusty be able to carve out enough time together to make their relationship work?

After just a few hours of sleep, Lucy opened her eyes and listened to the voices coming from the kitchen. She heard Sonya, Ramone and Dusty: the three most important people in her life. She peeked out her bedroom curtains and saw a faint dusting of snow on the ground, just as the weatherman had predicted. After taking a quick shower and dressing in a soft maroon sweater and jeans, she joined the others just as Sonya was starting to serve breakfast.

"About time, sleepy head," Sonya teased. " How in the world can you sleep in on Christmas morning?"

"Good morning, everyone," she said happily, planting a quick kiss on Dusty's cheek. "Merry Christmas!"

"I think everything is ready – sit down and eat while it's warm. We can do presents later."

"Presents? For me?" Lucy said teasingly. "I can't wait."

They talked and laughed as they shared their bountiful breakfast, then moved to the living room to open gifts.

"It was hard to know what to get you," Dusty said as he handed Lucy a beautifully wrapped gift. "Sonya gave me a few ideas, but mostly I had to wander around several stores to find just the right thing. I hope you like it."

Lucy's hands trembled a bit as she opened the lid to find a pale blue blouse made of the same organza as her premiere dress. Her fingers caressed the fabric then noticed a small velvet bag off to the side. Inside was a pair of diamond earrings that perfectly matched her tennis bracelet.

"Oh, Dusty, these are beautiful. The blouse is stunning, and the jewelry….you are starting to spoil me with all these diamonds!"

"I saw the blouse and realized it reminded me of such a special night, both for you and for us. The color is lovely on you. And as for the diamonds….I hope you don't mind if I continue buying them for you?"

"Of course not," she said as she kissed him again. Sonya and Ramone smiled at each other. Would an engagement ring be coming soon for Lucy, too?

The week flew by with sightseeing trips to the Opry and Ryman Theater, along with many quiet evenings playing board games and working on the 1000-piece puzzle Dusty gave to Sonya. On the 29th, Lucy had the opportunity to sing a few songs at The Stage in front of an enthusiastic audience, and Dusty was proud of how courteous she was when she interacted with her fans. New Year's Eve was spent downtown walking up and down Broadway and hearing various groups singing on the street corners. At midnight they stood along the river, watching the fireworks. They shared a kiss and a promise of an unforgettable year ahead. Lucy had never been happier.

Chapter 12

Dusty returned to Ohio, and Lucy's schedule continued at a frantic pace. Radio interviews, video shoots, TV appearances, and then the start of her second tour. Since it was winter in the northern part of the country, she travelled to numerous venues in Georgia, Kentucky, South Carolina and Florida. Sonya did not accompany her this time, as she was working and had totally recovered from her injuries. Ramone continued as a member of the security team and helped with videography at times.

The tour was a huge success, and before long she left on a western trip to Arizona, California, Utah and Colorado. Each venue seemed larger than the last, and the crowds continued to be enthusiastic and supportive. Her second album was released along with four new videos. They added another guitarist to her band, along with two backup singers. The lighting setup was more complex and needed an additional specialist to run. Her bus was crowded with these additional people, but they all got along well. She was recognized pretty much everywhere she went now, and she was learning to adjust.

The tour continued through South Dakota and Missouri as they made their way back to Nashville. The final show was in Springfield at Hammons Hall, which had over 2200 seats, most of which were filled. Knowing it was the last show on this leg of her spring/summer tour, the crowd was rowdy and demanded three encores.

The final bus ride turned into a pretty crazy party, with lots of drinking and dancing. Lucy had learned her lesson a long time ago not to drink on the bus, so she stuck to Diet Coke. They arrived safely back at the studio around six A.M. while Lucy was sleeping in her bunk. Ramone woke her and they drove back to the condos. She tried to sneak in quietly so as not to wake Sonya, but she was already up and getting ready for an early day at work.

"Welcome home!" she said. "I don't have a lot of time before I need to leave for work. Ramone texted me once you were just a few miles out of town. I missed you of course while you were gone, but I cannot wait to see Ramone. I stocked up the fridge yesterday and have some things planned for dinner. I'm sure you are exhausted. There is some mail on your nightstand, but nothing looked urgent. Oh, the flowers on the table are from Dusty – they came yesterday. OK, I'm out of here. Have a relaxing day. I should be home around four."

Lucy texted Dusty, telling him she was safely home and thanking him for the flowers. She told him she was heading to bed but would reach out to him later.

Lucy was almost asleep when her phone rang. Her father's name showed on the caller ID, and she answered it quickly.

"Hi, Dad. Your timing is perfect. We just got back into town a little bit ago and I'm about to crash. But it was a great tour, and we had so much fun! Each show and each crowd were better than the last."

"I'm glad you had a good tour and hate to be the bearer of bad news. Lucy, Honey, your mom went home to heaven just a few minutes ago. You know she had decided to stop the chemo after Christmas. We knew this day was coming, and now she is at peace. I'm sorry to have to do this over the phone."

"Oh, Dad! I wish I had made another trip down to see her."

"No, it's OK. She hadn't been responsive for quite a while now, much different from when you visited a few months ago. She is no longer in pain, and I'm at peace with her decision."

"So, what happens now?"

"I'll pack things up here and head back to St. Louis. I imagine we will have some sort of service later, but I haven't really thought much about it. I just talked to our pastor back home and he will work with me to plan something. I'll let you know."

"I'm so sorry, Dad. I know this will be very hard for you, going back to the old house alone."

"I figured I would just find an apartment to rent for a while. I really don't want to go back there without your mom. Or maybe I'll just stay here in Florida as there isn't really anything waiting for me back home."

Lucy hung up the phone and sat on the edge of her bed for a few minutes, allowing the memories and tears to flow. Her dear, sweet mother was with Jesus now.

Eventually she picked up her phone and sent texts to Dusty, Sonya and Ramone. She wanted to talk to Josh, and knew their conversation needed more than just a text.

"Good morning, Josh," she said when he answered. "Got a few minutes to talk?"

"Good morning, Lucy. I figured you would be sleeping in, enjoying some down time after that amazing tour. What's keeping you up?"

"Josh, I don't know how to say this. I just got a call from my dad – my mom passed away this morning. Even though we knew it was coming, I feel so unprepared. I don't know anything about a service schedule or things like that. I know you wanted to keep the momentum up as we take a short break between tours, but I'm not sure I can focus on anything right now."

"I totally understand, Lucy, and am so very sorry. I'll have Vicki Jo reach out to you and we'll put together something for your website and social media. We'll handle all the press for you. Lay low for a few days, don't answer any calls. Again, I'm so sorry."

Lucy curled up into a ball on her bed and covered herself with a blanket. She remembered one of her mom's favorite pictures which was of Jesus walking forward, his arms open wide, welcoming someone into heaven. She imagined that was what her mom saw, just an hour or so ago.

Her friends responded with texts and Sonya offered to come home from work early, but Lucy told her not to. Vicki Jo called, and after offering condolences on behalf of the studio, she asked Lucy for some basic information about her mom, how long her parents had been married, that type of thing. For just a second, Lucy thought about her pain pills and how they would take the edge off this emotional devastation. But instead, she called Dr. Todd, and they had a long conversation.

They cried together, and Lucy felt a sense of relief once the call ended. There was another *ping* on her phone, and she found a text from Vicki Jo with a link to the Star Records website. Once Lucy gave her approval, Vicki Jo would make the post live and put it on her social media.

"It is with great sadness that we announce the passing of Marissa (Lopez) Armando, beloved mother of Star Record's Lucy Armando. She passed away in Florida after a lengthy illness. Married to Antonio Armando for almost 27 years, Marissa was well-loved in her hometown just outside of St. Louis, Missouri. The Armando family would like to request privacy during this difficult time. In lieu of flowers, donations can be made to the American Cancer Society. Services are pending."

It seemed so final, seeing it in print like this. She gave her approval for the post, then decided she might as well get up and at least unpack and start some laundry. She ate a light breakfast and sat in front of the television. She turned to CMT and was shocked to see that they were already running a story about her mother and showing old family photos, probably taken from the archives of the *Rising Star* TV show. She was so beautiful before she got sick – how were she and her dad going to live without her?

Her phone started ringing almost immediately. This had certainly escalated quickly. She was about to turn her phone off when she recognized one of the names on the caller ID as Travis' family attorney Mr. Bobbenhouse. Today of all days – what did he want?

She answered the phone and was greeted by a receptionist who sounded familiar.

"Good morning Ms. Armando. My name is Stacy from attorney James Bobbenhouse's office. We met last year."

"Yes, I remember. How can I help you?"

"We have just heard from Travis Jones' manager that they will be releasing the duets album in the next few weeks. You were a part of that, I believe?"

"Yes, I was."

"The studio stated that royalties from the album were to be distributed to each of the artists who participated. We have been tasked with making those distributions and will need you to come into the office to fill out the related paperwork. When would you like to set up that appointment? You will need to meet with Mr. Bobbenhouse at that time as well while he reviews the options and stipulations of the agreement."

Lucy cringed at the mention of Travis' name. "Am I required to take the royalties in person, or can I donate my share of the proceeds directly to a charity?"

"I would imagine that a donation would be possible, but we would need to verify. If so, is there a charity you have in mind? I could go ahead and draw up that paperwork and have it ready for you to sign, if you were to choose that option."

"Yes, the American Cancer Society. My mother passed away from cancer just this morning."

"Oh, I am so very sorry. And my call could not have come at a worse time. Please accept my apology, and my condolences."

"Of course. You had no way of knowing. Let me check my schedule and I'll get back to you in a few days, if that's OK?"

"Absolutely. We will just hold your funds until a decision is made. Again, I'm sorry to have intruded this morning."

Lucy ended the call and closed her eyes. Even the grief she felt with losing her mother would now always be intertwined with Travis. Would she ever be able to escape the memories of that night?

Chapter 13

Sonya rushed into the condo and gave her best friend a big hug. "Oh, Honey, I am so sorry. Your mom was like a bonus mom to me when we were growing up. Her pecan cookies were the best, along with her enchiladas. Are you doing OK? What can I do to help?"

"As far as Mom is concerned, I'm doing better than I thought I would. I had a long talk with Dr. Todd today and she helped me put some things into perspective. But that actually wasn't the hardest part of my day."

"What could be worse? Or do I want to know?"

"Sit down next to me – I need to talk to you about a different call I got today."

"You are starting to scare me," Sonya said timidly as they sat together on the sofa.

"I had just finished talking to Vicki Jo about my social media post when I got a call from attorney James Bobbenhouse's receptionist. You remember who that is?"

"Of course, that's a hard name to forget. But why were they calling you today?"

"It seems that the duet album will be dropping soon, and per Travis' instructions to his manager, the proceeds from the sales and streaming are to be divided among everyone who performed on the album. I need to go to the office to sign paperwork to set up a direct deposit for my share."

Sonya started to tremble, and Lucy continued, "It will be OK. I don't plan to accept the money, but have it sent directly to a charity. I chose the American Cancer Society, of course, but I just had a brilliant idea. What if we had a portion sent to the Nashville Humane Society? No one would ever know why, but this would be a quiet way for you to be compensated for his actions against you. Not that it would ever be enough, but what do you think? If it's allowed, will you let me do this for you?"

Sonya closed her eyes and took a deep breath. She opened them and glanced around the living room. This is the room where she was attacked, where he kicked her ribs and face and called her nasty names. Where he would have raped her if he had not figured out his mistake at the last minute. This is the room where it all started, and this is the room where it was going to end.

"I think that would be perfect. He took so much from me, and I was injured and emotionally crippled for months. This isn't payback, or a way to even the score. That will never happen. But if the kittens and puppies that I love so much can benefit from all that happened, I'm fine with it. Yes, Lucy. If it can be arranged, I would be proud for our donation to be to the Humane Society."

Ramone opened the front door and came in carrying a large bouquet of roses and a stack of mail. "As soon as the word was out about your mom, the studio's phones began lighting up and your fans started showing up with cards and letters. I was in the office for a meeting with Josh, so he asked me to bring these to you. The flowers are from the studio. How are you doing? I'm so sorry that this has happened – I loved both of your parents, you know that."

"Yes, I do, and they loved you, loved both of you. Ramone, I have some other news to share with you. Can you sit for a minute?"

"Sure, what's up?"

Lucy shared with him about the call from the attorney's office and the distribution of royalties from the duets album. He approved of their decision to donate the money and offered to take Lucy to sign the papers whenever they set up the appointment.

"I don't want you to go alone," he said softly.

"I appreciate that, but I feel like I need to do this by myself. This whole situation is because of me, and I want to be the one to end it."

"No, it was because of *him*, but I do understand. Let me know if you change your mind."

"I originally planned a celebratory dinner for you, but with all that has happened, do you mind if we just order a pizza?" Sonya asked. "Or Ramone could pick up some BBQ?"

"Actually, I was hoping for some real food. You remember all the fast food we ate when you were on tour with us? Well, multiply that by 20. I need some real food for a change. Ramone, would you mind picking up some Italian? I'm craving something different, but special.

"I heard about a place called Caffé Nonna that is supposed to be good. I'll call and see if I can swing by and pick up a variety of dishes."

"Sounds great! Several combo platters would be wonderful. Josh told me to stay here in the condo as much as possible until the news settles down a bit. Mom was even on CMT this morning."

Ramone returned an hour later with several containers full of pasta, salad, soup and bread sticks. The food was wonderful and filling, and just what the group needed.

Three days later, Lucy drove to the attorney's office for her meeting with Mr. Bobbenhouse. He was a short, balding man about her father's age, and was quite curious about her relationship to Travis, although he knew better than to ask specific questions. He went over the details of the contract regarding her share of the royalties and wanted to be sure she understood the tax ramifications of her options. The papers had been drawn up for 75% of her royalties to go to the American Cancer Society, and the remaining 25% sent to the Nashville Humane Society. The album was due to be released at the start of the next week, and the goal was to have the paperwork in place before sales started being reported. She was relieved to put this part of her past with Travis behind her.

Dusty had been in constant contact with her since the mom's passing, but Lucy was still missing spending time with him. They were only able to squeeze in a short day here or there since New Year's, and for a few hours when she was in Missouri for her mom's funeral. Lucy hated the additional media scrutiny due to her fame, but her father was glad she was able to come.

He had made the decision to move to Florida in the spring, selling the house and most of their belongings.

The day the duets album was released, Lucy was inundated with calls for interviews and TV appearances. Her standard two-sentence response she had used when Travis passed away seemed inadequate, and she knew she needed to expand her comments. She decided to focus on the duet itself, and how helpful Travis had been during the recording process. She tried to avoid talking about him as a person but only about his music, which she had always admired.

When she talked to Dusty that evening, he thought she sounded a bit strange and uncomfortable during an interview that had been posted online. Was she OK? He was concerned about her.

"Is there any chance you can come down this weekend, even for a day? I really need to see you."

"Of course – I miss you, too. I'll let you know once I book a flight. I'm on a first-name basis with the attendants of my usual flight, I think."

That evening, Lucy and Sonya had finished dinner and were cleaning the kitchen when Lucy confessed that she wanted to tell Dusty the truth about Travis.

"I won't, if you don't want me to, but I feel like I need to be honest with him. I really don't want our relationship to get more serious with me keeping such a huge secret from him. How do you feel about it?"

"I don't want you keeping secrets, either. Enough time has passed, and I think he will understand our reasoning for handling it the way we did."

"Let's hope so. He's such an upstanding guy, always doing things by the book. I pray he won't be angry that we kept the truth from him all this time."

Dusty arrived late Friday afternoon, and the two couples enjoyed a quiet dinner at home. Knowing the difficult conversation Lucy was planning, Sonya and Ramone left to go see a late movie and to give her some privacy.

"It seems a bit late to go to a movie," Dusty said suspiciously. "Is something going on? Is everything OK?"

"I don't know – it all depends on how you react to what I have to tell you."

"Well, that's mysterious," he joked. Realizing she was completely serious, he said, "Lucy, talk to me. What's wrong?"

"I've been dreading telling you about something that happened a long time ago, even before I met you. But you mean so much to me, and I feel like I need to be completely honest with you now if we are to take our relationship further. Please forgive me for not trusting you with this earlier. I'm just not sure where to start."

Lucy took a deep breath and began telling him about her drive to Nashville after winning the contest, and how much she admired Travis and his music. She continued through the recording of the duets album and receiving flowers and other gifts from him.

"I'm still not sure where this is going," Dusty said. "But I'm listening."

Lucy started crying and she detailed for him Sonya's attack and learning that Travis had been responsible. Horror showed on Dusty's face as he realized what had happened, and what could have happened if Lucy had been home instead of Sonya. She concluded with their decision to keep the attack a secret once they learned that Travis had died in the river, but that all the feelings had resurfaced first with the discovery of Travis' box and then with the release of the album.

It took a few minutes for the entire story to register with Dusty. Travis Jones – the famous country singer – had attacked and was about to rape a girl he thought was Lucy. They learned later that he was a creepy stalker and extremely violent. But yet, the rest of the country music world mourned his passing and there was even talk of honoring him with a star on the Hollywood Walk of Fame. How was all of this possible? Oh, and then add the fact that her friends had kept this a secret from him, from the rest of the world, for over a year.

"It's going to take me some time to digest all of this. How in the world did you handle it all alone?"

"It wasn't easy, I won't lie. Sonya suffered the most, of course. But I have had such tremendous guilt. If she didn't look so much like me, she never would have been hurt."

"But he was out to hurt you, and probably would have succeeded eventually. This whole mess just sickens me, especially the way everyone else idolizes him."

"Please forgive me for not telling you sooner. We honestly just wanted to put it all behind us."

"I'm glad you did finally tell me, even though I am very angry. Not at you, obviously, but at him, and at the music industry as a whole. Surely you are not the only one he misbehaved with."

"I've often wondered about that, but of course we will never know unless someone else were to come forward, and after all this time, I doubt it."

The front door opened gently, and Sonya poked her head in. "Safe to come in?" she asked.

"Of course – I've told him everything," Lucy answered.

The couple came in and sat in chairs opposite the sofa where Dusty and Lucy were huddled. "First off, Sonya, I just want to say how very sorry I am about all that has happened this past year," Dusty said sadly. "I cannot imagine how difficult this has been for you, for all of you. I won't use the words I would like to describe that piece of trash. I have a couple of his CDs, but they will be going into the dumpster as soon as I get home. And Ramone, thank you so much for being such a support to both of these wonderful women. I owe you a lot."

"I wouldn't be anywhere else. On a much lighter note, Sonya and I have some good news to share with you," Ramone said with a smile. "We set a wedding date!"

"Oh, how exciting!" Lucy said brightly. "Give us the details!"

"We've been debating for quite a while when to have the ceremony, and where," Sonya chimed in. "We are both from large extended families, you know, but we don't what a huge extravaganza. We would prefer a simple ceremony with just the most important people in attendance. So, we have chosen September 17th for a small service at a place called Skinner Chapel. I was hoping that we could start looking for dresses this weekend while you are home?"

"Yes, of course. Let's get that date onto my calendar before Josh decides to send me to Alaska or someplace crazy. I am so very happy for both of you. You deserve all the happiness in the world."

Chapter 14

Lucy and Sonya spent the rest of the weekend looking at bridal magazines and discussing flowers and colors and invitations. They only had a few months to work out all the details, and Lucy was taking her job as Maid of Honor seriously. Dusty returned to Ohio, still struggling with his mixed emotions. While he was glad that Lucy finally confided in him, he had a growing distrust of the music industry. How many more creeps like Travis were walking around town, their fame hiding sinister motives and behaviors? Was the woman he loved still in danger?

Lucy was soon back on the road for the continuation of her summer tour, this time performing multiple shows in Iowa, Minnesota, Michigan and Wisconsin. She still loved performing before almost sellout crowds each night, but the tour bus life was starting to wear on her a bit. She was thankful that the longest she was on the road was 10 days before she got a few days off at home. There were times she had a random day off in a strange city, and she would sight see to sight see a bit but also just rest on the bus and strum her guitar. Adam and Blake were always at her side encouraging her to continue to write new songs, and Toby sent her emails about upcoming videos to film once she got back to town. Her time with Dusty was becoming even less frequent, although they did stay in touch each evening by phone or text.

The summer tour was about to wind down as Sonya's wedding day approached. The plans were ready, and Sonya's dress was stunning. Lucy couldn't wait for her best friends to be married.

Once back at the studio, the pace increased with more videos and album recording, and Josh was finalizing the trip to Hawaii as part of the Winter Showcase that was planned to run for five days. The logistics of getting everyone to Honolulu was daunting, and Lucy was glad she had a team of professionals to handle it.

The last day of the Showcase was scheduled for November 13th, the day before Dusty's 30th birthday. She hated being so far away from him, but then had a crazy idea. What if she hopped on a redeye immediately after her last show and flew to Ohio to surprise him? She could rent a car, get some balloons and a few gifts, and show up unannounced! She did some research and found flights that would work so she purchased the tickets. She would fly to Los Angeles and then catch a direct flight to Cincinnati. She shared her idea with Sonya who thought it sounded perfect. Lucy purchased the tickets and anticipated her surprise.

Late September in Nashville is often spectacular weather, but this year it was even more perfect. Sonya and Ramone's wedding went off without a hitch, and the newlyweds left for a short honeymoon in Toronto. Sonya had already emptied her room at Lucy's condo and moved her things to Ramone's. "Shortest move I ever made," she said laughingly, "but for the best reason by far!"

"I'll still keep my eye on your place while you are on tour," she continued. "It will give me something to do while both you are Ramone are out of town."

Lucy worried that she would feel nervous living alone again after being with Sonya for so long, but she found that she relished the privacy and freedom to come and go without worrying about anyone else's schedule. And she really didn't have all that much free time before her tour made another swing through the southwest and then on to Hawaii.

She had no idea the flight from Los Angeles to Honolulu would take so long – six hours! She was exhausted when they landed and struggled to adjust to the four-hour time zone change from Nashville. The weather was perfect, though, and everyone was excited to have a little free time to enjoy the sights and gorgeous beaches.

Overwhelmed by the number of talented musicians who were part of the Showcase, Lucy and her band took in as many performances as possible. Josh and Toby were on top of the world: meeting with other managers and videographers, working on potential collaborations, and introducing Lucy to the leading names in the music business. Josh never stopped networking, it seemed, and Lucy's calendar continued to fill.

On the day of her performance, Lucy wore a cowboy hat with her Hawaiian dress, and the crowd was dancing in the aisles. Changing into jeans and a ruffled shirt, she left most of her luggage with Josh and dashed to the airport. Sliding into a window seat in Row 2, she pulled a Kansas City Royals cap down over her eyes and tried to sleep. The flight was very uneventful, and before long they were approaching Los Angeles.

She only had a short layover between flights and was thrilled that the gates were close together. She still was the last one to board and again crashed into a first-class seat. As she was putting her bag into the overhead storage bin and the flight attendant found a place for her guitar, she noticed the couple sitting behind her. She wasn't sure why, but they looked very familiar. It took her a while, but she finally realized that the woman was Jean Miller, author of one of her favorite books '*Fountain of Love.*' Lucy introduced herself, and soon she and Jean were chatting about life and art and finding love. Jean and her husband Nathan had been in Los Angeles for the premiere of her book that had been made into a movie and were now on their way home to Ohio. They were excited to meet her, as they had followed her career on *Rising Star* and all her videos.

Lucy was very comfortable talking with Jean and found herself sharing stories about being on the road and her sudden fame, but that recognition was not all it was cracked up to be, especially when it came to knowing who she could trust. Just before the plane landed, Nathan handed her a picture he had drawn of her with her guitar. They promised to keep in touch, and Jean teased that maybe her next book would be about a rising country star.

The plane landed, and Lucy dashed to the car rental counter. She programmed Dusty's address into the GPS and drove out into the freezing night. Ohio was so much colder than the Hawaiian beaches she had just left hours ago!

After a quick stop at a CVS for balloons and a big card, she pulled onto Dusty's street. She was just about to open her car door when she saw movement in front of his house.

She immediately recognized Dusty's tall frame walking down the steps and heading toward his car. On his arm was a tall, long-legged blond who was looking up at him adoringly. They seemed very comfortable with each other, and when she slipped a bit on the icy steps, they laughed as he kept her from falling. Lucy lowered her car window just an inch so she could hear them speaking.

"Oh, Dusty!" the woman gushed between giggles. "Whatever would I do without you? You're my hero!" She stood on her tiptoes and whispered something into his ear. He laughed loudly and wrapped his arms around her.

Lucy wanted to gag at the fake flattery she was witnessing. But what was even more upsetting was how much Dusty was enjoying it.

"I've always been your hero, you know that! I'm so glad you are here with me tonight. I was dreading celebrating alone."

"It's horrible she left alone tonight, but I wouldn't miss your birthday for the world! Where are you taking me?"

"Shouldn't you be taking me out, since I'm the birthday boy? Thirty years is a big deal!"

"Well, you know all the best places to go. And I have a *very* special present waiting for you when we get home!"

They laughed again as Dusty opened her car door and gently helped her inside. Before long, they drove off into the night.

Lucy sat stunned by what she had just witnessed. Dusty – the man she had fallen in love with and who had professed growing feelings toward her – was wrapped in the arms of another woman; a woman it was obvious he had known a long time and was comfortable flirting with. Just the other day Lucy and Dusty had talked on the phone, and he told her how much he missed her and wanted to spend more time with her. Was this punishment for her being too busy with her career to be with him on his birthday? Did he ever truly care about her, had he been playing the field this whole time?

Several minutes went by before she decided what to do. She wrote a message inside the card, *"Dusty – Surprise. I came here to wish you a happy 30th birthday, but it is obvious you had other plans. I hope you and your blond had a nice evening. I loved you, but it's clear that you're not ready to settle down. I get that – who wants to be 'Mr. Armando' anyway?? I hope she gives you what I cannot. Lucy"* She got out and tied the balloons to his mailbox and placed the card inside. She returned to her car and drove off into the night.

Chapter 15

Lucy drove around for what seemed like hours before she pulled into a Hampton Inn and asked for a room. Her flight to Nashville was not for two days, and she just wanted a place to crash and be left alone.

She hung the 'do not disturb' sign on the door and crawled into bed. She tried to sleep, but all she could hear was the blond's voice over and over, "You are my hero, Dusty!" Frustrated, she climbed out of bed and took out her guitar.

She strummed a few chords, and that melody that had been haunting her for over a year suddenly turned into a song of heartbreak and pain.

I Guess You're Not Mine

Verse 1:
And here I thought we made the sweetest harmony
You matched me note for note, the perfect chord
You saw me and I saw you and I saw a dream come true
Turns out dreams were all I could afford.

Verse 2:

Here I thought I finally found the answer
Forever felt like more than just a song
You loved me and I loved you, but it wasn't quite enough
I guess I'll never know where we went wrong.

Chorus 1:

We could have gone down in history
But I guess we're going down in flames
Could've kissed me, now you've missed me
And isn't it such a shame
I'm gonna survive you,
But I won't lie,
You really made a mess of me this time,
So no, I'm not fine
'Cause I guess you're not mine.

Verse 3:

Here I thought the universe was on my side
That it finally game me someone I could trust
You changed me, thought I changed you,
But I guess I missed the mark
Just wishful thinking crumbling into dust.

Chorus 2:
We could have ridden into the sunset
But I guess we're gonna crash and burn
It was all set, then you said not yet
Now we've both got lessons to learn.
I'm gonna survive you,
But I won't lie,
You really took a toll on me this time.
I'm far from fine
'Cause I guess you're not mine.

Bridge:
Take your charm,
Take your blue skies, take your brown eyes,
Take your smile.
Take your sweet words, they were all lies
I really thought we'd go as far as we could go
But no, guess we'll never know.

Chorus 3:
We could have been a real-life fairy tale
But I guess it's just a tragedy
Thought we couldn't fail, couldn't go stale

But it was never meant to be.
I'm gonna survive you,
But I won't lie,
You really made a mess of me this time
So no, I'm not fine
'Cause I guess you're not mine.

It was well past midnight when she finished writing, worn out by the emotions that she had expressed. This song was very different from any she had ever written before but was probably the most raw and honest. She pressed the *record* button on her phone, and sang it again, this time barely making it through without crying. Now exhausted, she fell into a deep and dreamless sleep.

It was almost noon when she woke up the next day. Confused at first as to where she was, the memories of last night came rushing back. She took a shower and changed into casual pants and a sweater. She was hungry, but did not want to go out. She called down to the front desk and asked if any restaurants in the area would deliver lunch for her. Her options were pizza or Subway, and the clerk gave her their numbers. She called for a meat lover's pizza and a large bottle of diet coke, which was delivered to her room about 30 minutes later.

Her phone was full of text messages and voicemails from Dusty, but she refused to read them or listen. She didn't feel she could believe anything he said. She did text Josh to say she was safely in Ohio and would be back in the studio on Monday.

She had a new song she wanted to record as soon as possible and would be sending a file to Darren soon.

She spent the rest of the weekend rarely leaving her room. She put the finishing touches on her song and then recorded it one more time. She drove to the airport and returned her rental car. As she sat in the waiting area to board her flight to Nashville, she forwarded the file to Darren with the note to please meet her in the studio in the morning.

Several people on the plane recognized her and asked for autographs and pictures. She complied as best she could before the plane took off, then closed her eyes for the short flight home. Dusty had made this flight numerous times, and said the flight attendants knew him by name. But this time she was the one on the plane, and her heart was broken.

After landing, she called for an UBER to take her home. Ramone and the rest of the band were not coming back from Hawaii until tomorrow, and Sonya was at work. She knew the studio would be empty tomorrow, and for this song, she didn't want background musicians or singers, just herself and her guitar.

Once back in her condo, she unpacked her overnight bag and thumbed through the mail Sonya had left for her on her nightstand. A letter from Attorney Bobbenhouse caught her eye.

"Good morning Ms. Armando. As we agreed earlier, your share of Travis Jones' duets album is to be distributed between the two charities you selected. Enclosed is the first receipt of your royalties and documentation of these disbursements. If you have

any questions, please do not hesitate to contact our office. James R. Bobbenhouse."

Lucy unfolded another piece of paper to find a receipt for $10,287 which represented her share of royalties from the album. The breakdown between the two charities was included, and Lucy was thrilled to see that over $2,500 had been sent to the Humane Society. It would in no way compensate for all Sonya had gone through, but it would help with the healing a bit and help a cause she was so passionate about.

Her cellphone rang, and she saw that it was Darren. "Hey – you got the file I sent?" she said as she answered.

"Hello to you, too," he said with a smile in his voice. "I'm not going to ask what happened once you got to Ohio, but the song is….I don't even have the right words. I thought '*If Only*' was a look into your soul, but this………." His voice trailed off and she could tell he was on the verge of tears. "I'm so very sorry for whatever led to this. But I'm not sure I have ever heard a song with such deep emotion."

"It was a rough weekend, but it's over and I'm moving on. Do you think you can find a studio for me tomorrow so we can record? I really want this done as soon as possible."

"Actually, things are pretty slow right now due to the holidays. Yes, we can record. You're sure you don't want to wait for anyone else? Adam or Blake?"

"No, this is my story, my heartache. I need to do it alone."

"OK, then, I'll see you around nine tomorrow?"

"Fine, thanks Darren."

Lucy arrived promptly at nine the next morning. Darren was right about there not being many people in the office. Some were still on their way back from Hawaii, and others had taken an extended holiday. She walked into the studio reserved for her and opened her guitar case. She was determined to record this song in as few takes as possible and hoped she could keep the tears away until she was done.

Darren had talked to Josh while the group was in a layover in Los Angeles. He explained that Lucy had a new song to record, and it was perhaps the best song he had ever heard. He wanted to know how fast they could rush it out to have it considered for award season in the spring.

"Is it really that good? I trust you, always, of course. If you feel that strongly, I'll make some calls and see how fast we can get it released."

"I saw all the good press from Hawaii," Darren said. "It looks like there is no stopping her."

"Seems that way. There was so much talent there and they all want to collaborate with her."

"OK, I'm headed into the studio. When do you get to town?"

"Not until late this afternoon," Josh answered. "I'll check in later and see how things are going."

Lucy was set up and ready when Darren came into the recording booth.

"You're sure you want to do this by yourself?" he asked again.

"Just me. I hope you and Josh understand."

"Of course we do. Let's do a mic check and then get this started."

Lucy sat with her back to Darren and closed her eyes. She started softly strumming a haunting melody that spoke of loss and despair. Once she began singing, a tear trickled down her cheek and her voice broke a bit. She stopped and turned to Darren.

"Sorry, let's start over. I'm really trying to stay in control, but it's hard."

"I actually think it sounded fine, very natural and true to the lyrics. I think if it happens again, just try to keep going.

The second time through she stumbled on the lyrics a bit, so she tried a third time. Her voice cracked in places, but she kept going, and the result was a brutal song of love and loss. She opened her eyes, feeling exhausted yet free at the same time.

She looked at Darren, who had tears streaming down his cheeks. "Oh, Lucy. I don't know what to say. I know Josh will agree to releasing this as soon as possible so it can be considered for the CMA's in the spring. Are you OK with that?"

"Yes, that is fine. I'm not one who likes to capitalize on the pain of others, but this is my hurt this time. And I'm fine with sharing it as soon as we can."

As expected, the song rapidly climbed the charts and was an overnight success. Country radio stations played it nonstop and it went viral on the two major streaming services. When the award nominations were announced just after Christmas, Lucy was nominated for Newcomer of the Year and '*I Guess You're Not Mine*' was nominated for Song of the Year. How different this Christmas was compared to the last. Lucy was at the height of her popularity, but as brave as she pretended to be, her heart was still shattered. How could Dusty have done this to her?

She never replied to any of his texts, including those he sent to Ramone asking for answers. Eventually he stopped trying. Lucy worked to stay busy recording and making videos. Josh lined up an even bigger tour for her in the summer, including a trip to the UK and Germany. This is what she wanted, right? Then why did she feel so empty?

The night of the CMA's was another star-studded red-carpet event. She couldn't help but remember her first one two years ago with Dusty by her side. Had she really been so naive to believe he cared for her? Had he been playing her the entire time?

Arriving by limo and wearing a bright purple sequined gown, she was a far cry from the shy little girl in the blue organza dress, stars in her eyes and a handsome man on her arm. She was alone this time and felt so much more confident and mature, perhaps even a bit jaded. How foolish she had been to have trusted him.

She was excited to perform at the ceremony, and of course everyone wanted her to hear her nominated song live. The pain was not as sharp as it had been, but it was still excruciating for her to sing about Dusty and his betrayal. There is no way he could not know the song was about him, and a part of her hoped it hurt him just a fraction of what it hurt her.

After her performance and she was backstage changing, there was a knock on her dressing room door. "Flowers for you, Lucy," came a male voice that sounded familiar. The door opened and there was Dusty, holding a dozen roses.

"I don't want to talk to you," Lucy said rudely, turning her back to him. "I want you to leave."

"I'm not leaving until you hear me out. I don't know what you thought you saw that night when you came to surprise me, but I was not cheating on you."

"Oh, really? Then who was that tall blond who kept calling you her hero? Who giggled and said she had a 'special gift' for you after dinner? Who was so comfortable wrapped in your arms? I know what I saw and heard."

"What you saw and heard was my cousin Amanda. She didn't want me to celebrate alone while you were in Hawaii, so she and I got dressed up and were acting a bit silly. And yes, I was her hero when we were growing up. Even though we are the same age, it was like I was her big brother, her protector. I told you that we were very close. I tend to be overly serious, but she's goofy and silly and brings out the little kid in me. But she is *not* my girlfriend or even someone I'm dating on the side. She is my cousin."

"Your cousin?" she said, almost in shock. "You were arm in arm, and she was flirting with you. I don't believe you."

"Lucy, I have never lied to you. I love you! Amanda is my cousin."

Chapter 16

Silence hung over the dressing room as Lucy tried to grasp what Dusty had just told her. Had this really been just a giant misunderstanding?

There was a loud knock on the door followed by the stage manager telling Lucy that they were about to announce the winner of Song of the Year. She stood up, wiped a few tears from her cheeks, and walked toward the door. "I need some time to think about things. Please leave me alone now."

Lucy stood backstage and waited for the winner to be announced. "It's time, ladies and gentlemen, to announce the winner of one of our most anticipated categories," the host said. "Song of the Year!" He went through the list of nominated songs and then said, "And the winner is……………..'*I Guess You're Not Mine*', written and performed by Lucy Armando, produced by Star Records!"

Lucy stepped onto the stage amid thunderous applause. Her song was playing in the background as she was handed her trophy. She stood behind the podium and looked around the room to find Josh, Darren, and several others from the studio. Sonya and Ramone were a bit further back in the room but clapping loudly. She saw A-list celebrities standing on their feet applauding, and then she glanced off to the right wing and saw Dusty standing there. Dusty – the man she loved but who had broken her heart. The pain from that is what birthed this song, which was now Song of the Year!

She took a deep breath and said, "Thank you so much everyone. I am overwhelmed by the response to my song. I'd like to thank my manager Josh and producer Darren, and all the people at Star Records who work so hard every day to help me look good and sound even better. I would like to thank my dear friends Sonya and Ramone who have been with me since high school and who loved me even when I was a nerdy band geek. Most of you probably know that my mother passed away last year from cancer. She never got to see most of this," she said as she gestured around the theater, "but I know she was proud of me and would be so happy tonight. I want to thank the fans, of course, who have embraced me and cheered me on through bus accidents and other drama. I have learned a lot these past couple of years since winning *Rising Star* – things about myself, things about the music industry, and things about people. To all those kids at home who want to be music stars, my advice to you is to keep practicing, of course, but also to discover which values and morals are the most important to you and that you are willing to fight for. This industry is not easy and is not for the faint of heart! But if you can experience it with a few good friends by your side and a management team who cares for you as a person as well as a performer, you can find happiness and success. I love you all – thanks again!"

Lucy left the stage and stood beside Dusty.

"I'm so proud of you," he whispered. "The song was amazing, even though it was painful to know you were talking about us."

"Obviously, we have a lot to talk about, but I need to stay here several more hours. How long are you going to be in town?"

"As of now, just until tomorrow afternoon. But I could change it, if you want me to."

The TV station that was broadcasting the award show had gone to a commercial, and that was Lucy's signal to return to her seat. "Call me in the morning, OK?" she asked as an usher escorted her toward the main floor. "And thank you for the flowers. They are lovely."

Lucy returned to her place between Josh and Darren, carrying her roses and her award. "I'm so proud of you!" Darren whispered. "Where did the roses come from?"

"Dusty," she whispered, a confused look on her face.

"Dusty? He's here? I just figured...."

"You figured right. I haven't spoken a word to him since my trip to Ohio, that is, until just now."

"But he's here? Now? Why?"

"I can't talk about it now, Darren. Let's just enjoy the rest of the evening."

Although nominated for Newcomer of the Year, she didn't win, and she was OK with that. The ceremony ended and Lucy went with the others to an after-party. It was almost two A.M. when she finally made it back to her condo. She carried her flowers and award into the kitchen and placed them on the table. Too exhausted to even find a vase for the roses, she went to her bedroom and collapsed without getting undressed.

She woke up a few hours later and made her way to the bathroom. She stared at her reflection in the mirror, not sure she recognized the person looking back at her. Was Dusty telling the truth? Is it possible that she misinterpreted everything? Would she be able to trust her instincts ever again?

She was reading social media accounts of last night's awards when she got a text from Sonya. *"Awake? Can we come over?"*

"Sure," Lucy replied. *"About to make breakfast."*

"Wait for us – we have a surprise."

It only took a few minutes before there was a knock on the door. Ramone and Sonya came in with big smiles on their faces.

"First off, Congratulations! We are so very happy for you!"

"Thanks – it was a pretty big surprise, since the song had only been out for a few months."

"The trophy is so heavy!" Ramone admired it as he lifted it from the table. "But what's with the flowers? They look almost dead."

"That's a long story for later. What is your news? I'm so curious."

"Well, we've been keeping a secret for a few days," Sonya said with a huge smile on her face. "We didn't want to infringe on the CMA's. But we can't wait any longer – we're expecting a baby, due around the 1st of September!"

"Oh, my goodness! A baby! I'm so very happy for you! How are you feeling? Is everything OK?"

"I'm fine, except for some morning sickness. We weren't really planning for a baby this soon, but I couldn't be happier!"

"And I'm thrilled too, of course," Ramone smiled. "Imagine us as parents!"

They chatted a while, then Sonya said, "So, what's the deal with the flowers? Did you get them last night?"

"Yes, from Dusty."

"Dusty? How? Was he there last night?"

"Yes, he came backstage after my performance, and we talked a bit. I'm not sure what to think."

"I know you never wanted to go into details about what happened in Ohio, and I didn't want to pry," Sonya continued. "Can you talk about it now?"

"I guess," Lucy said sadly, and she then detailed the events of that November night when she saw Dusty leave his house with a blond on his arm. Ramone became visibly upset as he imagined her shock and sense of betrayal.

"So yes, I was very angry, and the song I wrote was in direct response to that hurt and disappointment. But tonight he told me that he had not been cheating, that the blond was actually his cousin Amanda."

"*His cousin?*" Ramone scoffed. "Typical excuse."

"I think maybe he was telling the truth. A long time ago he told me about a girl cousin who he was really close to. But they were certainly not acting like cousins that night, so of course I jumped to a conclusion."

"So, what happens now?" Sonya asked gently. "Do you want to talk to him and to try to work things out?"

"He's in town until this afternoon. I asked him to call me this morning sometime. I think I owe it to him, no, to both of us, to hear what he has to say."

"I am not nearly as forgiving as you are," Ramone said firmly, "but yes, I think you need to hear him out. I felt that you two had a lot of potential as a couple, and I would hate to see you call it quits if it really was a misunderstanding. Unless he is a total jerk, I really believed he cared for you."

After putting the flowers in water, Sonya said, "We'll leave and give you some privacy. I want to go shopping for nursery furniture."

Lucy hugged her friends and wished them well. Just a few minutes passed before her phone rang again.

"Hi, Lucy. Are you awake? I didn't want to call too early."

"Yes, I'm awake. In fact, Sonya and Ramone were just here."

"Oh, I can call later if you want," he said sadly.

"No, it's OK. They just left to go furniture shopping They told me this morning that they are expecting a baby!"

"Wow! Congratulations to them. They will make wonderful parents."

They were both silent, struggling with what to say next. Finally, Dusty asked, "Is it OK if I come over? I really want to try to explain again what you saw that night. Can we fix this somehow? I have missed you terribly."

"Yes, that's fine. But I cannot promise anything, I hope you understand."

About 30 minutes later, there was a gentle tap on the door. Lucy opened it to find Dusty looking tired and sad.

"Thanks for letting me come over. I have something I want to show you, if that's alright. I think it will help to explain everything."

"OK," Lucy said skeptically. "Let's sit at the table."

Dusty sat across from her and opened a small backpack. Inside was an old photo album that he put in front of Lucy.

"I had my dad go through some old boxes and ship this to me. It's photos of our family from when I was a kid."

Lucy thumbed through the pictures of Dusty as a young boy learning to ride a bike and singing in the school choir. There were pictures of his parents, and it was the first time she saw his mother – such a lovely woman. Lucy turned a page and froze as she saw pictures of him and a blond girl swimming at a lake and riding horses on a ranch. The girl looked identical to the blond from Ohio. In faded printing under the pictures were the words "Dusty and Amanda." His cousin Amanda was the same blond she saw the night of his birthday. Dusty had not been cheating, and Lucy had made a huge mistake.

Chapter 17

Lucy sat in silence, staring at the pictures of Dusty and Amanda. She had totally overreacted, and now wasn't sure what to do to make it right.

Dusty reached across the table and put his hand on hers. "Lucy, I won't lie and say it didn't hurt when you ghosted me without a chance to explain. Part of me understands, and I might have done the same thing if the places were reversed. But please come to me the next time you are concerned or hurt or worried. We have to talk these things out, not just run away. You can trust me. I never stopped loving you."

"I know, you're right. I guess it was the way the two of you were talking and she was looking at you that made me so jealous. Add that to my jet lag and guilt about being away so much….I really am sorry. Can you forgive me?"

"Already done. Please, come sit with me on the sofa. I have one more thing to talk to you about."

"Should I be worried?" she asked.

"No, it's good news, actually. I know that one of our biggest challenges is that we rarely get to see each other for more than a few hours at a time. I have the chance to fix that, if you are interested."

"Of course! Tell me!"

"I have the opportunity to do basically the same IT work I do now but for a company that is based here in Nashville. Ever heard of the Tennessee Titans football team?"

"Of course I have! You got a job with the Titans?"

"I haven't officially accepted, but yes, it is mine if I want it."

"And do you? Want it, I mean?"

"I know that I want to be with you, and the job at the Titans would help that to happen. I guess I could learn to tolerate the team if it means we can be together. You know I'll always be a Cowboys fan."

"I would love it if we could be together more. I'll still be touring and performing a lot but having you in the same area code would be so exciting."

"I love you Lucy – I have for a very long time. I hope you never again doubt my love for you."

"I love you, too, which is why this situation hurt so much. Please forgive me. Being in a relationship is very new to me, and I obviously handled this all wrong."

They talked a bit more before Dusty flew back to Ohio and made plans to accept the job with the Titans. Within six weeks he sold his house and moved into an apartment not far from the stadium. They enjoyed many evenings together watching movies, playing board games and just enjoying each other's company. Sonya and Ramone joined them often, and the two couples regularly went to shows or sporting events together. One of the perks of working for the Titans was access to a skybox where celebrities often hung out to watch the games. Lucy swore she would never go back to a regular seat again after enjoying the luxurious amenities it provided. She treasured their extra time together and knew their relationship was getting stronger every day.

Sonya's pregnancy went smoothly, and on September 2nd she gave birth to a baby boy they named Titus Ramone. Lucy relished her role as Auntie and did her best to spoil him.

Lucy and Dusty took dinner and gifts over to them about a week after they were home from the hospital. It was obvious that Sonya was exhausted and needed to rest, so they didn't stay long, but rather went back to Lucy's condo.

"He's such an adorable baby!" Lucy said as they snuggled on the sofa. "And did you see the way Ramone looked at him? What a happy little family they are."

"We never really talked about children," Dusty said softly. "What are your thoughts?"

"I always imagined myself as a mom to at least a few children. As an only child, it was lonely for me at times. What about you?"

"I feel the same. I would love at least two or three children, maybe more. And I would hope they have your eyes."

Their conversation lagged a bit, and then Dusty turned toward Lucy. "I know that sounded presumptive, but there is nowhere else I would rather be than to be with you, raising our children. Is that something you would want – to spend our lives together? Will you do me the honor of being my wife?"

Lucy's eyes grew large as he reached into his jeans pocket and pulled out a large princess cut diamond ring.

"I know things have not always been easy for us with crazy schedules, bus crashes and other difficult challenges, but I know in my heart that you are the one for me. I love you, Lucy Armando, and want to spend the rest of my life showing you how precious you are to me."

"Oh, Dusty, I love you, too. Yes! Yes! I will marry you!"

Dusty slipped the ring onto her finger and kissed her hand gently. "Let's call your dad and let him know, and then my dad. Who do you want to tell after that?"

"Sonya and Ramone, of course, and then everyone at the studio. Take a picture of the ring on my hand and I'll send it to Vicki Jo after we talk to our dads. How soon can we get married? I don't want to wait any longer than we have to."

"Well, that depends on your tour schedule, I'm sure. But I don't want to wait either. Where do you think we should live? My apartment is really small."

"Would you mind living here? I purchased it a year ago when my lease was up, and there is plenty of room for the two of us, plus a baby or two down the road."

"Perfect – now let's make those phone calls!"

Refrain

Lucy rested her head on Dusty's shoulder, inhaling his scent that she had loved since they first met. She smiled at the wedding ring on her finger, nestled next to her gorgeous engagement ring, the jewels sparking in the nearly dark car. Her wedding dress was tucked in around her, it's long train puddled on the floor. The wedding had been a media event, but now she cherished this time alone with him.

They were parked at their favorite place near the river, admiring the Nashville skyline reflected in the water at sunset. On her wrist was the tennis bracelet he had given her the night of her first red carpet, and she was wearing the earrings he gave her that special Christmas. Added just today was a matching diamond necklace that was his wedding gift to her.

"Do you know how much I love you?" she asked softly. He was so handsome in his tuxedo, even more than he was the night of the premiere. "I am so happy to be your wife. No more '*If Only*'… my dreams have come true."

"And you are the most beautiful bride. I'm the lucky one. Are you ready to go home, Mrs. Pierce?"

"I am very ready, Mr. Pierce. I cannot wait to begin our life together!"